Cecil Headlam, Laurie Magnus

Prayers from the poets

A calendar of devotion

Cecil Headlam, Laurie Magnus

Prayers from the poets
A calendar of devotion

ISBN/EAN: 9783337282202

Printed in Europe, USA, Canada, Australia, Japan

Cover: Foto ©Andreas Hilbeck / pixelio.de

More available books at **www.hansebooks.com**

Prayers from the Poets

A Calendar of Devotion.

COMPILED AND EDITED BY

LAURIE MAGNUS MA

AUTHOR OF 'A PRIMER OF
WORDSWORTH'. ETC

AND

CECIL HEADLAM, BA

AUTHOR OF 'PRAYERS OF
THE SAINTS'. 'THE STORY
OF NUREMBERG. ETC

WILLIAM BLACKWOOD AND SONS
EDINBURGH·AND·LONDON
MDCCCXCIX

PREFACE.

We are indebted to the following authors and publishers for permission to include copyright poems in our Anthology :—

To Mrs Coventry Patmore for the use of two odes by the late Coventry Patmore in 'The Unknown Eros'; to Mrs Meynell for "Veni, Creator," from her volume of 'Poems'; to Mrs Henry Lucas for several selections from her compilation, 'The Jewish Year'; to Miss Nina Davis for two of her translations from the Hebrew contributed to the 'Jewish Quarterly Review'; to the Poet Laureate for passages from 'Prince Lucifer,' 'The Tower of Babel,' and 'Madonna's Child' respectively; to Mr Rudyard Kipling and his publishers in this country and the United States (Messrs Macmillan and Co. and the Doubleday and M'Clure Co. of New York) for "L'Envoi" from 'Life's Handicap'; to Sir Lewis Morris for three selections from his collected 'Poetical Works'; to the Dean of Ely for two pieces from 'Bryhtnoth's Prayer and other Poems'; to Mr Robert Bridges for his "Pater Noster"; to Mr Theodore Watts-Dunton for his "John the Pilgrim"; to Mr P. J. Bailey for a passage from 'Festus'; to Mr W. E. Henley for "Out of the Pit," with the consent of Messrs David Nutt; to the Rev. H. C. Beeching for his "Prayer of a Boy"; to Mr Robert Whitelaw of Rugby and his publishers for passages from his translations of Sophocles; to Mr F. S. Ellis and Mr Cockerell, the trustees of the literary property of the late William Morris, for two passages from the 'Earthly Paradise'; to Messrs George Bell and Sons for a poem by the late Thomas Ashe; to Messrs Chatto and Windus for two poems by the late Arthur O'Shaughnessy; to Messrs Macmillan and Co., who more than any other one firm of publishers are associated with the poetry of the nineteenth century, for placing at our disposal the passages we coveted from the works of the Rossettis, of Matthew Arnold, and of Fitzgerald's 'Omar Khayyám'; and to Messrs Blackwood and Sons, the courteous publishers of this volume, for poems by George Eliot and the late Mrs Oliphant respectively.

To each and all of these we gladly take the present opportunity of recording our debt of hearty gratitude for the advantage which our work derives from their generous and ready assistance, accompanied in some instances by valuable letters of encouragement and advice.

We are further indebted to some private correspondents abroad, whose aid has enabled us to increase the examples from the devotional verse of foreign poets. Our rendering of a poem by the Hungarian writer, Zrinyi, is from a literal German version.

It was inevitable that the dues of copyright should occasionally have precluded our selection of certain poems, but if any which might claim a place in this volume have been unwittingly omitted, we shall be grateful for all suggestions which will help to increase its representative character.

THE EDITORS.

LONDON, *November* 1899.

PRAYERS FROM THE POETS.

JANUARY 1.

A PRAYER OF MOSES.

LORD, thou hast been our dwelling-place in all generations.

Before the mountains were brought forth, or ever thou hadst formed the earth and the world, from everlasting to everlasting, thou art God.

Thou turnest man to destruction; and sayest, Return, ye children of men.

For a thousand years in thy sight are but as yesterday when it is past, and as a watch in the night.

Thou carriest them away as with a flood; they are as a sleep: in the morning they are like grass which groweth up.

In the morning it flourisheth, and groweth up; in the evening it is cut down, and withereth.

For we are consumed by thine anger, and by thy wrath are we troubled.

Thou hast set our iniquities before thee, our secret sins in the light of thy countenance.

For all our days are passed away in thy wrath: we spend our years as a tale that is told.

A

The days of our years are threescore years and ten ;
and if by reason of strength they be fourscore years,
yet is their strength labour and sorrow ; for it is soon
cut off, and we fly away.

Who knoweth the power of thine anger ? even
according to thy fear, so is thy wrath.

So teach us to number our days, that we may apply
our hearts unto wisdom.

Return, O Lord, how long ? and let it repent thee
concerning thy servants.

O satisfy us early with thy mercy ; that we may
rejoice and be glad all our days.

Make us glad according to the days wherein thou
hast afflicted us, and the years wherein we have seen
evil.

Let thy work appear unto thy servants, and thy
glory unto their children.

And let the beauty of the Lord our God be upon
us : and establish thou the work of our hands upon us ;
yea, the works of our hands establish thou it.

Psalm xc.

THE sudden stormes that heave me to and fro,
   Had well near peirced faith, my guiding saile,
For I, that on the noble voyage go
   To succour truth and falshed to assaile,
Constrayned am to beare my sailes full low,
   And never could attaine some pleasant gaile :
For unto such the prosperous winds do blow
   As runne from port to port to seke availe :
This bred dispaire, whereof such doubts did grow
    That I gan fainte, and all my courage faile ;
      But now my blage, mine errour well I see,
      Such goodly light King David giveth me.

HENRY HOWARD, Earl of Surrey.

JANUARY 2.

WHILE brickle houre - glasse runs, guide Thou our
    panting pace :
Give us foresightful mindes : give us mindes to obey
What foresight tels : our thoughts upon thy know-
    ledge stay.
Let so our fruits grow up that Nature be maintained,
But so our hearts keepe downe, with vice they be not
    stain'd.
Let this assurèd hold our judgments overtake,
That nothing winnes the heaven but what doth earthe
    forsake.   SIR PHILIP SIDNEY.

JANUARY 3.

MISERERE, DOMINE.

O THOU unknown, Almighty Cause
    Of all my hope and fear !
In whose dread presence, ere an hour,
    Perhaps I must appear !

If I have wandered in those paths
    Of life I ought to shun ;
As something loudly in my breast
    Remonstrates I have done ;

Thou know'st that Thou hast formèd me
    With passions wild and strong ;
And list'ning to their witching voice
    Has often led me wrong.

Where human weakness has come short,
    Or frailty stept aside,

Do Thou, All-Good! for such Thou art,
    In shades of darkness hide.

When with intention I have err'd,
    No other plea I have,
But Thou art good; and goodness still
    Delighteth to forgive.

ROBERT BURNS.

God! Thou art love!   I build my faith on that
Even as I watch beside Thy tortured child,
Unconscious whose hot tears fall fast by him,
So doth Thy right hand guide us through the world
Wherein we stumble. . . .
                Or, say he erred—
Save him, dear God; it will be like Thee: bathe him
In light and life! Thou art not made like us;
We should be wroth in such a case: but Thou
Forgivest.

ROBERT BROWNING.

JANUARY 4.

QUA CURSUM VENTUS.

As ships becalmed at eve, that lay
    With canvas drooping, side by side,
Two towers of sail at dawn of day
    Are scarce long leagues apart descried:

When fell the night, upsprung the breeze,
  And all the darkling hours they plied,
Nor dreamt but each the self-same seas
  By each was cleaving, side by side :

E'en so—but why the tale reveal
  Of those whom, year by year unchanged,
Brief absence joined anew to feel,
  Astounded, soul from soul estranged ?

At dead of night their sails were filled,
  And onward each rejoicing steered ;
Ah, neither blame, for neither willed,
  Or wist, what first with dawn appeared.

To veer, how vain !   On, onward strain,
  Brave barks !   In light, in darkness too,
Through winds and tides one compass guides—
  To that and your own selves be true.

But O blithe breeze ! and O great seas,
  Though ne'er, that earliest parting past,
On your wide plain they join again,
  Together lead them home at last.

One port, methought, alike they sought,
  One purpose hold where'er they fare,—
O bounding breeze, O rushing seas !
  At last, at last, unite them there.

A. H. CLOUGH.

JANUARY 5.

O Thou great arbiter of life and death,
Nature's immortal, immaterial Sun !
Whose all prolific beam late called me forth
From darkness, teeming darkness, where I lay

The worm's inferior, and in rank beneath
The dust I tread on, high to bear my brow;
To drink the spirit of the golden day,
And triumph in existence; and couldst know
No motive but my bliss, and hast ordained
A rise in blessing with the Patriarch's joy,
Thy call I follow to the land unknown.
I trust in Thee, and know in whom I trust;
Or life, or death is equal: neither weighs!
All weigh in this—O let me live to Thee.

JAMES THOMSON.

JANUARY 6.

Holy Jesus! God of Love!
Look with pity from above!
Shed the precious purple tide
From Thine hands, Thy feet, Thy side;
Let Thy streams of comfort roll,
Let them please and fill my soul.
Let me thus for ever be,
Full of gladness, full of Thee.
This, for which my wishes pine,
Is the cup of love divine;
Sweet affections flow from hence,
Sweet above the joys of sense;
Blessed philtre! how we find
Its sacred worships! how the mind,
Of all the world forgetful grown,
Can despise an earthly throne;
Raise its thoughts to realms above,
Think of God and sing of love.

THOMAS PARNELL.

JANUARY 7.

PURGE Thou my heart, Omnipotent and Good!
Purge Thou my heart with hyssop, lest, like Cain,
I offer fruitless sacrifice and with gifts
Offend and not propitiate the adored.
Though Gratitude were blessed with all the powers
Her bursting heart could long for; though the swift,
The fiery-winged Imagination soar'd
Beyond Ambition's wish—yet all were vain
To speak Him, as He is, who is ineffable.
Yet still let Reason through the eye of Faith
View him with fearful love; let Truth pronounce,
And Adoration on her bended knee,
With heaven-directed hands, confess His reign,
And let the angelic, archangelic band
With all the hosts of Heaven, cherubic forms,
And forms seraphic with their silver trump
And golden lyres attend—" For Thou art holy,
For Thou art one, the Eternal, who alone
Exerts all goodness and transcends all praise!"

CHRISTOPHER SMART.

JANUARY 8.

THE PRAYER OF ABEL.

O GOD,

Who made us and who breathed the breath of life
Within our nostrils, who hath blessed us,
And spared, despite our father's sin, to make
His children all lost, as they might have been,
Had not Thy justice been so temper'd with
The mercy which is Thy delight, as to

Accord a pardon like a Paradise
Compared with our great crimes: Sole Lord of Light,
Of good and glory and eternity!
Without whom all were evil and with whom
Nothing can err, except to some good end
Of Thine omnipotent benevolence—
Inscrutable but still to be fulfilled—
Accept from out Thy humble first of shepherds
First of the first-born flocks—an offering
In itself nothing—as what offering can be
Aught unto Thee?—but yet accept it for
The thanksgiving of him who spreads it in
The face of Thy high heaven, bowing his own
Even unto the dust, of which he is, in honour
Of Thee and of Thy Name for evermore!

LORD BYRON.

JANUARY 9.

"CONSIDER HER WAYS, AND BE WISE."

THOU, who didst put to flight
Primæval silence, when the morning stars
Exulting shouted o'er the rising ball;
O Thou, whose word from solid darkness struck
That spark, the sun; strike wisdom from my soul!
My soul, which flies to Thee, her trust, her treasure,
As misers to their gold, while others rest.
  Through this opaque of Nature and of Soul,
This double night, transmit one pitying ray,
To lighten and to cheer. O lead my mind—
A mind that fain would wander from its woe—
Lead it through various scenes of Life and Death,
And from each scene the noblest truths inspire.
Nor less inspire my Conduct than my Song.

Teach my best reason, reason : my best will
Teach rectitude ; and fix my firm resolve
Wisdom to wed and pay her long arrear.
Nor let the phial of Thy vengeance, pour'd
On this devoted head, be pour'd in vain.

EDWARD YOUNG.

JANUARY 10.

THE DYING PAGAN TO HIS SOUL.

My pretty soul, my fleeting soul,
   Who guest and comrade wert to me,
To what dim, undiscover'd goal,
   Pale little spectre, now wilt flee,
On timid wings of frigid fear,
Forgetting all thy wonted cheer ?

EMPEROR HADRIAN.
(Trs. Editors.)

THE DYING CHRISTIAN TO HIS SOUL.

VITAL spark of heavenly flame !
Quit, oh quit this mortal frame !
   Trembling, hoping, lingering, flying,
   Oh, the pain, the bliss of dying !
Cease, fond Nature, cease thy strife,
And let me languish into life !

Hark ! they whisper ; angels say,
Sister spirit, come away !
   What is this absorbs me quite,
   Steals my senses, shuts my sight,
Drowns my spirit, draws my breath ?
Tell me, my soul, can this be death ?

The world recedes; it disappears!
Heaven opens on my eyes! my ears
  With sounds seraphic ring:
Lend, lend your wings! I mount! I fly!
O Grave! where is thy victory?
  O Death! where is thy sting?

ALEXANDER POPE.

JANUARY 11.

THE HEBREW TO HIS SOUL.

O THOU, who springest gloriously
  From thy Creator's fountain blest,
  Arise, depart, for this is not thy rest!
The way is long, thou must preparèd be,
  Thy Maker bids thee seek thy goal—
  Return then to thy rest, my soul,
For bountifully has God dealt with thee.

Behold! I am a stranger here,
  My days like fleeting shadows seem.
  When wilt thou, if not now, thy life redeem?
And when thou seek'st thy Maker have no fear,
  For if thou have but purified
  Thy heart from stain of sin and pride,
Thy righteous deeds to Him shall draw thee near.

O thou in strength who treadest, learn
  To know thyself, cast dreams away!
  The goal is distant far, and short the day.
What canst thou plead th' Almighty's grace to earn?
  Would thou the glory of the Lord
  Behold, O soul? with prompt accord
Then to thy Father's house, return, return!

JEHUDAH HALEVI.
(Trs. Mrs Henry Lucas.)

JANUARY 12.

VENI CREATOR SPIRITUS.

CREATOR SPIRIT, by whose aid
The world's foundations first were laid,
Come visit every pious mind ;
Come pour Thy joys on human kind,
From sin and sorrow set us free
And make Thy temples worthy Thee.
  O source of uncreated light,
Thy Father's promis'd Paraclete !
Thrice holy fount, thrice holy fire,
Our hearts with heavenly love inspire,
Come, and Thy sacred unction bring
To sanctify us while we sing.
  Plenteous of grace, descend from high
Rich in Thy sevenfold energy !
Thou strength of His Almighty hand
Whose power does heaven and earth command,
Proceeding Spirit, our defence,
Who dost the gift of tongues dispense,
And crown'st Thy gifts with eloquence !
  Refine and purge our earthly parts ;
But, oh, inflame and fire our hearts !
Our frailties help, our vice control,
Submit the senses to the soul :
And when rebellious they are grown,
Then lay Thy hand and hold them down.
Chase from our minds the infernal foe,
And peace, the fruit of love, bestow.
And lest our feet should step astray,
 Protect and guide us in the way.
  Make us eternal truths receive,
And practise all that we believe.

Give us Thyself, that we may see
The Father and the Son by Thee.
    Immortal honour, endless fame,
Attend the Almighty Father's name,
The Saviour Son be glorified
Who for lost man's redemption died ;
And equal adoration be,
Eternal Paraclete, to Thee.

JOHN DRYDEN.

JANUARY 13.

IN MEMORIAM.

THE One remains, the many change and pass ;
Heaven's light forever shines, Earth's shadows fly ;
Life, like a dome of many coloured glass,
Stains the white radiance of Eternity,
Until Death tramples it to fragments.   Die,
If thou wouldst be with that which thou dost seek !
Follow where all is fled ! Rome's azure sky,
Flowers, ruins, statues, music, words are weak
The glory they transfuse with fitting truth to speak.

Why linger, why turn back, why shrink, my Heart ?
Thy hopes are gone before : from all things here
They have departed : thou shouldst now depart !
A light is past from the revolving year,
And man and woman ; and what still is dear
Attracts to crush, repels to make thee wither.
The soft sky smiles,—the low wind whispers near ;
'Tis Adonais calls ! oh, hasten thither,
No more let Life divide what Death can join together.

That light whose smile kindles the Universe,
That Beauty in which all things work and move,
That Benediction which the eclipsing Curse
Of birth can quench not, that sustaining Love
Which through the web of being blindly wove
By man and beast and earth and air and sea,
Burns bright or dim, as each are mirrors of
The fire for which all thirst; now beams on me,
Consuming the last clouds of cold mortality.

The breath whose might I have invoked in song
Descends on me; my spirit's bark is driven
Far from the shore, far from the trembling throng
Whose sails were never to the tempest given;
The massy earth and spherèd skies are riven!
I am borne darkly, fearfully, afar;
Whilst burning through the inmost veil of Heaven,
The soul of Adonais, like a star,
Beacons from the abode where the Eternal are.

P. B. SHELLEY.

JANUARY 14.

DE PROFUNDIS.

O THOU Great Being! what Thou art
    Surpasses me to know:
Yet sure I am that known to Thee
    Are all Thy works below.

Thy creature here before Thee stands
    All wretched and distrest;
Yet sure those ills that wring my soul
    Obey Thy high behest.

Sure Thou, Almighty, canst not act
    From cruelty or wrath !
Oh, free my weary eyes from tears,
    Or close them fast in death !

But if I must afflicted be,
    To suit some wise design ;
Then man my soul with firm resolves
    To bear and not repine !

ROBERT BURNS.

JANUARY 15.

CALL NO MAN HAPPY TILL HIS DEATH.

MAN ought his future happiness to fear
If he be always happy here ;
He wants the bleeding mark of grace,
The circumcision of the chosen race.
If no one part of him supplies
The duty of a sacrifice,
He is (we doubt) reserv'd entire
As a whole victim for the fire.
Besides, ev'n in this world below,
To those who never did ill-fortune know,
The good does nauseous or insipid grow.
Consider man's whole life, and you'll confess
The sharp ingredient of some bad success
Is that which gives the taste to all his happiness.
But the true method of felicity
Is when the worst
Of human life is plac'd the first,
And when the child's correction proves to be
The cause of perfecting the man.
Let our weak days lead up the van ;

Let the brave second and Triarian band
Firm against all impression stand :
The first we may defeated see,
The virtue and the force of these are sure of victory.

ABRAHAM COWLEY.

JANUARY 16.

GRACIOUS GOD ! presumptuous man,
With random guesses, makes pretence
To sound Thy searchless providence,
From which he first began ; . . .
Thy patient thunder he defies,
Lays down false principles, and moves
By what his vicious choice approves,
And when he's vainly wicked thinks he's wise.
  Return, return, too long misled !
With filial fear adore thy God :
Ere the vast deep of heav'n was spread,
Or bodies first in space abode,
Glories ineffable adorned his head. . . .
  On the vast ocean of his wonders here,
We momentary bubbles ride,
Till, crush'd by the tempestuous tide,
Sunk in the parent flood we disappear :
We, who so gaudy on the waters shone,
Proud, like the showery bow, with beauties not our own.
  But, at the signal giv'n, this earth and sea
Shall set their sleeping vassals free,
And the belov'd of God,
The faithful and the just,
Like Aaron's chosen rod,
Tho' dry, shall blossom in the dust :
Then, gladly bounding from their dark restraints,
The skeletons shall brighten into saints,

And, from mortality refin'd, shall rise
To meet their Saviour coming in the skies.
Instructed then by intuition, we
Shall the vain efforts of our wisdom see;
Shall then impartially confess
Our demonstration was but guess;
That knowledge, which from human reason flows,
Unless Religion guides its course,
And Faith her steady mounds oppose,
Is ignorance at best, and often worse.

ELIJAH FENTON.

JANUARY 17.

O do not use me
After my sinnes! look not on my desert,
But on Thy glorie; then Thou wilt reform,
And not refuse me; for Thou onely art
The mighty God, but I a sillie worm:
        O, do not bruise me!

O do not urge me;
For what account can Thy ill steward make?
I have abus'd Thy flock, destroy'd Thy woods,
Suckt all Thy magazens; my head did ake,
Till it found out how to consume Thy goods:
        O, do not scourge me!

O, do not fill me
With the turn'd viall of Thy bitter wrath!
For Thou hast other vessels full of blood,
A part whereof my Saviour empti'd hath,
Ev'n unto death: since He died for my good,
        O, do not kill me!

But O, reprieve me !
For Thou hast life and death at Thy command ;
Thou art both Judge and Saviour, feast and rod,
Cordiall and corrosive : put not Thy hand
Into the bitter box ; but, O my God,
      My God, relieve me !

GEORGE HERBERT.

JANUARY 18.

THE PILGRIMAGE.

As travellers, when the twilight's come,
    And in the sky the stars appear,
The past day's accidents do summe,
    With "Thus wee saw there and thus here,"

Then, Jacob-like, lodge in a place—
    A place, and no more, is set down—
Where, till the day restore the race,
    They rest and dream homes of their own,

So for this night I linger here,
    And, full of tossings to and fro,
Expect still when Thou wilt appear
    That I may get me up and go.

I long and groan and grieve for Thee,
    For Thee my words, my tears do gush ;
Oh ! that I were but where I see !
    Is all the note within my bush.

As birds robbed of their native wood,
    Although their diet may be fine,
Yet neither sing nor like their food,
    But with the thought of home do pine ;

So do I mourn and hang my head,
  And, though Thou dost me fulness give,
Yet look I for far better bread,
  Because by this man cannot live.

O feed me then ! and since I may
  Have yet more days, more nights to count,
So strengthen me, Lord, all the way,
  That I may travel to Thy mount.

HENRY VAUGHAN.

JANUARY 19.

AVE.

MOTHER of the Fair Delight,
Thou handmaid perfect in God's sight,
Now sitting fourth beside the Three,
Thyself a woman—Trinity,—
Being a daughter born to God,
Mother of Christ from stall to rood,
And wife unto the Holy Ghost :—
Oh, when our need is uttermost,
Think that to such as death may strike,
Thou once wert sister, sister-like !
Thou headstone of humanity,
Groundstone of the great Mystery,
Fashioned like us, yet more than we ! . . .
  Soul, is it Faith, or Love or Hope
That lets me see Her standing up
Where the light of the Throne is bright ?
Unto the left, unto the right,
The cherubim, succinct, conjoint,
Float inward to a golden point,

And from between the seraphim
The glory issues for a hymn.
O Mary Mother, be not loth
To listen,—Thou whom the stars clothe,
Who seëst and mayst not be seen!
Hear us at last, O Mary Queen!
Into our shadow bend thy face,
Bowing thee from the secret place,
O Mary Virgin, full of grace!

W. M. ROSSETTI.

JANUARY 20.

SAINT AGNES' EVE.

DEEP on the convent-roof the snows
    Are sparkling to the moon:
My breath to heaven like vapour goes:
    May my soul follow soon!
The shadows of the convent-towers
    Slant down the snowy sward,
Still creeping with the creeping hours
    That lead me to my Lord;
Make Thou my spirit pure and clear
    As are the frosty skies,
Or this first snowdrop of the year
    That in my bosom lies.

As these white robes are soil'd and dark
    To yonder shining ground;
As this pale taper's earthly spark
    To yonder argent round;
So shows my soul before the Lamb,
    My spirit before Thee;
So in mine earthly house I am,
    To that I hope to be.

Break up the heavens, O Lord ! and far,
  Thro' all yon starlight keen,
Draw me, Thy bride, a glittering star,
  In raiment white and clean.

He lifts me to the golden doors,
  The flashes come and go ;
All heaven bursts her starry floors,
  And shows her lights below,
And deepens on and up ! the gates
  Roll back, and far within
For me the Heavenly Bridegroom waits,
  To make me pure of sin.
The sabbaths of Eternity—
  One sabbath deep and wide—
A light upon the shining sea—
  The Bridegroom with his bride.

ALFRED, LORD TENNYSON.

JANUARY 21.

Drop, drop, slow tears
  And bathe those beauteous feet
Which brought from Heaven
  The news and Prince of Peace :
Cease not, wet eyes,
  His mercies to entreat :
To cry for vengeance
  Sin doth never cease :
In your deep floods
  Drown all my faults and fears ;
Nor let his eye
  See sin, but through my tears.

PHINEAS FLETCHER.

SCEPTRE and Star divine,
  Who in Thine inmost shrine
Hast made us worshippers, O claim Thine own ;
  More than Thy seers we know—
  O teach our love to grow
Up to Thy heavenly light, and reap what Thou hast
  sown.
JOHN KEBLE.

JANUARY 22.

MEDITATION OF THE SAGE.

THE gusts of appetite, the clouds of care,
  And storms of disappointment, all o'erpast,
Henceforth no earthly hope with Heav'n shall share
  This heart, where peace serenely shines at last.
  And if for me no treasure be amass'd,
And if no future age shall hear my name,
  I lurk the more secure from fortune's blast,
And with more leisure feed this pious flame,
Whose rapture far transcends the fairest hopes of fame.

The end and the reward of toil is rest.
  Be all my prayer for virtue and for peace.
Of wealth and fame, of pomp and power possess'd,
  Who ever felt his weight of wo decrease ?
  Ah ! what avails the lore of Rome and Greece,
The lay heaven-prompted, and harmonious string,
  The dust of Ophir, or the Tyrian fleece,
All that art, fortune, enterprise can bring,
If envy, scorn, remorse, or pride the bosom wring ?

Let vanity adorn the marble tomb
  With trophies, rhymes, and scutcheons of renown,
In the deep dungeon of some Gothic dome,
  Where night and desolation ever frown.

Mine be the breezy hill that skirts the down;
Where a green grassy turf is all I crave,
  With here and there a violet bestrown,
Fast by a brook, or fountain's murmuring wave;
And many an evening sun shine sweetly on my grave.

And thither let the village swain repair;
  And, light of heart, the village maiden gay,
To deck with flowers her half-dishevel'd hair,
  And celebrate the merry morn of May.
  There let the shepherd's pipe the livelong day
Fill all the grove with love's bewitching wo;
  And when mild evening comes in mantle gray,
Let not the blooming band make haste to go;
No ghost, nor spell, my long and last abode shall know.

For tho' I fly to 'scape from Fortune's rage,
  And bear the scars of envy, spite, and scorn,
Yet with mankind no horrid war I wage,
  Yet with no impious spleen my breast is torn:
  For virtue lost, and ruin'd man, I mourn.
O man! creation's pride, Heav'n's darling child,
  Whom Nature's best, divinest gifts adorn,
Why from thy home are truth and joy exil'd,
And all thy favourite haunts with blood and tears
    defil'd?

Along yon glittering sky what glory streams!
  What majesty attends Night's lovely queen!
Fair laugh our valleys in the vernal beams;
  And mountains rise, and oceans roll between,
  And all conspire to beautify the scene.
But in the mental world, what chaos drear;
  What forms of mournful, loathsome, furious mien!
O when shall that eternal morn appear,
These dreadful forms to chase, this chaos dark to
    clear?

O Thou, at whose creative smile, yon Heaven,
  In all the pomp of beauty, life, and light
Rose from th' abyss; when dark Confusion, driven
  Down, down the bottomless profound of night,
  Fled, where he ever flies thy piercing sight!
O glance on these sad shades one pitying ray,
  To blast the fury of oppressive might,
Melt the hard heart to love and mercy's sway,
And cheer the wandering soul, and light him on the
    way.   JAMES BEATTIE.

JANUARY 23.

DANTE BESEECHES DEATH FOR THE LIFE OF BEATRICE.

DEATH, if indeed thou smite this gentle one
  Whose outward work but tells the intellect
    How wondrous is the intellect within,—
Thou biddest Virtue rise up and begone,
  Thou dost away with Mercy's best effect,
    Thou spoil'st the mansion of God's sojourning.
    Yea unto nought her beauty thou dost bring,
Which is above all other beauties, even
In so much as befitteth one whom Heaven
  Sent upon earth in token of its own.
Thou dost break through the perfect trust which hath
Been alway her companion in Love's path:
    The light once darkened which was hers alone,
Love needs must say to them he ruleth o'er,
" I have lost the noble banner that I bore."

Death, have some pity then for all the ill
  Which cannot choose but happen if she die,
    And which will be the sorest ever known.

Slacken the string, if so it be thy will,
  That the sharp arrow leave it not,—thereby
    Sparing her life, which if it flies is flown.
    O Death, for God's sake, be some pity shown!
Restrain within thyself, even at its height,
The cruel wrath which moveth thee to smite
    Her in whom God hath set so much of grace.
Show now some ruth, if 'tis a thing thou hast!
I seem to see Heaven's gate, that is shut fast,
    Open, and angels filling all the space
About me,—come to fetch her soul whose laud
Is sung by saints and angels before God.

           DANTE (*Trs.* by W. M. Rossetti).

JANUARY 24.

TO ADVERSITY.

DAUGHTER of Jove, relentless power,
  Thou tamer of the human breast,
Whose iron scourge and torturing hour
  The bad affright, afflict the best!
Bound in thy adamantine chain
The proud are taught to taste of pain,
And purple tyrants vainly groan
With pangs unfelt before, unpitied and alone. . . .

Oh! gently on thy suppliant's head,
  Dread goddess, lay thy chast'ning hand!
Not in thy Gorgon terrors clad,
  Not circled with the vengeful band
(As by the impious thou art seen);
With thundering voice and threatening mien,
With screaming Horror's funeral cry,
Despair and fell Disease and ghastly Poverty:

Thy form benign, O goddess, wear,
  Thy milder influence impart,
Thy philosophic train be there
  To soften, not to wound my heart.
The gen'rous spark extinct revive,
Teach me to love and to forgive,
Exact my own defects to scan,
What others are to feel and know myself a Man.

Thomas Gray.

JANUARY 25.

Weary of myself, and sick of asking
  What I am, and what I ought to be,
  At this vessel's prow I stand, which bears me
  Forwards, forwards o'er the starlit sea.
And a look of passionate desire
  O'er the sea and to the stars I send :
  'Ye who from my childhood up have calm'd
      me,
  Calm me, ah, compose me to the end !
'Ah, once more,' I cried, ' ye stars, ye waters,
  On my heart your mighty charm renew ;
  Still, still let me, as I gaze upon you,
  Feel my soul becoming vast like you ! '
From th' intense, clear, star-sown vault of heaven,
  Over the lit sea's unquiet way,
  In the rustling night-air came the answer :
  ' Wouldst thou *be* as these are ?   *Live* as they.
' Unaffrighted by the silence round them,
  Undistracted by the sights they see,
  These demand not that the things without
      them
  Yield them joy, amusement, sympathy.

'And with joy the stars perform their shining,
  And the sea its long moon-silver'd roll;
  For self-poised they live, nor pine with noting
  All the fever of some differing soul.
'Bounded by themselves, and unregardful
  In what state God's other works may be,
  In their own task all their powers pouring,
  These attain the mighty life you see.'
O air-born voice! long since, severely clear,
  A cry like thine in mine own heart I hear:
  'Resolve to be thyself; and know, that he
  Who finds himself, loses his misery!'

MATTHEW ARNOLD.

JANUARY 26.

[General Gordon died at Khartoum, 1885.]

" This is he
That every man in arms should wish to be."

WHO is the happy warrior? Who is he
That every man in arms should wish to be?
It is the generous spirit, who, when brought
Among the tasks of real life, hath wrought
Upon the plan that pleased his boyish thought:
Whose high endeavours are an inward light
That makes the path before him always bright:
Who, with a natural instinct to discern
What knowledge can perform, is diligent to learn;
Abides by this resolve, and stops not there,
But makes his moral being his prime care;
Who, doomed to go in company with Pain,
And Fear, and Bloodshed, miserable train!
Turns his necessity to glorious gain; . . .
More skilful in self-knowledge, even more pure,
As tempted more; more able to endure,

As more exposed to suffering and distress ;
Thence also more alive to tenderness. . . .
Who, if he rise to station of command,
Will rise by open means, and there will stand
On honourable terms, or else retire,
And in himself possess his own desire ; . . .
Whose powers shed round him in the common
        strife,
Or mild concerns of ordinary life,
A constant influence, a peculiar grace ;
But who, if he be called upon to face
Some awful moment, to which Heaven has joined
Great issues, good or bad, for humankind,
Is happy as a Lover ; and attired
With sudden brightness, like a Man inspired ; . .
He who, though thus endued as with a sense
And faculty for storm and turbulence,
Is yet a Soul whose master-bias leans
To home-felt pleasures and to gentle scenes ; . . .
Who, not content that former worth stand fast,
Looks forward, persevering to the last,
From well to better, daily self-surpast :
Who, whether praise of him must walk the earth
For ever, and to noble deeds give birth,
Or he must fall, and sleep without his fame,
And leave a dead unprofitable name—
Finds comfort in himself and in his cause ;
And, while the mortal mist is gathering, draws
His breath in confidence of Heaven's applause.

W. WORDSWORTH.

JANUARY 27.

LET US GO TO BETHLEHEM.

CARRY me, babe! to Bethlehem now,
  For I would look on Thee, my God!
Thou art alone my goal,—and Thou,
  Thou to that goal the only road.

From my deep slumbers bid me wake,
  Call me,—no evil shall betide me;
  Give me Thy heavenly hand to guide me,
And I shall not heaven's way mistake.
  So shall I straight to Bethlehem go,
    Where I shall look on Thee, my God!
Thou art alone my goal,—and Thou,
  Thou to that goal the only road.

Though I'm oppressed with want and woe,
  Though I am clad in garments torn,
  Though I'm a wanderer lost and lorn,
Guide me, my God! where'er I go!
  Bring me, I pray, to Bethlehem now,
    Where I may look on Thee, my God!
Thou art alone my goal,—and Thou,
  Thou to that goal my only road.

ANON.

(Trs. from the Spanish by Sir John Bowring.*)*

JANUARY 28.

THE POET'S PRAYER.

TO APOLLO ON THE PALATINE.

What is it that the Poet implores
The shrined Apollo, when he pours
  The first-fruits of the grape with prayer?
Not broad Sardinia's wealth of corn,
Nor herds from lush Calabria borne,
  Nor gold of Ind, nor ivory rare,
Nor orchards silent as the grave
Where Liris pours her greedy wave.
  Let others wield the pruning-knife,
And render lavish Fortune thanks
Who cast their lot on Cales' banks;
  And let the merchant owe his life
To Heaven itself, who boldly dares
To cross the ocean with his wares
  Some three or four times every year;
From golden goblets though he drain
The precious vintage of his gain,
  For me the price were all too dear.
Light olives feed me, and such fare
As my own garden-plot will bear;
  My present goods are my desire,
While strength remains, and I would find,
Latona's son, with stable mind,
  An honour'd eld and trusty lyre.

Horace (Trs. Editors).

JANUARY 29.

MERCY PRAYETH FOR MANKIND IN HEAVEN.

HE was but dust, why fear'd he not to fall?
  And being fall'n, how can he hope to live?
Cannot the hand destroy him, that made all?
  Could He not take away, as well as give?
  Should man deprave, and shall not God deprive?
  Was it not all the world's deceiving spirit,
  (That puffèd up with pride of his own merit,
Fell in his rise) that him of heav'n did disinherit?

He was but dust: how could he stand before him?
  And being fall'n, why should he fear to die?
Cannot the hand that made him first, restore him?
  Depraved by sin, should he deprivèd lie
  Of grace?—Can he not hide infirmity,
  Who gave him strength? Unworthy the forsaking
  He is, who ever weighs, without mistaking,
Or maker of the man, or manner of his making.

Who shall bring incense to Thy temple more?
  Or on Thy altar crown the sacrifice;
Or strew with idle flow'rs the hallow'd floor?
  Or why should prayer deck with herbs and spice
  Her vials, breathing orisons of price?
  If all must pay, that which all cannot pay,
  Oh! first begin with me, and Mercy flay.
And Thy thrice-honoured Son, who now beneath doth
    stray.

But if or He or I may live and speak,
  And heav'n rejoice to see a sinner weep,
Oh! let not Justice' iron sceptre break

A heart already broke ; that low doth creep,
And with humility her feet's dust doth sweep.
Must all go by desert ? is nothing free ?
Ah ! if but chose, who only worthy be,
None should Thee ever see, none should Thee ever see !

What hath man done, that man shall not undo,
 Since God to him is grown so near akin ?
Did his foe slay him ?　He shall slay his foe :
 Hath he lost all ?　He all again shall win :
 Is sin his master ?　He shall master sin ;
 Too hardy soul, with sin the field to try ;
 The only way to conquer, was to fly :
But thus long death hath liv'd, and now death's self
  shall die.

Christ is a path,—if any be misled ;
 He is a robe,—if any naked be ;
If any chance to hunger,—He is bread ;
 If any be a bondman, he is free ;
 If any be but weak,—how strong is He ?
 To dead men, life He is ; to sick men health ;
 To blind men, sight ; and to the needy, wealth ;
A pleasure without loss ;—a treasure without stealth.

GILES FLETCHER.

JANUARY 30.

[Execution of Charles I., 1649.]

THE VANITY OF KINGS.

   Of comfort no man speak ;
Let's talk of graves, of worms, and epitaphs ;
Make dust our paper, and with rainy eyes
Write sorrow on the bosom of the earth.

Let's choose executors, and make our wills :
And yet not so,—for what have we to bequeath
Save our deposèd bodies to the ground ?
Our lands, our lives, and all, are Bolingbroke's,
And nothing can we call our own but death,
And that small model of the barren earth
Which serves as paste and cover to our bones.
For God's sake, let us sit upon the ground
And tell sad stories of the death of kings,—
How some have been deposed, some slain in war,
Some haunted by the ghosts they have deposed,
Some poison'd by their wives, some sleeping killed,—
All murdered.—For within the hollow crown
That rounds the mortal temples of a king
Keeps Death his court ; and there the antic sits,
Scoffing his state, and grinning at his pomp,
Allowing him a breath, a little scene
To monarchize, be feared, and kill with looks,
Infusing him with self and vain conceit,
As if this flesh, which walls our mortal life,
Were brass impregnable,—and, humour'd thus,
Comes at the last, and with a little pin
Bores through his castle walls,—and farewell, king !
Cover your heads, and mock not flesh and blood
With solemn reverence ; throw away respect,
Tradition, form, and ceremonious duty,
For you have but mistook me all this while ;
I live with bread like you, feel want, taste grief,
Need friends ;—subjected thus,
How can you say to me—I am a king ?

WILLIAM SHAKESPEARE.

JANUARY 31.

PARAPHRASE.   ISAIAH XII.

O LIVING LORD, I still will laud Thy name,
  For though Thou wert offended once with me,
Thy heavy wrath is turned from me again,
  And graciously Thou now dost comfort me.

Behold, the Lord is my salvation,
  I trust in Him, and fear not any power:
He is my song, the strength I lean upon,
  The Lord God is my loving Saviour.

Therefore with joy out of the Well of Life
  Draw forth sweet water which it doth afford;
And in the day of trouble and of strife
  Call on the name of God, the living Lord.

Extol His works and wonders to the sun;
  Unto all people let His praise be shown:
Record in song the marvels He hath done,
  And let His glory through the world be blown.

Cry out aloud, and shout on Zion's hill,
  I give thee charge that this proclaimèd be:
The great and mighty King of Israel
  Now only dwelleth in the midst of thee.

MICHAEL DRAYTON.

C

FEBRUARY 1.

VENI CREATOR.

So humble things Thou hast borne for us, O God,
Left'st Thou a path of loneliness untrod ?
Yes, one, till now ; another Olive-Garden.
For we endure the tender pain of pardon,—
One with another we forbear.   Give heed,
Look at the mournful world Thou hast decreed.
The time has come.   At last we hapless men
Know all our haplessness all through.   Come, then,
Endure undreamed humility : Lord of Heaven,
Come to our ignorant hearts and be forgiven.

ALICE MEYNELL.

FEBRUARY 2.

ABOU BEN ADHEM.

ABOU BEN ADHEM (may his tribe increase !)
Awoke one night from a deep dream of peace,
And saw, within the moonlight in his room,
Making it rich, and like a lily in bloom,
An Angel writing in a book of gold :—
Exceeding peace had made Ben Adhem bold,
And to the Presence in the room he said,
" What writest Thou ? "—The Vision raised its head,
And with a look made of all sweet accord
Answer'd, " The names of those who love the Lord."

"And is mine one?" said Abou.　"Nay, not so,"
Replied the Angel.　Abou spake more low,
But cheerily still; and said, "I pray Thee, then,
Write me as one that loves his fellow-men."
　　The Angel wrote, and vanish'd.　The next night
It came again with a great wakening light,
And show'd the names whom love of God had bless'd,
And, lo! Ben Adhem's name led all the rest.

LEIGH HUNT.

FEBRUARY 3.

THE WISDOM OF THE EAST.

THE Moving Finger writes; and, having writ,
Moves on: nor all thy Piety nor Wit
　　Shall lure it back to cancel half a Line,
Nor all thy Tears wash out a Word of it.

And that inverted Bowl we call the Sky,
Whereunder crawling coop't we live and die,
　　Lift not thy hands to *It* for help—for It
Rolls impotently on as Thou or I. . . .

Oh Thou who didst with Pitfall and with Gin
Beset the Road I was to wander in,
　　Thou wilt not with Predestination round
Enmesh me, and impute my Fall to Sin?

Oh Thou who Man of baser Earth didst make,
And who with Eden didst devise the Snake;
　　For all the sin wherewith the Face of Man
Is blacken'd, Man's Forgiveness give—and take!

OMAR KHAYYÁM.
(*Trs.* E. Fitzgerald.)

FEBRUARY 4.

EARL BRYHTNOTH'S THANKSGIVING.

THANKS be to Thee, God,
Wielder of Nations,
Lord everlasting !
For all the joy of life
Winsome and wealthful,
Bairns' love and Wife's love,
Heart-trust of comrades,
War-weal and hearth-gear,
All I have here below
Fared for or gotten,
Now, oh my Maker mild,
Most need have I that Thou
Good-speed my ghost :
Yea, that my Soul to Thee
Safely may journey,
Safe to Thy Kingdom,
Lord of the Angels !

DEAN STUBBS.
(*From the Anglo-Saxon.*)

DREAD Searcher of the hearts,
Thou who didst seal by Thy descending Dove
Thy servants' choice, O help us in our parts,
Else helpless found, to learn and teach Thy love.

JOHN KEBLE.

FEBRUARY 5.

"*WHERE IS THY VICTORY?*"

THEY are all gone into the world of light !
    And I alone sit lingering here ;
Their very memory is fair and bright,
    And my sad thoughts doth clear.

It glows and glitters in my cloudy breast
    Like stars upon some gloomy grove,
Or those faint beams in which this hill is drest
    After the sun's remove.

I see them walking in an air of glory,
    Whose light doth trample on my days ;
My days, which are at best but dull and hoary,
    Mere glimmering and decays.

O holy Hope ! and high Humility,
    High as the heavens above !
These are your walks, and you have show'd them me
    To kindle my cold love.

Dear, beauteous Death ! the jewel of the just,
    Shining nowhere but in the dark ;
What mysteries do lie beyond thy dust
    Could man outlook that mark !

He that hath found some fledg'd bird's nest may know,
    At first sight, if the bird be flown ;
But what fair well or grove he sings in now,
    That is to him unknown.

And yet as angels in some brighter dreams
    Call to the soul, when man doth sleep:
So some strange thoughts transcend our wonted themes,
    And into glory peep. . . .

O Father of eternal life, and all
    Created glories under Thee !
Resume Thy spirit from this world of thrall
    Into true liberty.

Either disperse these mists, which blot and fill
    My perspective—still—as they pass ;
Or else remove me hence unto that hill
    Where I shall need no glass !

HENRY VAUGHAN.

FEBRUARY 6.

Γνῶθι σεαυτόν.

Let others proudly stand, and for a while,
    The giddy danger to beguile
With joy and with disdain, look down on all,
    Till their heads turn and down they fall.
Me, O ye Gods, on earth, or else so near
    That I no fall to earth may fear,
And, O ye Gods, at a good distance seat
    From the long ruins of the great.
Here, wrapt in the arms of Quiet, let me lie,
    Quiet, Companion of Obscurity !
Here let my life with as much silence slide
    As Time, that measures it, does glide ;
Nor let the breath of infamy or fame
    From town to town echo about my name.

Nor let my homely death embroidered be
  With scutcheon or with elegy.
    An old plebeian let me die,
Alas! all then are such as well as I.
    To him, alas, to him I fear
The face of death will terrible appear,
Who in his life flattering his senseless pride
By being known to all the world beside,
Does not himself, when he is dying, know,
Nor what he is nor whither he's to go.

SENECA.
(Trs. Abraham Cowley.)

FEBRUARY 7.

O LORD, Thy face I never saw,
  Nor ever heard Thy human voice:
My life beneath an iron law
  Moves on without my choice.

No memory of a happier time
  When in Thine arms, perchance, I slept,
In some lost ante-natal clime
  My mortal frame hath kept;

And all is dark—before—behind,
  I cannot reach Thee, where Thou art,
I cannot bring Thee to my mind,
  Nor clasp Thee to my heart.

And this is why, by night and day,
  Still with so many an unseen tear,
These lonely lips have learned to pray
  That God would spare me here,

While yet my doubtful course I go
    Along the vale of mortal years,
By Life's dull stream, that will not flow
    As fast as flow my tears,

One human hand, my hand to take,
    One human heart, my own to raise :
One loving human voice, to break
    The silence of my days.

Saviour, if this wild prayer be wrong,
    And what I seek I may not find,
Oh, make more hard and stern and strong
    The framework of my mind !

Or, nearer to me, in the dark
    Of life's low hours, one moment stand,
And give me keener eyes to mark
    The moving of Thy hand.

THE EARL OF LYTTON
(OWEN MEREDITH).

FEBRUARY 8.

A PARENT'S PRAYER.

OH, drinking deep of slumber's holy wine,
    Whence may the smile that lights thy countenance be ?
We seek in vain the mystery divine ;
    For in thy dim unconscious infancy
No games as yet, no play-fellows are thine,
    To stir in waking hours such thoughts of glee,
As recollected in thine innocent dream
Might shed across thy face a happy gleam.

It may be, though small notice thou canst take,
  'Thou feelest that an atmosphere of love
Is ever round thee, sleeping or awake :
  Thou wakest, and kind faces from above
Bend o'er thee—when thou sleepest, for thy sake
  All sounds are hush'd, and each doth gently move :
And this dim consciousness of tender care
Has caused thy cheek this light of joy to wear.

Or it may be thoughts deeper than we deem
  Visit an infant's slumbers—God is near,
Angels are talking to them in their dream,
  Angelic voices whispering sweet and clear ;
And round them lies that region's holy gleam,
  But newly left, and light which is not here :
And thus has come that smile upon thy face,
As tidings brought thee from thy native place.

But whatsoe'er the causes which beguiled
  That dimple on thy countenance, it is gone ;
Fair is the lake disturbed by ripple mild,
  And not less fair when ripple it has none :
And now what deep repose is thine, dear child,
  What smoothness thy unruffled cheek has won !
Oh ! who that gazed upon thee could forbear
The silent breathing of an heart-felt prayer ?

RICHARD CHENEVIX TRENCH.

FEBRUARY 9.

GOD, that madest earth and heaven,
  Darkness and light ;
Who the day for toil hast given,
  For rest the night—

May Thine angel-guards defend us ;
Slumbers sweet Thy mercy send us :
Holy dreams and hopes attend us,
    This livelong night.

Guard us waking, guard us sleeping ;
    And when we die,
May we in Thy mighty keeping
    All peaceful lie.
When the last dread trump shall wake us,
Do not Thou, O Lord, forsake us,
But to reign in glory take us
    With Thee on high.

ARCHBISHOP WHATELEY.

FEBRUARY 10.

O HOLY, blessed, glorious Trinitie
Of persons, still one God in unitie,
The faithful man's beleeved mysterie,
    Helpe, helpe to lift

Myselfe up to Thee, harrowéd, torne, and bruised
By sinne and Sathan : and my flesh misused,
As my heart lies in peeces, all confused,
    O take my gift,

All gracious God, the sinner's sacrifice.
A broken heart Thou wert not wont despise,
But 'bove the fat of rammes or bulls to prize
    An off'ring meet

For Thy acceptance. O, behold me right
And take compassion on my grievous plight.
What odour can be than a heart contrite
    To Thee more sweet ?

Eternall Father, God, who didst create
This All of nothing, gavest it forme and fate,
And breath'd into it life and light, with state
    To worship Thee.

Eternall God the Sonne, who not denyd'st
To take our nature : becam'st man and dyd'st
To pay our debts upon thy crosse and cryd'st
    " All's done in me."

Eternall Spirit, God from both proceeding,
Father and Sonne ; the Comforter, in breeding
Pure thoughts in man : with fiery zeale them feeding
    For acts of grace.

Increase those acts, O glorious Trinitie
Of persons, still one God in unitie,
Till I attain the long'd-for mysterie
    Of seeing your face,

Beholding one in three and three in one,
A Trinitie, to shine in unitie ;
The gladdest light darke man can thinke upon ;
    O grant it me !

Father and Sonne and Holy Ghost, you three
All coeternal in your majestie,
Distinct in persons, yet in unitie
    One God to see.

My Maker, Saviour, and my Sanctifier,
To heare, to meditate, and sweeten my desire
With grace, with love, with cherishing intire,
    O, then how blest ;

Among Thy saints elected to abide,
And with Thy angels placèd side by side,
But in Thy presence, truly glorified
    Shall I there rest ?

BEN JONSON.

FEBRUARY 11.

PARAPHRASE. PSALM CXXX.

From depth of sin, and from a deep despair,
  From depth of death, from depth of heart's sorrów,
From this deep cave of darkness deep repair,
  Thee have I called, O Lord! to be my borrów.
Thou in my voice, O Lord! perceive and hear
  My heart, my hope, my plaint, my overthrow,
My will to rise; and let, by grant, appear
  That to my voice Thine ears do well entend.
No place so far that to Thee is not near,
  No depth so deep that Thou ne mayst extend
Thine ear therto.   Hear, then, my woful plaint,
  For, Lord, if Thou do observe what men offend,
And put Thy native mercy in restraint,
  If just exaction demand reconipence,
Who may endure, O Lord! who shall not faint
  At such accompt? dread, and not reverence
Should so reign large: but Thou seek'st rather love;
  For in Thy hand is Mercy's residence,
By hope whereof Thou dost our heartés move.
  I in the Lord have set my confidence;
My soul such trust doth evermore approve.
  Thy Holy Word of eterne excellence,
Thy mercy's promise that is alway just,
  Have been my stay, my pillar, and pretence.
My soul in God hath more desirous trust
  Than hath the watchman looking for the day,
By the relief to quench of sleep the thrust.
  Let Israel trust unto the Lord alway;
For grace and favour are His property:
  Plenteous ransom shall come with Him, I say,
And shall redeem all our iniquity.

Sir Thomas Wyat.

FEBRUARY 12.

"THE EVENING AND THE MORNING WERE THE FIRST DAY."

O BLEST Creator of the light,
  Who, bringing forth the light of days,
With the first work of splendour bright
  The world didst to beginning raise ;

Who morn with evening join'd in one
  Commandedst should be call'd the day :
The foul confusion now is gone ;
  O hear us when with tears we pray :

Lest that the mind, with fears full fraught,
  Should lose best life's eternal gains,
While it hath no immortal thought,
  But is enwrapt in sinful chains.

O may it beat the inmost sky,
  And the reward of life possess !
May we from hurtful actions fly,
  And purge away all wickedness !

WILLIAM DRUMMOND of Hawthornden.

FEBRUARY 13.

SHALL I, for fear of feeble man,
Thy Spirit's course in me restrain ?
Or undismay'd in deed and word,
Be a true witness to my Lord ?

Awed by a mortal's frown, shall I
Conceal the Word of God most high?
How then before Thee shall I dare
To stand, or how Thy anger bear?

No; let man rage! since Thou wilt spread
Thy shadowing wings around my head:
Since in all pain Thy tender love
Will still my sweet refreshment prove.

Saviour of men! Thy searching eye
Does all my inmost thoughts descry:
Doth aught on earth my wishes raise?
Or the world's favour, or its praise?

The love of Christ does me constrain,
To seek the wand'ring souls of men:
With cries, entreaties, tears to save,
To snatch them from the gasping grave.

For this let men revile my name,
No cross I shun, I fear no shame:
All hail, reproach, and welcome pain!
Only Thy terrors, Lord, restrain.

My life, my blood I here present,
If for Thy truth they may be spent:
Fulfil Thy sov'reign counsel, Lord:
Thy will be done! Thy name ador'd!

Give me Thy strength, O God of power!
Then let winds blow, or thunders roar,
Thy faithful witness will I be—
'Tis fix'd! I can do all through Thee!

GEORGE WHITEFIELD.

FEBRUARY 14.

[St Valentine's Day.]

Love hath taught me to obey
All His precepts, and to say,
" Not to-morrow, but to-day."

What He wills, I say, " I must " ;
What I must, I say, " I will " ;
He commanding, it is just,
What He would, I should fulfil ;
Whilst He biddeth, I beleeve ;
What He calls for, He will give ;
To obey Him is—to live.

His commandments grievous are not
Longer than men think them so ;
Though He send me forth, I care not,
Whilst He gives me strength to goe.
When or whither, all is one ;
On His bus'nesse, not mine owne,
I shall never goe alone.

If I be compleat in Him,—
And in Him all fulnesse dwelleth,—
I am sure aloft to swim
Whilst that ocean overswelleth ;
Having Him that's All in All,
I am confident I shall
Nothing want for which I call.

Christopher Harvey.

FEBRUARY 15.

Eternal Scheme,
　　Great Lord of all,
　　August, Supreme,
　　Prostrate we fall,
We cannot know Thy working, nor its end,
Nor by what hidden paths Thy Perfect Will may tend.

　　But if one word
　　　　Might come, or sign,
　　Our souls were stirred
　　　　To growths divine,
No longer should we walk in fear and doubt,
Like children in dark ways, before the stars come out.

　　Ah no ! the word
　　　　The soul can hear
　　Is only heard
　　　　By the inner ear,
No outward light it is which can illume
The spiritual eye, and pierce the enshrouding gloom.

　　An inborn light,
　　　　An inner voice,
　　Which burneth bright,
　　　　Which doth rejoice,
A Faith in things unseen, an inward sight
Which through a wrecked world sees the victory of
　　Right.

　　With this our guide,
　　　　Our strength, our stay,
　　No more aside
　　　　Our footsteps stray.
Fulfil Thyself, Great Scheme, Eternal Plan,
Work out—we ask no word—the Destiny of Man.

　　　　　　　　　　Sir Lewis Morris.

FEBRUARY 16.

BENEDICTION.

My God, how endless is Thy love !
Thy gifts are every evening new;
And morning mercies from above
Gently distil the early dew.

Thou spread'st the curtains of the night,
Great Guardian of my sleeping hours ;
Thy sovereign word restores the light,
And quickens all my drowsy pow'rs.

I yield my pow'rs to Thy command,
To Thee I consecrate my days ;
Perpetual blessings from Thine hand
Demand perpetual songs of praise.

Isaac WATTS.

FEBRUARY 17.

Dear Jesus, give me patience here,
And faith to see my crown as near,
And almost reached, because 'tis sure,
If I hold fast, and slight the lure.
Give me humility and peace,
Contented thoughts, innoxious ease,
A sweet, revengeless, quiet minde,
And, to my greatest haters, kinde.
Give me, my God ! a heart as milde
And plain as when I was a childe.
That when "Thy throne is set" and all
These "conquerors" before it fall,

I may be found, preserved by Thee,
Amongst that chosen company,
Who by no blood—here—overcame
But the blood of the blessed Lamb.

HENRY VAUGHAN.

FEBRUARY 18.

To Mercy, Pity, Peace, and Love
 All pray in their distress,
And to these virtues of delight
 Return their thankfulness.

For Mercy, Pity, Peace, and Love
 Is God our Father dear ;
And Mercy, Pity, Peace, and Love
 Is man, His child and care.

For Mercy has a human heart,
 Pity a human face ;
And Love, the human form divine,
 And Peace, the human dress.

Then every man, of every clime,
 That prays in his distress,
Prays to the human form divine :
 Love, Mercy, Pity, Peace.

And all must love the human form,
 In heathen, Turk, or Jew.
Where Mercy, Love, and Pity dwell,
 There God is dwelling too.

WILLIAM BLAKE.

FEBRUARY 19.

THE PALACE OF MAN.

My God, I heard this day
That none doth build a stately habitation
  But he that means to dwell therein.
  What house more stately hath there been,
Or can be, than is Man? to whose creation
    All things are in decay.

    For Man is ev'rything,
And more: he is a tree, yet bears more fruit;
  A beast, yet is, or should be, more:
  Reason and speech we only bring:
Parrots may thank us if they are not mute,
    They go upon the score.

    Man is all symmetry,
Full of proportions, one limb to another,
  And all to all the world besides;
  Each part may call the farthest brother,
For head with foot hath private amity,
    And both with moons and tides.

    Nothing hath got so far
But Man hath caught and kept it as his prey;
  His eyes dismount the highest star;
  He is in little all the sphere;
Herbs gladly cure our flesh, because that they
    Find their acquaintance there.

    For us the winds do blow,
The earth resteth, heaven moveth, fountains flow;
  Nothing we see but means our good,
  As our delight or as our treasure;
The whole is either our cupboard of food
    Or cabinet of pleasure.

The stars have us to bed,
Night draws the curtain, which the sun withdraws;
    Music and light attend our head;
    All things unto our flesh are kind
In their descent and being, to our mind
        In their ascent and cause.

    Each thing is full of duty:
Waters united are our navigation;
    Distinguishéd, our habitation;
    Below, our drink; above, our meat;
Both are our cleanliness.   Hath one such beauty?
        Then how are all things neat!

    More servants wait on Man
Than he'll take notice of: in every path
    He treads down that which doth befriend him
    When sickness makes him pale and wan.
O mighty love! Man is one world, and hath
        Another to attend him.

    Since then, my God, Thou hast
So brave a palace built, O dwell in it,
    That it may dwell with Thee at last!
    Till then afford us so much wit,
That, as the world serves us, we may serve Thee,
        And both Thy servants be.
                    GEORGE HERBERT.

FEBRUARY 20.

PRAYER FOR PRAYER.

Now, dear Priest, I pray thee,
For Goddés love, thou pray for me,
More I pray that thou me myng [1]
In thy mass when thou dost sing;

---

[1] Remember.

And yet I pray thee, levé [1] brother,
Read this oft, and so let other;
Hide it not in hodymoke, [2]
Let other mo readé this boke;
The mo therein doth read and learn
The mo to meed it shalé turn;
It is i-madé them to shown
That have no bookés of their own,
And others that beth of mean lore
That woldé fain conné more;
And thou that herein learnest most
Thanke trierné the Holy Ghost,
That giveth wit to eaché mon
To do the godé that he con,
And by his travail and his deed
Giveth him Heaven to his meed.
The meed and the joy of Heaven light
God us granté for his might.

JOHN MIRK.

FEBRUARY 21.

'Tis but vanity and folly
On the world to settle wholly.
All the joys of all this life
Are but toys, annoys, and strife.
O God, only wise and stable,
   To establish me in Thee,
Give me, Thou that art all-able,
   Wisdom with true constancy.

JOSHUA SYLVESTER.

1 Dear.   2 Confusion.

FEBRUARY 22.

I cannot do an act which Earth disdains not ;
I cannot think a thought which Earth corrupts not ;
I cannot speak a word which Earth profanes not ;
I cannot make a vow Earth interrupts not :
If I but offer up an early groan,
Or spread my wings to Heaven's long longed-for throne,
She darkens my complaints, and drags my off'ring down.

E'en like the hawk, whose keeper's wary hands
Have made a pris'ner to her weath'ring stock,
Forgetting quite the pow'r of her fast bands,
Makes a rank bate [1] from her forsaken block ;
But her too faithful leash doth soon retain
Her broken flight, attempted oft in vain ;
It gives her loins a twitch, and tugs her back again.

So, when my soul directs her better eye
To Heaven's bright palace, where my treasure lies,
I spread my willing wings, but cannot fly ;
Earth holds me down—I cannot, cannot rise :
When I but strive to mount the least degree,
Earth gives a jerk, and foils me on my knee ;
Lord, how my soul is racked betwixt the World and
    Thee !

Great God, I spread my feeble wings in vain ;
In vain I offer my extended hands ;
I cannot mount till Thou unlock my chain ;
I cannot come till Thou release my bands ;
Which if Thou please to break, and then supply
My wings with spirit, th' eagle shall not fly
A pitch that's half so fair, nor half so swift as I.

FRANCIS QUARLES.

[1] Beating of the wings for flight.

FEBRUARY 23.

THE BROTHER'S FAREWELL.

By many peoples, many waters pass'd,
Brother, I stand by thy sad tomb at last,

To crown thee with the final dues of death,
And stir thy silent dust with empty breath;

For Fate hath parted me from thee, from thee,
Alas, poor Brother! filched away from me.

But ere I go, take, in our fathers' wise,
These gloomy funerals my rainy eyes

With many tears have moisten'd thro' and thro',
And ever, Brother, fare thee well.   Adieu,
                    Adieu!
              CATULLUS (*Trs.* Editors).

FEBRUARY 24.

"WHERE THE WICKED CEASE FROM TROUBLING."

THOUGH to the vilest things beneath the moon
For poor Ease' sake I give away my heart,
And for the moment's sympathy let part
My sight and sense of truth, Thy precious boon,
My painful earnings lost, all lost, as soon,
Almost, as gained; and though aside I start,
Belie Thee daily, hourly—still Thou art,
Art surely as in heaven the sun at noon;

How much soe'er I sin, whate'er I do
Of evil, still the sky above is blue,
The stars look down in beauty as before:
It is enough to walk as best we may,
To walk and sighing dream of that blest day
When ill we cannot quell shall be no more.

A. H. CLOUGH.

FEBRUARY 25.

TO KEEP A TRUE LENT.

Is this a fast, to keep
    The larder lean?
      And clean
From fat of veals and sheep?

Is it to quit the dish
    Of flesh, yet still
      To fill
The platter high with fish?

Is it to fast an hour,
    Or ragg'd to go,
      Or show
A downcast look and sour?

No: 'tis a fast to dole
    Thy sheaf of wheat,
      And meat,
Unto the hungry soul.

It is to fast from strife,
From old debate
And hate ;
To circumcise thy life.

To show a heart grief-rent ;
To starve thy sin,
Not bin ;
And that's to keep thy Lent.

R. HERRICK.

FEBRUARY 26.

TO GOD, MY GOD.

SINCE I am coming to that holy room
  Where with the quire of saints for evermore
I shall be made Thy music ; as I come,
  I tune the instrument here at the door,
  And what I must do then, think here before.

Whilst my physicians by their lore are grown
  Cosmographers, and I their map, who lie
Flat on this bed, that by them may be shown
  That this is my south-west discovery—
  Per fretum febris—by these straits to die :

I joy, that in those straits I see my West,
  For though those currents yield return to none,
What shall my West hurt me ?   As west and east
  In all flat maps (and I am one) are one,
  So death doth touch the Resurrection.

Is the Pacific Sea my home ? or are
  The eastern riches ? is Jerusalem ?
Anyan and Magellan and Gibraltar are
  All straits, and none but straits are ways to them,
  Whether where Japhet dwelt or Ham or Shem.

We think that Paradise and Calvarie,
  Christ's cross and Adam's tree, stood in one place :
Look, Lord, and find both Adams met in me !
  As the first Adam's sweat surrounds my face,
  May the last Adam's blood my soul embrace.

So, in His purple wrapp'd, receive me, Lord !
  By these His thorns, give me His other crown !
And as to others' souls I preached Thy Word,
  Be this my text, my sermon to mine own :—
  Therefore that He may raise, the Lord throws down.

JOHN DONNE.

FEBRUARY 27.

LA CONVALESCENCE D'ÉZÉCHIAS.

I HAVE seen this life of tears
  Toward its night declining ;
At the high noon of my years
  Dimly my sun was shining.
For lo ! gaunt Death his wings outspread,
And straight, with their eternal shade,
  Cloaked the light that I adore.
And in the darkness of that night
I sought in vain the vanished light
  Of the days that were no more.

God! has Thy hand requirèd
  The guerdon I was winning?
Yea! it comes to slit the thread
  Of life that it was spinning!
See, for me the last sun riseth!
For I am hurried by Thy breath
  From my happy home, the world,
And, like a lone leaf, witherèd,
That from the living stem is shed,
  Plaything of the winds, am hurl'd.

Thus, with cries and coward fears
  My sickness seems increasing,
And my eyes, that swim with tears,
  To open now are ceasing.
And to the gloomy night I call,
"O Night, within thy sombre pall
  Thou'lt envelope me always."
And loud I cry unto the morn,
"This, the day that now is born,
  Is the last day of my days!"

My senses are benumbed with fear,
  My soul in darkness crying,
Answer, just God, hear, O hear!
  I call upon Thee, dying!
Oh God! at last Thy hand it is
Has saved me from the precipice
  Yawning sheer beneath my feet.
Thy succour gives me back my life,
And yields my soul, amid the strife
  Fought with Death, a comfort sweet.

J.-B. Rousseau (Trs. Editors).

FEBRUARY 28.

Lord, what am I ?   A worm, dust, vapour, nothing !
  What is my life ?   A dream, a daily dying !
What is my flesh ?   My soul's uneasie clothing !
  What is my time ?   A minute ever flying !
    My time, my flesh, my life, and I :
    What are we, Lord, but vanity ?

Where am I, Lord ?   Downe in a vale of Death :
  What is my trade ?   Sin my dear God offending :
My sport sin, too ; my stay a puffe of breath :
  What end of sin ?   Hell's horrour never ending :
    My way, my trade, sport, stay and place
    Help up to make my doleful case.

Lord, what art Thou ? pure life, power, beauty, bliss :
  Where dwell'st Thou ? up above in perfect light :
What is Thy time ? eternity it is :
  What state ? attendance of each glorious spirit :
    Thyself, Thy place, Thy dayes, Thy state
    Pass all the thoughts of powers create.

How shall I reach Thee, Lord ?   Oh, soar above,
  Ambitious soul !   But which way should I flie ?
Thou, Lord, art way and end.   What wings have I ?
  Aspiring thoughts of faith, of hope, of love,
    Oh, let these wings that way alone
    Present me to Thy blissful throne.

BISHOP HALL.

FEBRUARY 29.

A HEBREW PRAYER.

O Lord, I call on Thee when sore dismayed,
And Thou wilt hear my voice and lend me aid,
Nor shall I be of myriads afraid,
    For Thou wilt ever be
The portion of my lot,—Thou savest me.

In troubled times Thy mercy's plenteous store
Is full to overflowing evermore,
And when in straitness I my plaint outpour,
    With words entreating Thee,
Then with enlargement Thou dost answer me.

Make known Thy love to those that trust and pray,
To those who hold Thy name their keep and stay,
Waiting for Thy salvation day by day.
    Yea, who, O Lord, but Thee,
Shall make me glad, who else deliver me?

Do Thou from heavenly heights my pain behold,
And lead me back unto Thy sheltering fold,
That I may answer scorners as of old:
    Yea, though my dwelling be
In darkest night, God is a light to me.

ABRAHAM IBN EZRA.
(*Trs.* Mrs Henry Lucas.)

MARCH 1.

[St David's Day.]

I ADORE the Supreme, Lord of all animation—
Him that supports the Heavens, Ruler of every extreme,
Him that made the water good for all,
Him that has bestowed each gift and blesses it ;—
May abundance of mead be given to Maelgwn of
    Anglesey, who supplies us,
From his foaming meadhorns, with the choicest pure
    liquor.
Since bees collect and do not enjoy,
We have sparkling distilled mead, which is universally
    praised.
The multitude of creatures which the earth nourishes
God made for man with a view to enrich him ;—
Some are violent, some are mute : He enjoys them ;
Some are wild, some are tame : the Lord makes
    them ;—
Part of their produce becomes clothing ;
For food and beverage till doom will they continue.
I entreat the Supreme, Sovereign of the region of peace,
To liberate Elphin from banishment,
The man who gave me wine and ale and mead,
With large princely steeds, of beautiful appearance :
May he yet give me : and at the end
May God of His good will grant me, in honour,
A succession of numberless ages, in the retreat of
    tranquillity.
Elphin, knight of mead, late be thy dissolution !

TALIESIN (Trs. from the Welsh by
Lady Charlotte Guest).

MARCH 2.

"FOR THOU ART WITH ME, I WILL NOT FEAR."

O MAY my constant feet not fail
Walking in paths of righteousness,
Sinless in word and deed—
True to those eternal laws
That scale forever the high steep
Of heaven's pure ether, whence they sprang :
For only in Olympus is their home,
Nor mortal wisdom gave them birth,
And, howsoe'er men may forget,
They will not sleep ;
For the might of the God within them grows not old.
Rooted in pride the tyrant grows :
But pride that with its own too-much
Is rashly surfeited,
Heeding not the prudent mean,
Down the inevitable gulf
From its high pinnacle is hurled,
Where use of feet or foothold there is none.
But, O kind gods, the noble strength,
That struggles for the state's behoof,
Unbend not yet :
In the gods have I put my trust—I will not fear.

SOPHOCLES.
(*Trs.* R. Whitelaw.)

MARCH 3.

AGNUS DEI, QUI TOLLIS PECCATA MUNDI.

O Lamb of God, that takest away the sins of the world,
  Give me peace, give me peace !
The mists are round me, rolled and curled,
  The dark and dangers of the way increase.
    I cannot pray,
      Pray as of old.
  My thoughts are like a flock astray,
  Wilt Thou not call them back,
  Back to the heavenly track,
    Unto the trodden pathway of Thy fold ?
  Bid these strange tumults cease !
    Thyself upon my heart enthrone !
    Make me Thine own, Thine own !
  Give me peace, give me peace !

ALFRED AUSTIN.

MARCH 4.

THE MEDIATION OF CHRIST IN HEAVEN.

Father, Thy word is passed, Man shall find grace ;
And shall Grace not find means, that finds her way,
The speediest of Thy wingèd messengers,
To visit all Thy creatures, and to all
Comes unprevented, unimplored, unsought ?
Happy for Man, so coming !   He her aid
Can never seek, once dead in sins and lost—
Atonement for himself, or offering meet,
Indebted and undone, hath none to bring.

Behold *me*, then : me for him, life for life,
I offer ; on me let Thine anger fall ;
Account me Man : I for his sake will leave
Thy bosom, and this glory next to Thee
Freely put off, and for him lastly die
Well pleased ; on me let Death wreak all his rage.
Under his gloomy power I shall not long
Lie vanquished.   Thou hast given me to possess
Life in myself for ever ; by Thee I live ;
Though now to Death I yield, and am his due,
All that of me can die, yet, that debt paid,
Thou wilt not leave me in the loathsome grave
His prey, nor suffer my unspotted soul
For ever with corruption there to dwell ;
But I shall rise victorious, and subdue
My vanquisher, spoiled of his vaunted spoil.
Death his death's wound shall then receive, and stoop
Inglorious, of his mortal sting disarmed ;
I through the ample air in triumph high
Shall lead Hell captive maugre Hell, and show
The powers of Darkness bound.   Thou, at the sight
Pleased, out of Heaven shalt look down and smile,
While, by Thee raised, I ruin all my foes—
Death last, and with his carcase glut the grave ;
Thou, with the multitude of my redeemed,
Shall enter Heaven, long absent, and return,
Father, to see Thy face, wherein no cloud
Of anger shall remain, but peace assured
And reconcilement : wrath shall be no more
Thenceforth, but in Thy presence joy entire.

JOHN MILTON.

E

MARCH 5.

GREAT Prince of Shepherds, than Thy heavens more
  high,
 Low as our earth, here serving, ruling there ;
Who taught'st our death to live, Thy life to die ;
 Who, when we broke Thy bonds, our bonds wouldst
   bear ;
  Who reignedst in Thy heaven, yet felt'st our
   hell ;
  Who (God) bought'st man, whom man (tho'
   God) did fell,
Who in our flesh, our graves, and, worse, our hearts,
  wouldst dwell.

Great Prince of Shepherds, Thou who late didst deign
 To lodge Thyself within this wretched breast
(Most wretched breast, such guest to entertain,
 Yet oh most happy lodge in such a guest !)
  Thou first and last, inspire Thy sacred skill ;
  Guide Thou my hand, grace Thou my artless
   quill ;
So shall I first begin, so last shall end Thy will.

       PHINEAS FLETCHER.

MARCH 6.

KING JOVINIAN PRAYETH:

" Create a fresh heart within us, O Lord !"

O LORD GOD, give me back myself again !
E'en if therewith I needs must die straightway.
Indeed I know that since upon this earth
I first did go, I ever day by day

Have grown the worse, who was of little worth
E'en at the best time since my helpless birth. . . .
Why am I hated so of everyone?
Wilt Thou not let me live my life again,
Forgetting all the deeds that I have done,
Forgetting my old name, and honours vain,
That I may cast away this lonely pain?
Yet if Thou wilt not, help me in this strife,
That I may pass my little span of life,
Not made a monster by unhappiness.
What shall I say?   Thou mad'st me weak of will,
Thou wrapped'st me in ease and carelessness,
And yet, as some folk say, Thou lov'st me still:
Look down! of folly I have had my fill,
And am but now as first Thou madest me,
Weak, yielding clay to take impress of Thee.

WILLIAM MORRIS.

MARCH 7.

A PSALM FOR THE SONS OF KORAH.

How amiable are thy tabernacles, O Lord of Hosts!

My soul longeth, yea, even fainteth, for the courts of the Lord; my heart and my flesh cryeth out for the living God.

Yea, the sparrow hath found an house, and the swallow a nest for herself, where she may lay her young, even thine altars, O Lord of Hosts, my King and my God.

Blessed are they that dwell in thy house: they will be still praising thee.

Blessed is the man whose strength is in thee; in whose heart are the ways of them:

Who passing through the valley of Baca make it a
well; the rain also filleth the pools.

They go from strength to strength; every one of them
in Zion appeareth before God.

O Lord God of Hosts, hear my prayer; give ear,
O God of Jacob.

Behold, O God, our shield, and look upon the face
of thine anointed.

For a day in thy courts is better than a thousand.
I had rather be a doorkeeper in the house of my God,
than to dwell in the tents of wickedness.

For the Lord God is a sun and shield: the Lord will
give grace and glory: no good thing will he withhold
from them that walk uprightly.

O Lord of Hosts, blessed is the man that trusteth in
thee.

Psalm LXXXIV.

TO THE PSALMIST.

O servant of God's holiest charge,
The minister of praise at large,
  Which thou may'st now receive;
From thy blessed mansion hail and hear,
From topmost eminence appear
  To this the wreath I weave.

Christopher Smart.

MARCH 8.

AN ACT OF HOPE.

Sweet Hope is soveraigne comfort of our life :
Our joy in sorrow and our peace in strife ;
The dame of beggers and the queene of kings :
Can these delight in height of prosperous things
Without expecting still to keep them sure ?
Can those the weight of heavy wants endure
Unless persuasion instant paine allay,
Reserving spirit for a better day ?
Our God, who planted in His creature's brest
This stop, on which the wheeles of passion rest,
Hath rays'd, by beames of His abundant grace,
This strong affection to a higher place.
It is the second vertue which attends
That soule, whose motion to His sight ascends.
Rest here, my mind, thou shalt no longer stay
To gaze upon these houses made with clay :
Thou shalt not stoope to honours or to lands,
Nor golden balles, where sliding fortune stands ;
If no false colours draw thy steps amisse,
Thou hast a palace of eternal blisse,
A paradise from care and feare exempt,
An object worthy of the best attempt.
Who would not for so rich a country fight ?
Who would not runne that sees a goal so bright ?
O Thou, who art our Author and our End,
On whose large mercy chaines of hope depend ;
Lift me to Thee by Thy propitious hand,
For lower I can find no place to stand.

Sir John Beaumont.

MARCH 9.

PRAYER TO THE HOLY SPIRIT.

O LIVING Spirit, O falling of God-dew,
O grace which does console us and renew,
O vital light, O breath of angelhood,
O generous ministration of things good,
Creator of the visible, and best
Upholder of the great unmanifest
Power infinitely wise, new boon sublime
Of science and of art, constraining might,
In whom I breathe, live, speak, rejoice, and write,—
Be with us in all places, for all time !

MANUEL PHILE.
(*Trs.* E. Barrett Browning.)

MARCH 10.

DE PROFUNDIS.

Out of my soule's depth to Thee my cryes have
    sounded :
Let Thine eares my plaints receive, on just feare
    grounded.
Lord, shouldst Thou weigh our faults, who's not
    confounded ?

But with grace Thou censur'st Thine when they have
    erred,
Therefore shall Thy blessed Name be lov'd and feared.
Ev'n to Thy throne my thoughts and eyes are reared.

Thee alone my hopes attend, on Thee relying;
In Thy sacred word Ile trust, to Thee fast flying,
Long ere the watch shall breake, the morne descrying.

In the mercies of our God who live secured,
May of full redemption rest in Him assured;
Their sinne-sicke soules by Him shall be recured.

DR THOMAS CAMPION.

MARCH 11.

O THOU! the unseen, the all-seeing! Thou whose
    ways
Mantled with darkness mock all finite gaze,
Before whose eyes the creatures of Thy hand,
Seraph and man, alike in weakness stand,
And countless ages, trampling into clay
Earth's empires on their march, are but a day;
Father of worlds unknown, unnumbered! Thou
With whom all time is one eternal *now*,
Who know'st no past nor future — Thou whose
    breath
Goes forth and bears to myriads life or death,
Look on us, guide us! wanderers of a sea
Wild and obscure, what are we, reft of Thee?
A thousand rocks, deep hid, elude our sight,
A star may set—and we are lost in night:
A breeze may waft us to the whirlpool's brink,
A treacherous song allure us—and we sink!
Oh! by His love who, veiling Godhead's light,
To moments circumscribed the Infinite,
And Heaven and earth disdained not to ally
By that dread union—Man with Deity;
Immortal tears o'er mortal woes who shed,
And, ere He raised them, wept above the dead;

Save, or we perish !   Let Thy word control
The earthquakes of that universe—the soul ;
Pervade the depths of passion—speak once more
The mighty mandate, guard of every shore,
" Here shall thy waves be stayed " in grief, in pain
The fearful poise of reason's sphere maintain,
Thou, by whom suns are balanced !—Thus secure
In Thee shall Faith and Fortitude endure :
Conscious of Thee, unfaltering shall the just
Look upward still, in high and holy trust,
And, by affliction guided to Thy shrine,
The first, last thoughts of suffering hearts be Thine.

Mrs Hemans.

MARCH 12.

AN HYMNE OF HEAVENLY BEAUTIE.

Vouchsafe, then, O Thou most Almightie spright !
From whom all guifts of wit and knowledge flow,
To shed into my breast some sparkling light
Of Thine eternall truth, that I may show
Some little beames to mortall eyes below
Of that immortal Beautie, there with Thee,
Which in my weak distraughted mynd I see ;

That with the glorie of so goodly sight
The hearts of men, which fondly here admyre
Faire seeming showes and feed on vaine delight,
Transported with celestiall desyre
Of those faire formes, may lift themselves up hyer,
And learne to love, with zealous humble dewty,
Th' Eternall Fountaine of that heavenly Beauty.

Then looke, who list thy gazefull eyes to feed
With sight of that is faire, looke on the frame
Of this wyde universe, and therein reed
The endlesse kinds of creatures which by name
Thou canst not count, much less their natures aime ;
All which are made with wondrous wise respect
And all with admirable Beautie deckt.

These thus in faire each other farre excelling,
As to the Highest they approach more near,
Yet is that Highest farre beyond all telling,
Fairer than all the rest which there appeare,
Though all their beauties joyned together weare ;
How then can mortall tongue hope to expresse
The image of such endlesse perfectnesse ?

Cease then, my tongue, and lend unto my mynd
Leave to bethinke how great that Beautie is,
Whose utmost parts so beautifull I fynd ;
How much more those essentiall parts of His,
His truth, His love, His wisedome, and His blis,
His grace, His doome, His mercy, and His might,
By which He lends us of Himselfe a sight !

Those unto all He daily doth display
And shew Himselfe in th' image of His grace,
As in a looking-glasse, through which He may
Be seene of all His creatures vile and base,
That are unable else to see His face,
His glorious face ! which glistereth else so bright,
That th' angels selves can not endure His sight !

But we, fraile wights ! whose sight cannot sustaine
The sun's bright beames when he on us doth shyne,
But that their points rebutted backe againe
Are duld, how can we see with feeble eyne
The glory of that Maiestie Divine,
In sight of whom both sun and moone are darke,
Compared to His least resplendent sparke ?

The meanes, therefore, which unto us is lent
Him to behold, is on His workes to looke,
Which He hath made in beauty excellent,
And in the same, as in a brasen booke,
To read enregistred in every nooke
His goodnesse, which His Beautie doth declare;
For all that's good is beautifull and faire.

EDMUND SPENSER.

MARCH 13.

A PRAYER IN JOY OR GRIEF.

IF the soft hand of winning Pleasure leads
By living waters, and through flowery meads,
Where all is smiling, tranquil, and serene,
And vernal beauty paints the flattering scene,
O ! teach me to elude each latent snare,
And whisper to my sliding heart,—Beware !
With caution let me hear the Siren's voice,
And, doubtful, with a trembling heart rejoice.
    If friendless in a vale of tears I stray,
Where briars wound, and thorns perplex my way,
Still let my steady soul Thy goodness see,
And, with strong confidence, lay hold on Thee;
With equal eye my various lot receive,
Resign'd to die, or resolute to live;
Prepared to kiss the sceptre or the rod,
While God is seen in all, and all in God.

ANNA LETITIA BARBAULD.

MARCH 14.

IN MEMORIAM.

Thou that know'st for whom I mourne
   And why these teares appeare,
That keep'st account till he returne
   Of all his dust left here,
As easily Thou might'st prevent
   As now produce, these teares,
And add unto that day he went
   A faire supply of yeares.
But 'twas my sin that forced Thy hand
   To cull this primrose out,
That by Thy early choice forewarned
   My soule might look about.
O what a vanity is man !
   How like the eye's quick winke
His cottage failes ; whose narrow span
   Begins even at the brink !
Nine months Thy hands are fashioning us,
   And many yeares, alas !
Ere we can lisp or aught discusse
   Concerning Thee, must pass :
Yet have I knowne Thy slightest things,
   A feather or a shell,
A stick, or rod, which some chance brings,
   The best of us excell ;
Yea, I have known these shreds outlast
   A fair-compacted frame,
And for one twenty we have past
   Almost outlive our name.
Thus hast Thou placed in man's outside
   Death to the common eye,
That heaven within him might abide
   And close eternitie.

Hence youth and folly, man's first shame,
   Are put into the slaughter,
And serious thoughts begin to tame
   The wise man's madness, laughter.
Dull, wretched worms! that would not keepe
   Within our first faire bed,
But out of Paradise must creepe
   For every foot to tread!
Yet had our Pilgrimage been free
   And smooth without a thorne,
Pleasure had soiled Eternitie
   And tares had choaked the corne.
Thus by the cross Salvation runnes,
   Affliction is a mother
Whose painful throes yield many sons,
   Each fairer than the other.
A silent teare can pierce Thy throne
   When loud joyes want a wing;
And sweeter airs stream through a groan
   Than any arted string.
Thus, Lord, I see my gain is great,
   My losse but little to it;
Yet something more I must intreate,
   And only Thou canst do it;
O let me, like him, know my end!
   And be as glad to find it:
And, whatsoe'er Thou shalt commend
   Still let Thy servant mind it!
Then make my soule white as his owne,
   My faith as pure and steady,
And deck me, Lord, with the same crowne
   That has crownd him already!

HENRY VAUGHAN.

MARCH 15.

UNIVERSAL PRAYER.

FATHER of all ! in every age,
  In every clime adored,
By Saint, by Savage, and by Sage,
  Jehovah, Jove, or Lord !

Thou Great First Cause, least understood,
  Who all my sense confined
To know but this, that Thou art good
  And that myself am blind :

Yet gave me, in this dark estate,
  To see the good from ill,
And binding nature fast in fate,
  Left free the human will.

What conscience dictates to be done,
  Or warns me not to do,
This teach me more than hell to shun,
  That more than heaven pursue.

What blessings Thy free bounty gives
  Let me not cast away,
For God is paid when man receives,
  To enjoy is to obey.

Yet not to earth's contracted span
  Thy goodness let me bound,
Or think Thee Lord alone of man
  When thousand worlds are round.

Let not this weak, unknowing hand
  Presume Thy bolts to throw,
And deal damnation round the land
  On each I judge my foe.

If I am right, Thy grace impart
  Still in the right to stay ;
If I am wrong, oh teach my heart
  To find that better way.

Save me alike from foolish pride
  Or impious discontent,
At aught Thy wisdom has denied
  Or aught Thy goodness lent.

Teach me to feel another's woe,
  To hide the fault I see,
That mercy I to others show
  That mercy show to me.

Mean though I am, not wholly so,
  Since quickened by Thy breath,
O lead me wheresoe'er I go
  Through this day's life or death.

This day be bread and peace my lot,
  All else beneath the sun
Thou know'st if best bestow'd or not,
  And let Thy will be done.

To Thee, whose temple is all space,
  Whose altar, earth, sea, skies,
One chorus let all Being raise,
  All nature's incense rise !

ALEXANDER POPE.

MARCH 16.

ARTHUR'S PRAYER.

THE old order changeth, yielding place to new,
And God fulfils Himself in many ways,
Lest one good custom should corrupt the world.
Comfort thyself: what comfort is in me?
I have lived my life, and that which I have done
May He within Himself make pure! but thou,
If thou shouldst never see my face again,
Pray for my soul.   More things are wrought by prayer
Than this world dreams of.   Wherefore, let thy voice
Rise like a fountain for me night and day.
For what are men better than sheep or goats,
That nourish a blind life within the brain,
If, knowing God, they lift not hands of prayer
Both for themselves and those who call them friend?
For so the whole round earth is every way
Bound by gold chains about the feet of God.
But now farewell.   I am going a long way
With these thou seëst—if indeed I go—
(For all my mind is clouded with a doubt)
To the island-valley of Avilion,
Where falls not hail, or rain, or any snow,
Nor ever wind blows loudly; but it lies
Deep-meadow'd, happy, fair with orchard-lawns
And bowery hollows crown'd with summer sea,
Where I will heal me of my grievous wound.

ALFRED, LORD TENNYSON.

MARCH 17.

[St Patrick's Day.]

O THOU fair Island, with thy Sister Isle
Indissolubly link'd for weal and woe ;
    Partaker of her present power,
      Her everlasting fame ;
Dear pledges hast thou render'd and received
Of that eternal union ! Bedell's grave
    Is in thy keeping ; and with thee
Deposited, doth Taylor's holy dust
      Await the Archangel's call.
O land profuse of genius and of worth,
Largely hast thou received, and largely given !

      Green Island of the west,
The example of unspotted Ormond's faith
      To thee we owe ; to thee
      Boyle's venerable name :
      Berkeley, the wise and good :
    And that great Orator, who first
Unmask'd the harlot sorceress, Anarchy,
What time, in Freedom's borrowed form profaned,
      She to the Nations round
      Her draught of witchcraft gave :
      And him who in the field
O'erthrew her giant offspring in his strength,
      And brake the iron rod.
        Proud of such debt,
    Rich to be thus indebted, these,
      Fair Island, Sister Queen
Of Ocean, Ireland, these to thee we owe.

Shall I then imprecate
A curse on them that would divide
Our union ?   Far be this from me, O Lord !
Far be it !   What is man,
That he should scatter curses ? . . . King of Kings,
Father of all, Almighty, Governor
Of all things ! unto Thee
Humbly I offer up our holier prayer !
I pray Thee, not in wrath
But in Thy mercy, to confound
These men's devices, Lord !
Lighten their darkness with Thy Gospel light,
And thus abate their pride,
Assuage their malice thus !

ROBERT SOUTHEY.

MARCH 18.

LORD, in this dust Thy sovereign voice
First quickened love divine ;
I am all Thine,—Thy care and choice,
My very praise is Thine.

I praise Thee, while Thy Providence
In childhood frail I trace,
For blessings given, ere dawning sense
Could seek or scan Thy grace ;

Blessings in boyhood's marvelling hour,
Bright dreams and fancyings strange ;
Blessings, when reason's awful power
Gave thought a bolder range ;

Blessings of friends, which to my door
Unask'd, unhoped, have come ;
And choicer still a countless store
Of eager smiles at home.

Yet, Lord, in memory's fondest place
    I shrine those seasons sad,
When looking up I saw Thy face
    In kind austereness clad.

I would not miss one sigh or tear,
    Heart-pang or throbbing brow ;
Sweet was the chastisement severe,
    And sweet its memory now.

Yes ! let the fragrant scars abide,
    Love tokens in Thy stead,
Faint shadows of the spear-pierced side
    And thorn-encompassed head.

And such Thy tender force be still
    When self would swerve or stray,
Shaping to truth the froward will
    Along Thy narrow way.

Deny me wealth : far, far remove
    The lure of power or name ;
Hope thrives in straits, in weakness love,
    And faith in this world's shame.

CARDINAL NEWMAN.

MARCH 19.

THOU art the source and centre of all minds,
Their only point of rest, Eternal Word !
From Thee departing they are lost, and rove
At random without honour, hope, or peace.
From Thee is all that soothes the life of man,
His high endeavour, and his glad success,

His strength to suffer, and his will to serve.
But, O Thou bounteous giver of all good,
Thou art of all Thy gifts Thyself the crown!
Give what Thou canst, without Thee we are poor ;
And with Thee rich, take what Thou wilt away.

WILLIAM COWPER.

MARCH 20.

TO THE HOLY GHOST.

O FIRY sentence, enflamed with all grace,
Enkyndling hertes with brandes charitable,
The endlesse rewarde of pleasure and solace,
To the Father and the Son Thou art communicable,
In unitate, which is inseparable.
O Water of lyfe, O wel of consolacion,
Against al suggestions deadly and dampnable
Rescu me, Good Lorde, by your preservacion.

To whom is appropryed the Holy Ghost by name,
The third parson, one God in Trinitie,
Of perfyt love Thou art the ghostlye flame,
O mirrour of mekenes, peace, and tranquilitye.
My comfort, my counsel, my parfit charity,
O Water of lyfe, O wel of consolacion,
Against all storms of hard adversitie
Rescu me, Good Lorde, by Thy preservacion.

JOHN SKELTON.

MARCH 21.

I LOOK FOR THE LORD.

Our wealth has wasted all away,
  Our pleasures have found wings ;
The night is long until the day ;
  Lord give us better things—
A ray of light in thirsty night
  And secret water-springs.

Our love is dead, or sleeps, or else
  Is hidden from our eyes :
Our silent love, while no man tells
  Or if it lives or dies.
Oh, give us love, O Lord, above
  In changeless Paradise.

Our house is left us desolate,
  Even as Thy Word hath said.
Before our face the way is great,
  Around us are the dead.
Oh guide us, save us from the grave,
  As Thou Thy saints hast led.

Lead us where pleasures evermore
  And wealth indeed are placed,
And home on an eternal shore,
  And love that cannot waste ;
Where joy Thou art unto the heart,
  And sweetness to the taste.

Christina Rossetti.

MARCH 22.

HYMN.

And dost Thou, holy Shepherd, leave
  Thine unprotected flock alone,
Here, in this darksome vale, to grieve,
  While Thou ascend'st Thy glorious throne?

O, where can they their hopes now turn
  Who never liv'd but on Thy love?
Where rest the hearts for Thee that burn,
  When Thou art lost in light above?

How shall those eyes now find repose
  That turn, in vain, Thy smile to see?
What can they hear save mortal woes,
  Who lose Thy voice's melody?

And who shall lay his tranquil hand
  Upon the troubled ocean's might,
Who hush the winds by his command,
  Who guide us thro' this starless night?

For Thou art gone!—that cloud so bright,
  That bears Thee from our love away,
Springs upward thro' the dazzling light,
  And leaves us here to weep and pray.

Luis Ponce de Leon.
(*Trs.* George Ticknor.)

MARCH 23.

"ARISE, SHINE, FOR THY LIGHT IS COME."

STERN Daughter of the Voice of God !
  O Duty ! if that name thou love,
Who art a light to guide, a rod
  To check the erring, and reprove ;
Thou who art victory and law
When empty terrors overawe ;
  From vain temptations dost set free,
And calm'st the weary strife of frail humanity.

There are who ask not if thine eye
  Be on them ; who, in love and truth,
Where no misgiving is, rely
  Upon the genial sense of youth :
Glad hearts ! without reproach or blot
Who do thy work, and know it not ;
  Oh ! if through confidence misplaced
They fail, thy saving arms, great Power ! around them
        cast. . . .

I, loving freedom, and untried,
  No sport of every random gust,
Yet being to myself a guide,
  Too blindly have reposed my trust :
And oft, when in my heart was heard
Thy timely mandate, I deferred
  The task in smoother walks to stray ;
But thee I now would serve more strictly, if I may.

Through no disturbance of my soul,
  Or strong compunction in me wrought,
I supplicate for thy controul ;
  But in the quietness of thought ;

Me this unchartered freedom tires ;
I feel the weight of chance desires :
    My hopes no more must change their name ;
I long for a repose which ever is the same.

Stern Lawgiver ! yet thou dost wear
    The Godhead's most benignant grace ;
Nor know we anything so fair
    As is the smile upon thy face :
Flowers laugh before thee on their beds,
And fragrance in thy footing treads ;
    Thou dost preserve the stars from wrong,
And the most ancient heavens, through thee, are fresh
        and strong.

To humbler functions, awful Power !
    I call thee : I myself commend
Unto thy guidance from this hour ;
    O, let my weakness have an end !
Give unto me, made lowly wise,
The spirit of self-sacrifice ;
    The confidence of reason give,
And in the light of Truth Thy Bondman let me live !

W. WORDSWORTH.

MARCH 24.

GRACE rules below and sits enthroned above,
How few the sparks of wrath ! how slow they move
And drop and die in boundless seas of love !

But me, vile wretch, should pitying Love embrace
Deep in its ocean, Hell itself would blaze,
And flash and burn me through the boundless seas.

Yea, Lord, my guilt, to such a vastness grown,
Seems to confine Thy choice to wrath alone,
And calls Thy power to vindicate Thy throne.

Thine honour bids " avenge Thine injured name,"
Thy slighted loves a dreadful glory claim,
While my moist tears might but incense Thy flame.

Should Heaven grow black, almighty thunder roar,
And vengeance blast me, I could plead no more,
But own Thy justice dying, and adore.

Yet can those bolts of Death, that cleave the flood
To reach a rebel, pierce this sacred shroud
Tinged in the vital stream of my Redeemer's blood.

Isaac Watts (from the French).

MARCH 25.

COMFORT.

Speak low to me, my Saviour, low and sweet
   From out the hallelujahs, sweet and low,
   Lest I should fear and fall, and miss Thee so
Who art not missed by any that entreat.
Speak to me as to Mary at Thy feet !
   And if no precious gums my hands bestow,
   Let my tears drop like amber while I go
In reach of Thy divinest voice complete

In humanest affection—thus, in sooth,
   To lose the sense of losing.   As a child,
   Whose bird-song seeks the wood for evermore,
Is sung to in its stead by mother's mouth
   Till, sinking on her breast, love-reconciled,
   He sleeps the faster that he wept before.

E. Barrett Browning.

MARCH 26.

THE bird let loose in Eastern skies
    When hastening fondly home,
Ne'er stoops to earth her wing, nor flies
    Where idle warblers roam.
But high she shoots, through air and light,
    Above all low delay,
Where nothing earthly bounds her flight
    Nor shadow dims her way.

So grant me, God, from every care
    And stain of passion free,
Aloft, through virtue's purer air,
    To hold my course to Thee !
No sin to cloud, no lure to stay
    My soul, as home she springs,
Thy sunshine on her joyful way,
    Thy freedom in her wings !

THOMAS MOORE.

MARCH 27.

THE DEFEAT OF PAIN.

SINCE 'tis God's will, Pain, take your course,
Exert on me your utmost force—
I well God's truth and promise know.
He never sends a woe,
But His supports divine
In due proportion with the affliction join.

Though I am frailest of mankind,
And apt to waver as the wind—
Though me no feeble bruised reed
In weakness can exceed—
My soul on God relies,
And I your fierce, redoubled shocks despise.

Patient, resigned, and humble wills
Impregnably resist all ills.
My God will guide me by His light,
Give me victorious might:
No pang can me invade
Beneath His wing's propitious shade.

BISHOP KEN.

MARCH 28.

[Rafael's Birthday.]

O Mary Mother, full of grace,
Above all other women blest,
Thro' whose pure womb our erring race
Beholds its sin-born doom redressed,
     Pray for us!
Thou by the Holy Ghost that wert
With every heavenly gift begirt,
Thou who canst shield us from all hurt,
     Pray for us, pray for us!
Tower of David, Ivory Tower,
Vessel of Honour, House of Gold,
Mystical Rose, unfading Flower,
Sure refuge of the unconsoled,
     Pray for us!
Mirror of Justice, Wisdom's Seat,
Celestial shade for earthly heat,
The sinner's last and best retreat,
     Pray for us, pray for us!

O Thou of Heaven that art the gate,
That to the feeble strength dost bear,
To whom no outcast turns too late,
E'en when Thy Son is deaf to prayer,
      Pray for us!
O Morning Star, to chase the dark,
Cause of our joy through care and cark,
Thou of the Covenant the Ark,
      Pray for us, pray for us!
Bright Queen of the angelic choir,
Of patriarchs, prophets, worshipped Queen!
Queen of the martyrs proved by fire,
And Queen of confessors serene;
Queen of the apostolic train,
Queen that o'er all the saints doth reign,
O Queen conceived without a stain,
      Pray for us, pray for us!

           ALFRED AUSTIN.

MARCH 29.

O ALL-SUFFICIENT, all beneficent,
Thou God of goodness and of glory, hear!
Thou who to lowest minds dost condescend,
Assuming passions to enforce Thy laws,
Adopting jealousy to prove Thy love,
Thou who resigned humility uphold'st,
Ev'n as the florist props the drooping rose,
But quell'st tyrannic pride with peerless pow'r,
Ev'n as the tempest rives the stubborn oak:
O all-sufficient, all-beneficent,
Thou God of goodness and of glory, hear!
Bless all mankind and bring them in the end
To heav'n, to immortality and Thee.

           CHRISTOPHER SMART.

MARCH 30.

TE DEUM.

THEE, Sovereign God, our grateful accents praise :
We own Thee Lord and bless Thy wondrous ways ;
To Thee, Eternal Father, earth's whole frame
With loudest trumpets sounds immortal fame.
Lord God of Hosts ! for Thee the heavenly powers
With sounding anthems fill the vaulted towers.
Thy Cherubim's thrice Holy, Holy, Holy, cry :
Thrice Holy all the Seraphims reply,
And thrice returning echoes endless songs supply.
Both heaven and earth Thy majesty display :
They owe their beauty to Thy glorious ray.
Thy praises fill the loud apostles' choir ;
The train of prophets in the song conspire.
Legions of martyrs in the chorus shine,
And vocal blood with vocal music join.
By these Thy Church, inspired by heavenly art,
Around the world maintains a second part,
And tunes her sweetest notes, O God, to Thee,
The Father of unbounded majesty,
The Son, adored co-partner of Thy seat,
And equal everlasting Paraclete.
Thou King of Glory, Christ, of the most high,
Thou co-eternal filial Deity ;
Thou who, to save the world's impending doom,
Vouchsaf'st to dwell within a virgin's womb ;
My God, my God, let me for once look on Thee
As though nought else existed, we alone !
And as creation crumbles, my soul's spark
Expands till I can say,—Even from myself
I need Thee and I feel Thee and I love Thee.

I do not plead my rapture in Thy works
For love of Thee, nor that I feel as one
Who cannot die : but there is that in me
Which turns to Thee, which loves or which should love.

R. BROWNING.

MARCH 31.

OLD Giant Death, disarmed, before Thee flew
The bolts of Heaven, and back the foldings drew
To give access and make Thy faithful way ;
From God's right hand Thy filial beams display.
Thou art to judge the living and the dead :
Then spare those souls for whom Thy veins have bled.
O take us up amongst Thy blessed above,
To share with them Thy everlasting love.
Preserve, O Lord ! Thy people and enhance
Thy blessing on Thine own inheritance.
For ever raise their hearts and rule their ways.
Each day we bless Thee and proclaim Thy praise.
No age shall fail to celebrate Thy name,
No hour neglect Thy everlasting fame.
Preserve our souls, O Lord, this day from ill ;
Have mercy on us, Lord, have mercy still ;
As we have hoped do Thou reward our pain ;
We've hoped in Thee—let not our hope be vain !

JOHN DRYDEN.

APRIL 1.

GRETCHEN'S PRAYER.

INCLINE, incline
That sorrow-laden face of Thine
  Unto my need, and pity me!
  Woes thousandfold,
Like swords, have pierced Thee, and, behold!
  Thine eyes gaze ever toward Calvary.
    Thou lift'st Thine eyes
Toward the Father, and Thy sighs
  Bear tidings of His need and Thine!
    Who shall assuage
    The fiery rage
Of sorrow in this frame of mine?
All the fears my poor heart thronging,
All its trembling, all its longing,
    To Thee are known,
    To Thee alone!
    Wheresoe'er I go,
    Ah, woe, woe, woe,
With woe's my bosom shaking!
    And I am scarce alone,
    I moan, I moan, I moan,
    My heart is breaking! . . .
  Save me from death and misery!
    Incline, incline
That sorrow-laden face of Thine
Unto my need, and rescue me!

GOETHE.　(Trs. Editors.)

APRIL 2.

THE prayers I make will then be sweet indeed
    If Thou the spirit give by which I pray :
    My unassisted heart is barren clay,
That of its native self can nothing feed :
Of good and pious works Thou art the seed,
    That quickens only where Thou say'st it may ;
    Unless Thou show to us Thine own true way
No man can find it.   Father ! Thou must lead.

Do Thou, then, breathe those thoughts into my mind
    By which such virtue may in me be bred
    That in Thy holy footsteps I may tread ;
The fetters of my tongue do Thou unbind,
    That I may have the power to sing of Thee,
    And sound Thy praises everlastingly.

MICHAEL ANGELO.
(Trs. William Wordsworth.)

APRIL 3.

HOW EXCELLENT IS THY NAME.

O LORD, our Lord, how excellent is thy name in
all the earth ! who hast set thy glory above the
heavens.

Out of the mouth of babes and sucklings hast thou
ordained strength, because of thine enemies ; that thou
mightest still the enemy and the avenger.

When I consider thy heavens, the work of thy
fingers ; the moon, and the stars, which thou hast
ordained ;

What is man, that thou art mindful of him ? and the son of man, that thou visitest him ?

For thou hast made him a little lower than the angels, and hast crowned him with glory and honour.

Thou madest him to have dominion over the work of thy hands ; thou hast put all things under his feet :

All sheep and oxen, yea, and the beasts of the field ;

The fowl of the air, and the fish of the sea, and whatsoever passeth through the paths of the seas.

O Lord, our Lord, how excellent is thy name in all the earth !

PSALM VIII.

APRIL 4.

O THOU, whose balance does the mountains weigh,
Whose will the wild tumultuous seas obey,
Whose breath can turn those wat'ry worlds to flame,
That flame to tempest and that tempest tame ;
Earth's meanest son, all trembling, prostrate falls,
And on the bounties of Thy goodness calls.
　O give the winds all past offence to sweep,
To scatter wide, or bury in the deep.
Thy power, my weakness may I ever see,
And wholly dedicate my soul to Thee !
Reign o'er my will, my passions ebb and flow
At Thy command, nor human motive know !
If anger boil, let anger be my praise,
And sin the graceful indignation raise.
My love be warm to succour the distressed,
And lift the burden from the soul oppressed.
O may my understanding ever read
This glorious volume which Thy wisdom made,
Who decks the maiden Spring with flow'ry pride?
Who calls forth Summer like a sparkling bride ?

Who joys the mother Autumn's bed to crown ?
And bids old Winter lay her honours down ?
May sea and land and earth and heaven be joined
To bring the Eternal Author to my mind.

EDWARD YOUNG.

APRIL 5.

TO HIS DEAR GOD.

ILE hope no more
For things that will not come ;
And, if they do, they prove but cumbersome.
Wealth brings much woe ;
And, since it fortunes so,
'Tis better to be poor
Than so t'abound
As to be drown'd
Or overwhelm'd with store.

Pale care, avant,
Ile learn to be content
With that small stock thy bounty gave or lent.
What may conduce
To my most healthful use,
Almighty God, me grant !
But that, or this,
That hurtful is,
Deny Thy suppliant.

R. HERRICK.

APRIL 6.

ON HIS BLINDNESS.

When I consider how my light is spent
  Ere half my days in this dark world and wide;
  And that one talent which is death to hide,
Lodged with me useless, though my soul more bent
To serve therewith my Maker, and present
  My true account, lest He returning chide;
  Doth God exact day labour, light deny'd,
I fondly ask? but Patience, to prevent
That murmur, soon replies, God doth not need
Either man's works or His own gifts; who best
  Bear His mild yoke, they serve Him best: His state
Is kingly; thousands at His bidding speed,
And post o'er land and ocean without rest;
  They also serve who only stand and wait.

John Milton.

APRIL 7.

DE PROFUNDIS.

From depth of doole wherein my soule doth dwell,
From heavy hart which harbours in my breast,
From troubled sprite which sildom taketh rest,
From hope of heaven, from dreade of darksome hell,
O gracious God, to Thee I crye and yell.
My God, my Lorde, my lovely Lorde, aloane
To Thee I call, to Thee I make my moane.
And Thou, good God, vouchsafe in gree to take
  This woeful plaint,
  Wherein I faint,
O, hearé me then for Thy great mercie's sake.

Oh bende Thine eares attentively to heare,
Oh, turne Thine eyes, behold me how I wayle,
Oh, hearken Lord, give eare for mine availe,
O marke in minde the burdens that I beare ;
See howe I sinke in sorrowes everye where.
Beholde and see what dollors I endure,
Give eare and marke what plaintes I put in ure.
Bende willing eare : and pittie therewithall
   My wayling voyce,
   Which hath no choyce
But evermore upon Thy name to call.

I look for Thee (my lovely Lord) therefore,
For Thee I wayte, for Thee I tarry styll,
Mine eyes do long to gaze on Thee my fyll.
For Thee I watch, for Thee I prye and pore.
My Soule for Thee attendeth evermore.
My Soule doth thyrst to take of Thee a taste,
My Soule desires with Thee for to bee plaste.
And to Thy worde, which can no man deceyve,
   Myne onely trust,
   My love and lust
In confidence continuallye shall cleave.

GEORGE GASCOIGNE.

APRIL 8.

   THILKE love, whiche that is
   Within a mannes herte affirmed,
   And stante of charitee confirmed :
   Suche love is goodly for to have,
   Suche love maie the body save,
   Suche love maie the soul amende,
   The highe God such love us sende

Forthwith the remenaunt of grace,
So that above in thilke place,
Where resteth love and all pees
Our joye maie be endelees.

JOHN GOWER.

APRIL 9.

THE MEASURE.

"*He comprehended the dust of the earth in a measure* (שליש)."—ISAIAH XL.
"*Thou givest them tears to drink in a measure* (שליש)."[1]
—PSALM LXXX.

GOD the Creator, with a pulseless hand
Of unoriginated power, hath weighed
The dust of earth and tears of man in one
　　Measure, and by one weight:
　　So saith His holy book.

Shall we, then, who have issued from the dust
And there return,—shall we, who toil for dust,
And wrap our winnings in this dusty life,
　　Say, "No more tears," Lord God!
　　"The measure runneth o'er"?

Oh, Holder of the balance, laughest Thou?
Nay, Lord, be gentler to our foolishness,
For His sake who assumed our dust and turns
　　On Thee pathetic eyes
　　Still moistened with our tears.

1 "I believe that the word occurs in no other part of the Hebrew
Scriptures."—Author's note.

And teach us, O our Father, while we weep,
To look in patience upon earth and learn,—
Waiting, in that meek gesture, till at last
    These tearful eyes be filled
    With the dry dust of death.

        E. BARRETT BROWNING.

APRIL 10.

THE REQUEST.

O THOU who didst deny to me
This world's adored felicity,
And every big imperious lust
Which fools admire in sinful dust,
With those fine subtle twists, that tie
Their bundles of foul gallantry,—
Keep still my weak eyes from the shine
Of these gay things which are not Thine!
And shut my ears against the noise
Of wicked, though applauded, joyes.
For Thou in any land hast store
Of shades and coverts for Thy poor.
Where from the busy dust and heat,
As well as storms, they may retreat.
A rock or bush are downy beds,
When Thou art there, crowning their heads
With secret blessings, or a tire
Made of the Comforter's live-fire.
And when Thy goodness, in the dress
Of anger, will not seem to bless,
Yet dost Thou give them Thy rich rain,
Which, as it drops, clears all again.

O what kind visits daily pass
"Twixt Thy great Self and such poor grass !
With what sweet looks doth Thy love shine
On those low violets of Thine,
While the tall tulip is accurst,
And crowns imperial dye with thirst.
O give me still those secret meals,
Those rare repasts which Thy love deals !
Give me that joy, which none can grieve
And which in all griefs doth relieve.
This is the portion Thy child begs ;
Not that of rust and rags and dregs.

HENRY VAUGHAN.

APRIL 11.

THE CRUCIFIX.

[From the Hungarian.]

MAKER of man, still canst Thou man regard,
    So greatly wrongèd by his unbelief,
For favours, numberless as sand, who dar'd
    Nail Thee, Lord, to the Cross, like robber, thief ?

And yet Thou wert a faithful shepherd there,
    Over the stray'd flock a watch didst set,
Didst move their Father for their sins with prayer,
    And all our trespasses Thou wouldst forget.

Thy limbs were rack'd with mortal agony,
    Thine eyes were bathèd with a rain of tears,
Pangs, sharp as poison, wrung Thy mouth awry,—
    Heroic, Lord, Thy strife with Death appears !

Thou God of heroes, on the cross-tree bound,
 Victorious Captain of an endless line,
Where was Thine arm, Thy shield, Thy strength
  renown'd,
 That Angel-arm? where were Thy dues divine?

All those, O Lord, Thou then didst leave escape,
 Nought of Thy great divinity didst show;
Thou didst reclothe Thyself in human shape,
 That drop by drop Thy blood for us might flow.

Thou sawest, we were bow'd, and sunk in hell,
 Our soul's salvation an eternal loss,
Therefore Thou cam'st from Heav'n, where Thou dost
  dwell,
 And let'st Thy body die upon the Cross.

O great Jehovah, Sovereign fount of grace,
 All-gracious Eloïm, Son unsurpass'd,
Lord of the hosts, King of Judæa's race,
 Source of all good, O Thou the First and Last—

A trail of ants upon a rocky floor
 Our merits mark,—like leaves upon the tree,
Or flight of birds, or sands upon the shore,
 Our sins are told, and deep as th' depths o' th' sea!

But, lo! Thy mercy's greater than them all,
 And Thine unmeasured mercy is our stay;
O, why take count of worms?—We are too small,
 That Thou with might of arms shouldst make
  display.

We are like chaff that's driv'n before the wind,
 When Thou against us lettest loose Thy blame;
Thy lovingkindness, Lord, no wrath should bind,
 Give wings to grace, and win more lasting fame!

Lord, not for us, nor for our merit's sake,
   But for Thy lovingkindness' sake be kind;
Thy Son's blood-sacrifice be pleased to take,
   Who on the Crucifix redeem'd mankind.

Zrinyi.
(Trs. Editors.)

APRIL 12.

O Lord, my God, do Thou Thy holy will—
   I will lie still;
I will not stir, lest I forsake Thine arm,
   And break the charm
Which lulls me, clinging to my Father's breast,
   In perfect rest.

Wild fancy, peace! thou must not me beguile
   With thy false smile:
I know thy flatteries and thy cheating ways;
   Be silent, Praise,
Blind guide, with siren voice, and blinding all
   That hear thy call.

Come, Self-devotion, high and pure,
Thoughts that in thankfulness endure,
Though dearest hopes are faithless found,
And dearest hearts are bursting round.
Come, Resignation, spirit meek,
And let me kiss thy placid cheek,
And read in thy pale eye serene
Their blessing, who by faith can wean
Their hearts from sense, and learn to love
God only, and the joys above. . . .

"O Father ! not My will, but Thine be done———"
          So spake the Son.
Be this our charm, mellowing Earth's ruder noise
          Of griefs and joys ;
That we may cling for ever to Thy breast
          In perfect rest !

JOHN KEBLE.

APRIL 13.

FEAR CAST OUT.

Wilt Thou forgive that sin, where I begun,
     Which was my sin though it were done before ?
Wilt Thou forgive that sin, through which I run
     And do run still, though still I do deplore ?
When Thou hast done, Thou hast not done,
                    For I have more.

Wilt Thou forgive that sin which I have won
     Others to sin and made my sins their door ?
Wilt Thou forgive that sin which I did shun
     A year or two, but wallowed in a score ?
When Thou hast done, Thou hast not done,
                    For I have more.

I have a sin of fear that, when I've spun
     My last thread, I shall perish on the shore ;
But swear by Thyself, that at my death Thy Son
     Shall shine, as He shines now and heretofore :
And, having done that, Thou hast done :
                    I fear no more.

JOHN DONNE.

APRIL 14.

"LEST WE FORGET."

When Israel, of the Lord beloved,
   Out from the land of bondage came,
Her father's God before her moved,
   An awful guide in smoke and flame.
By day, along the astonished lands
   The cloudy pillar glided slow;
By night, Arabia's crimsoned sands
   Returned the fiery column's glow.

There rose the choral hymn of praise,
   And trump and timbrel answered keen;
And Zion's daughters poured their lays,
   With priest's and warrior's voice between.
No portents now our foes amaze,
   Forsaken Israel wanders lone;
Our fathers would not know Thy ways,
   And Thou hast left them to their own.

But, present still, though now unseen,
   When brightly shines the prosperous day,
Be thoughts of Thee a cloudy screen,
   To temper the deceitful ray.
And oh, when stoops on Judah's path
   In shade and storm the frequent night,
Be Thou, long-suffering, slow to wrath,
   A burning and a shining light.

Our harps we left by Babel's streams,
   The tyrant's jest, the Gentile's scorn;
No censer round our altar beams,
   And mute are timbrel, trump, and horn.
But Thou hast said, The blood of goat,
   The flesh of rams, I will not prize;
A contrite heart, a humble thought,
   Are mine accepted sacrifice.

                    Sir Walter Scott.

APRIL 15.

"LOVE IS THE LESSON."

MOST glorious Lord of Life, that on this day
  Didst make Thy triumph over Death and Sin;
And, having harrow'd hell, didst bring away
  Captivity thence captive, us to win:

This joyous day, dear Lord, with joy begin,
  And grant that we, for whom Thou diddest die,
Being with Thy dear blood clean wash'd from sin,
  May live for ever in felicity;

And that Thy love we weighing worthily,
  May likewise love Thee for the same again:
And for Thy sake, that all like dear didst buy,
  With love may one another entertain.

So let us love, dear Love, like as we ought,
Love is the lesson which the Lord us taught.

EDMUND SPENSER.

APRIL 16.

AT EASTER.

THOU Love of God! or let me die
Or grant what shall seem heaven almost!
Let me not know that all is lost,
Though lost it be—leave me not tied
To this despair, this corpse-like bride!
Let that old life seem mine—no more—
With limitation as before,

With darkness, hunger, toil, distress;
Be all the earth a wilderness !
Only let me go on, go on
Still hoping ever and anon
To reach one eve the Better Land.

ROBERT BROWNING.

APRIL 17.

SAVIOUR of mankind !   Man Emmanuel !
Who sinless died for sin, who vanquished Hell,
The first-fruits of the grave, whose life did give
Light to our darkness, in whose death we live—
O strengthen Thou my faith, correct my will,
That mine may Thine obey; protect me still,
So that the latter death may not devour
My soul sealed with Thy seal : so in the hour
When Thou, whose body sanctified Thy tomb,
Unjustly judged, a glorious judge shall come
To judge the world with justice; by that sign
I may be known and entertained for Thine.

WILLIAM DRUMMOND of Hawthornden.

APRIL 18.

THE NIGHT PIECE.

HARK ! the prophetic raven brings
My summons on his boding wings;

The birds of night my fate foretel,
The prescient death-watch sounds my knell.

A solemn darkness spreads the tomb,
But terrors haunt the midnight gloom ;

Methinks a browner horrour falls,
And silent spectres sweep the walls.

Tell me, my soul, oh tell me why
The faltering tongue, the broken sigh ?

Thy manly cheeks bedew'd with tears,
Tell me, my soul, from whence these fears ? . . .

Had I a firm and lasting faith
To credit what the Almighty saith,

I could defy the midnight gloom,
And the pale monarch of the tomb.

Though tempests drive me from the shore,
And floods descend, and billows roar ;

Though death appears in every form,
My little bark should brave the storm.

Then if my God required the life
Of brother, parent, child, or wife,

Lord, I should bless the stern decree,
And give my dearest friend to Thee.

Amid the various scenes of ills,
Each stroke some kind design fulfils ;

And shall I murmur at my God,
When sovereign love directs the rod ?

Peace, rebel thoughts—I'll not complain,
My Father's smiles suspend my pain ;

Smiles—that a thousand joys impart,
And pour the balm that heals the smart.

Though Heaven afflicts, I'll not repine,
Each heart-felt comfort still is mine;

Comforts that shall o'er death prevail,
And journey with me thro' the vale.

Dear Jesus, smooth that rugged way,
And lead me to the realms of day,

To milder skies, and brighter plains,
Where everlasting sunshine reigns.

Dr Nathaniel Cotton.

APRIL 19.

GOOD MORROW.

You that have spent the silent night,
    In sleepe and quiet rest,
And joye to see the cheerefull lyght
    That ryseth in the East:
Now cleare your voyce, now chere your hart,
    Come help me nowe to sing;
Each willing wight come beare a part
    To prayse the heavenly King.

The Rainbowe bending in the skye,
    Bedeckt with sundry hewes,
Is like the seate of God on hye
    And seemes to tell these newes;
That as therby He promised
    To drowne the world no more,
So by the blood which Christ hath shed,
    He will our helth restore.

The Carrion Crowe, that lothsome beast,
    Which cries against the rayne,
Both for her hue and for the rest,
    The Devill resembleth playne :
And as with gunnes we kill the crowe
    For spoyling our releefe,
The Devill we must overthrowe
    With gunshot of beleefe.

The little byrds which sing so swete,
    Are lyke the angells' voyce,
Which render God his prayses mete
    And teach us to rejoyce :
And as they more esteem that myrth
    Than dread the night's annoy,
So much we deeme our days on earth
    But hell to heavenly joye.

Unto which joyes for to attayne,
    God graunt us all His grace,
And sende us after worldly payne
    In heaven to have a place.
Where we maye still enjoy that light
    Which never shall decaye ;
Lorde, for Thy mercy lend us might,
    To see that joyfull daye !

GEORGE GASCOIGNE.

APRIL 20.

AN HYMNE OF HEAVENLY LOVE.

O HUGE and most unspeakable impression
Of Love's deep wound, that pierst the piteous hart
Of that deare Lord with so entyre affection,
And, sharply launcing every inner part,
Dolours of death into His soule did dart,

Doing Him die that never it deserved,
To free His foes, that from His heast had swerved !

What hart can feel least touch of so sore launch,
Or thought can think the depth of so deare wound ?
Whose bleeding sourse their streames yet never staunch,
But stil do flow and freshly still redownd
To heal the sores of sinfull soules unsound,
And cleanse the guilt of that infected crime
Which was enrooted in all fleshly slyme.

O blessed Well of Love ! O Floure of Grace !
O glorious Morning Starre ! O Lampe of Light !
Most lively image of Thy Father's face,
Eternal King of Glorie, Lord of Might,
Meeke Lambe of God, before all worlds behight,
How can we Thee requite for all this good ?
Or what can prize that Thy most precious blood ?

Yet nought Thou ask'st in lieu of all this love,
But love of us, for guerdon of Thy paine :
Ay me ! what can us lesse than that behove ?
Had He required life for us againe,
Had it beene wrong to ask His owne with gaine ?
He gave us life, He it restorèd lost ;
Then life were least, that us so little cost.

But He our life hath left unto us free,
Free that was thrall, and blessed that was band,
Ne ought demaunds but that we loving bee,
As He Himselfe hath lov'd us afore-hand,
And bound therto with an eternall band,
Him first to love that was so dearely bought,
And next our brethren, to His image wrought.

EDMUND SPENSER.

APRIL 21.

THE OLD STOIC.

Riches I hold in light esteem
   And Love I laugh to scorn;
And lust of fame was but a dream,
   That vanished with the morn:

And if I pray, the only prayer
   That moves my lips for me
Is, "Leave the heart that now I bear,
   And give me liberty!"

Yes, as my swift days near their goal,
   'Tis all that I implore;
In life and death, a chainless soul,
   With courage to endure.

Emily Brontë.

APRIL 22.

FATHER FRANCIS' PRAYER.

Ne gay attire, ne marble hall,
Ne arched roof, ne pictured wall;
Ne cooks of Fraunce, ne dainty board
Bestowed with pies of Perigord;
Ne power, ne such-like idle fancies,
Grant, O sweet Lord, to Father Francis!
Let me ne more myself deceive,
Ne more regret the toys I leave,
The world I quit, the proud, the vain,
Corruption's and Ambition's train,
But not the good, perdie, nor fair,
'Gainst them I make ne vow, ne prayer:

But such aye welcome to my cell,
And oft, not always, with me dwell.
Then cast, sweet Lord, a circle round
And bless from fools this holy ground,
From all the woes to worth and truth,
From wanton old and homely youth,
The gravely dull and pertly gay,
Oh! banish there, and, by my fay,
Right well I ween that in this age
Mine house shall prove an hermitage.

GILBERT WEST.

APRIL 23.

[St George's Day.]

PRAYER FOR STATE AND CHURCH.

HAIL to the crown by Freedom shaped—to gird
An English Sovereign's brow! and to the throne
Whereon he sits! whose deep foundations lie
In veneration and the people's love;
Whose steps are equity, whose seat is law.
Hail to the State of England! And conjoin
With this a salutation as devout,
Made to the spiritual fabric of her Church;
Founded in truth; by blood of Martyrdom
Cemented; by the hands of Wisdom reared
In beauty of holiness, with ordered pomp,
Decent and unreproved. The voice, that greets
The majesty of both, shall pray for both;
That, mutually protected and sustained,
They may endure, long as the sea surrounds
This favoured Land, or sunshine warms her soil.

WILLIAM WORDSWORTH.

[Shakespeare's Birthday.]

ABOVE the goodly land, more his than ours,
He sits supreme, enthroned in skyey towers,
And sees the heroic brood of his creation
Teach larger life to his ennobled nation.
A shaping brain !   O flashing fancy's hues !
A boundless heart, kept fresh by pity's dews !
A wit humane and blithe ! O sense sublime
For each dim oracle of mantled Time !
Transcendent Form of Man ! in whom we read
Mankind's whole tale of Impulse, Thought, and Deed,
Amid the expanse of years beholding thee,
We know how vast our world of life may be :
Wherein, perchance, with aims as pure as thine,
Small tasks and strengths may be no less divine.

JOHN STERLING.

APRIL 24.

HYMN TO ZEUS.

MIGHTIEST of the Immortals, all-praised and all-
      powerful for ever,
Zeus, the Creator, who rulest the world Thou hast
      fashion'd with law,
Thine be the fruit of the lips, who permittest all flesh
      to address Thee.
For we are Thine offspring,[1] made in Thine image, who
      dwell on the earth.
Therefore to Thee be my hymn, Thy strength be my
      song evermore.

[1] Cp. : "As certain also of your own poets have said, For we are also
His offspring."—Acts xvii. 28.

Lo! the high heavens are Thine, and the lights of the
    heavens, Thy servants,
Circle the earth at Thy bidding; Thou guidest their
    motions in order.
In Thine hand is the power: in Thy right hand are
    the lightnings,
Two-edged, terrible, fiery, swift, and from everlasting.
Thine is the frost, and Thine is the snow, Thou sovran
    Disposer,
Lord of the great lights, Lord of the small, and King
    above all things.
Neither is anything done on the earth without Thy
    commandment,
Nor in the heavens above, nor in the waters below,
Save what the wicked do, by following after their folly.
But Thou hast understanding to set straight even the
    crooked,
Out of the void bringest form, and out of the alien
    kinship,
So Thou hast fashioned in one the good and the evil
    together,
That Thy Word should be One-in-All through all
    generations.
Woe unto them who flee that Word, woe, woe to the
    wicked,
Ever pursuing desires of their heart, and a good which
    is not good,
Blind are their eyes to Thy light, and their ears are
    deaf to Thy precepts,
Blind and deaf to the signs which lead to victorious
    living;
They are a guide to themselves; each erreth alone and
    in darkness;
Vain is unbridled ambition, and vain is the counsel of
    fools,
Vain are the lusts of the flesh,—and all who seek them
    shall perish.

But oh, bountiful Zeus! oh, Cloud-girt! clothed with
    the thunder,
Cleanse Thou man from his faults, scatter the seeds from
    his soul,
Plant Thy wisdom within, which ruleth all things
    rightly,
That we may give Thee glory, wherewith Thou hast
    glorified us !—
Praising the work of Thy hands, since praise becometh
    Thy children,—
Thou art the Law and the Life : praised be Thy
    name evermore !

CLEANTHES (Trs. Editors).

APRIL 25.

THESE hours and that which hovers o'er my end,
Into Thy hands and heart, Lord, I commend.

Take both to Thine account, that I and mine
In that hour and in these may be all Thine;

That as I dedicate my devoutest breath
To make a kind of life for my Lord's death :

So from his living and life-giving death
My dying life may draw a new and never-fleeting breath.

    O my dear Saviour, make me see
    How dearly Thou hast paid for me,
    That lost again, my life may prove
    As then in death, so now in love.

RICHARD CRASHAW.

APRIL 26.

HYMN.

Eternal Mover, whose diffusèd glory,
To show our grovelling reason what Thou art,
Unfolds itself in clouds of nature's story,
Where man, Thy proudest creature, acts his part,
Whom yet, alas, I know not why, we call
The world's contracted sum, the little all;

For what are we but lumps of walking clay?
Why should we swell? whence should our spirits rise?
Are not brute beasts as strong, and birds as gay,—
Trees longer lived, and creeping things as wise?
Only our souls were left an inward light,
To feel our weakness, and confess Thy might.

Thou then, our strength, Father of life and death,
To whom our thanks, our vows, ourselves we owe,
From me, Thy tenant of this fading breath,
Accept these lines which from Thy goodness flow,
And Thou, that wert Thy legal Prophet's muse,
Do not Thy praise in weaker strains refuse!

Let these poor notes ascend unto Thy throne,
Where majesty doth sit with mercy crowned,
Where my Redeemer lives, in whom alone
The errors of my wandering life are drowned;
Where all the choir of heaven resound the same,
That only Thine, Thine is the saving name!

Well then, my soul, joy in the midst of pain;
Thy Christ, that conquered hell, shall from above
With greater triumph yet return again,
And conquer His own justice with His love;
Commanding earth and seas to render those
Unto His bliss, for whom He paid His woes.

Now have I done; now are my thoughts at peace;
And now my joys are stronger than my grief;
I feel those comforts, that shall never cease,
Future in hope, but present in belief;
Thy words are true, Thy promises are just,
And Thou wilt find Thy dearly-bought in dust!

Sir Henry Wotton.

APRIL 27.

THE MAGNET.

Thou hast made me, and shall Thy work decay?
Repair me now; for now mine end doth haste,
I run to Death, and Death meets me as fast,
And all my pleasures are like yesterday.

I dare not move my dim eyes any way,
Despair behind and Death before doth cast
Such terror, and my feeble flesh doth waste
By sin in it, which it towards Hell doth weigh.

Only Thou art above, and when towards Thee
By Thy leave I can look, I rise again;
But our old subtle foe so tempteth me,
That not one hour myself I can sustain.

Thy grace may wing me to prevent his art,
And Thou like adamant draw mine iron heart.

John Donne.

APRIL 28.

DISCIPLINE.

Throw away Thy rod,
Throw away Thy wrath ;
        O my God,
Take the gentle path.

For my heart's desire
Unto Thine is bent ;
        I aspire
To a full consent.

Not a word or look
I affect to own,
        But by book,
And Thy book alone.

Though I fail, I weep ;
Though I halt in pace,
        Yet I creep
To the throne of grace.

Then let wrath remove ;
Love will do the deed ;
        For with love
Stony hearts will bleed.

Love is swift of foot ;
Love's a man of war
        And can shoot,
And can hit from far.

Who can 'scape his bow ?
That which wrought on Thee
          Brought Thee low,
Needs must work on me.

Throw away Thy rod ;
Though man frailties hath,
          Thou art God ;
Throw away Thy wrath.

GEORGE HERBERT.

APRIL 29.

THE THRESHING-FLOOR.

THE world's a floor, whose swelling heaps retain
  The mingled wages of the ploughman's toil ;
The world's a heap, whose yet unwinnow'd grain
  Is lodged with chaff and buried in her soil ;
All things are mix'd, the useful with the vain ;
  The good with bad, the noble with the vile ;
    The world's an ark, wherein things pure and gross
    Present their lossful gain, and gainful loss
Where ev'ry pound of gold contains a pound of dross.

The worldly wisdom of the foolish man
  Is like a sieve, that does alone retain
The grosser substance of the worthless bran :
  But thou, my soul, let thy brave thoughts disdain
So coarse a purchase : O be thou a fan
    To purge the chaff, and keep the winnow'd grain ;
    Make clean thy thoughts, and dress thy mix'd
      desires :
    Thou art heav'n's tasker ; and thy God requires
The purest of thy flow'r, as well as of thy fires.

Let grace conduct thee to the paths of peace,
    And wisdom bless the soul's unblemish'd ways;
No matter, then, how short or long's the lease,
    Whose date determines thy self-number'd days:
No need to care for wealth's or fame's increase,
    Nor Mars his palm, nor high Apollo's bays.
        Lord, if Thy gracious bounty please to fill
        The floor of my desires, and teach me skill
To dress and choose the corn, take those the chaff
        that will.   FRANCIS QUARLES.

APRIL 30.

THY WILL BE DONE.

WHAT is this passing scene?
    A peevish April day!
A little sun, a little rain,
And then night sweeps along the plain,
        And all things fade away;
            Man (soon discuss'd)
            Yields up his trust,
And all his hopes and fears lie with him in the
    dust. . . .

        Then, since this world is vain,
            And volatile, and fleet,
Why should I lay up earthly joys
Where rust corrupts, and moth destroys,
        And cares and sorrows eat?
            Why fly from ill
            With cautious skill,
When soon this hand will freeze, this throbbing heart
    be still?

Come, Disappointment, come !
Thou art not stern to me ;
Sad monitress ! I own thy sway,
A votary sad in early day,
I bend my knee to thee.
From sun to sun
My race will run ;
I only bow, and say, My God, Thy will be done !

KIRKE WHITE.

MAY 1

INVOCATION.

Strong Son of God, immortal Love,
   Whom we, that have not seen Thy face,
   By faith, and faith alone, embrace,
Believing where we cannot prove;

Thine are these orbs of light and shade;
   Thou madest Life in man and brute;
   Thou madest Death; and lo, Thy foot
Is on the skull which Thou hast made.

Thou wilt not leave us in the dust:
   Thou madest man, he knows not why;
   He thinks he was not made to die;
And Thou hast made him: Thou art just.

Thou seemest human and divine,
   The highest, holiest manhood, Thou:
   Our wills are ours, we know not how;
Our wills are ours, to make them Thine.

Our little systems have their day;
   They have their day and cease to be:
   They are but broken lights of Thee,
And Thou, O Lord, art more than they.

We have but faith : we cannot know ;
  For knowledge is of things we see ;
  And yet we trust it comes from Thee,
A beam in darkness : let it grow.

Let knowledge grow from more to more,
  But more of reverence in us dwell ;
  That mind and soul, according well,
May make one music as before,

But vaster.   We are fools and slight ;
  We mock Thee when we do not fear :
  But help Thy foolish ones to bear ;
Help Thy vain worlds to bear Thy light.

ALFRED, LORD TENNYSON.

MAY 2.

"THANK GOD OF ALL."

By a way wandering as I went
  Well sore I sorrowed, for sighing sad,
Of hardé haps that I had hent,
  Mourning me made almost mad,
'Till a letter all one me had
  That well was written on a wall,
A blissful word that on I rad,
  That alway said "Thank God of all !"

And yet I read furthermore,
  Full good intent I took theretill,
Christ may well your state restore,
  Nought is to strive against His will;
He may us spare and also spill,
  Think right well we ben His thrall,
What sorrow we suffer, loud or still,
  Alway thank God of all.

What divers sonde that God thee send,
  Here or in any other place,
Také it with good intent,
  The sooner God will send His grace;
Though thy body be brought full bas,
  Let not thy heart adown fall,
But think thee God is where he was,
  And alway thank God of all.

For Christés love be not so wild
  But rule thee by reason within and without,
And take in good heart and mild
  The sonde that God sent all about;
Then dare I say withouten doubt,
  That in Heaven is made thy stall,
Rich and poor that low will lout,
  Alway thank God of all.

JOHN LYDGATE.

MAY 3.

Little lamb, who made thee?
Dost thou know who made thee,
Gave thee life, and bid thee feed
By the stream and o'er the mead:

Gave thee clothing of delight,
Softest clothing, woolly, bright :
Gave thee such a tender voice,
Making all the vales rejoice ?
  Little lamb, who made thee ?
  Dost thou know who made thee ?

Little lamb, I'll tell thee ;
Little lamb, I'll tell thee :
He is callèd by thy name
For He calls Himself a Lamb,
He is meek and He is mild,
He became a little child :
I a child and thou a lamb
We are callèd by His name.
  Little lamb, God bless thee !
  Little lamb, God bless thee !

WILLIAM BLAKE.

MAY 4.

*"Great God! I'd rather be
A Pagan suckled in a creed outworn !
So might I, standing on this pleasant lea,
Have glimpses that would make me less forlorn."*

O THOU, whose mighty palace-roof doth hang
From jagged trunks, and overshadoweth
Eternal whispers, glooms, the birth, life, death
Of unseen flowers in heavy peacefulness ;
Who lovest to see the Hamadryads dress
Their ruffled locks where meeting hazels darken ;
And through whole solemn hours dost sit and hearken

The dreary melody of bedded reeds—
In desolate places where dank moisture breeds
The pipy hemlock to strange overgrowth,
Bethinking thee how melancholy loth
Thou wast to lose fair Syrinx—do thou now,
By thy love's milky brow,
By all the trembling mazes that she ran,
Hear us, great Pan!

O Thou, for whose soul-soothing quiet, turtles
Passion their voices cooingly 'mong myrtles,
What time thou wanderest at eventide
Through sunny meadows, that outskirt the side
Of thine enmossèd realms; O thou, to whom
Broad-leavèd fig-trees even now foredoom
Their ripen'd fruitage; yellow-girted bees
Their golden honeycombs; our village leas
Their fairest-blossom'd beans and poppied corn;
The chuckling linnet its five young unborn
To sing for thee; low-creeping strawberries
Their summer coolness; pent-up butterflies
Their freckled wings; yea, the fresh-budding year
All its completions—be quickly near,
By every wind that nods the mountain pine,
O forester divine! . . .

O Hearkener to the loud-clapping shears,
While ever and anon to his shorn peers
A ram goes bleating: Winder of the horn
When snouted wild-boars routing tender corn
Anger our huntsman: Breather round our farms
To keep off mildew, and all weather harms:
Strange ministrant of undescribèd sounds,
That come a-swooning over hollow grounds,
And wither drearily on barren moors:
Dread Opener of the mysterious doors

Leading to universal knowledge—see
Great son of Dryope,
The many that are come to pay their vows
With leaves about their brows!

Be still the unimaginable lodge
For solitary thinkings: such as dodge
Conception to the very bourne of heaven,
Then leave the naked brain: be still the haven
That spreading in this dull and clodded earth
Gives it a touch ethereal—a new birth:
Be still a symbol of immensity:
A firmament reflected in a sea:
An element filling the space between:
An unknown—but no more: we humbly screen
With uplift hands our foreheads, lowly bending,
And giving out a shout most heaven-rending,
Conjure thee to receive our humble Pæan,
Upon thy Mount Lycean!

JOHN KEATS.

MAY 5.

MORNING PRAYER IN EDEN.

THESE are Thy glorious works, Parent of good,
Almighty! Thine this universal frame,
Thus wondrous fair: Thyself how wondrous then!
Unspeakable! who sitt'st above these heavens
To us invisible, or dimly seen
In these Thy lowest works; yet these declare
Thy goodness beyond thought, and power divine.
Speak, ye who best can tell, ye Sons of Light,
Angels—for ye behold Him, and with songs

J

And choral symphonies, day without night,
Circle His throne rejoicing—ye in Heaven ;
On Earth join, all ye creatures, to extol
Him first, Him last, Him midst, and without end. . . .
Ye Mists and Exhalations, that now rise
From hill or steaming lake, dusky or gray,
Till the sun paint your fleecy skirts with gold,
In honour to the World's great Author rise ;
Whether to deck with clouds the uncoloured sky,
Or wet the thirsty earth with falling showers,
Rising or falling, still advance His praise.
His praise, ye Winds, that from four quarters blow,
Breathe soft or loud ; and wave your tops, ye Pines,
With every Plant, in sign of worship wave.
Fountains, and ye that warble, as ye flow,
Melodious murmurs, warbling tune His praise.
Join voices, all ye living Souls.   Ye Birds,
That, singing, up to Heaven-gate ascend,
Bear on your wings and in your notes His praise.
Ye that in waters glide, and ye that walk
The earth, and stately tread, or lowly creep,
Witness if *I* be silent, morn or even,
To hill or valley, fountain, or fresh shade,
Made vocal by my song, and taught His praise.
Hail, universal Lord !   Be bounteous still
To give us only good : and, if the night
Have gathered aught of evil, or concealed,
Disperse it, as now light dispels the dark.

JOHN MILTON.

MAY 6.

O HOLY LORD, who with the Children Three
        Didst walk the piercing flame,
Help, in those trial hours, which, save to Thee
        I dare not name:
Nor let these quivering eyes and sickening heart
Crumble to dust beneath the Tempter's dart.

Thou, who didst once Thy life from Mary's breast
        Renew from day to day,
Oh, might her smile, severely sweet, but rest
        On this frail clay!
Till I am Thine with my whole soul; and fear,
Not feel a secret joy, that Hell is near.

CARDINAL NEWMAN.

MAY 7.

JESUS, I love.   Come, dearest name,
Come and possess this heart of mine;
I love, tho' 'tis a fainter flame
And infinitely less than Thine.

O, if my Lord would leave the skies
Drest in the rays of mildest grace,
My soul should hasten to my eyes,
To meet the pleasures of His face.

How would I feast on all His charms,
Then round His lovely feet entwine!
Worship and love in all their forms
Should honour beauty so divine.

In vain the tempter's flattering tongue
The world in vain shall bid me move,
In vain : for I should gaze so long
Till I were all transformed to love.

Then, mighty God, I'd sing and say,
" What empty names are crowns and kings !
Amongst them give these worlds away,
These little despicable things."

I would not ask to climb the sky,
Nor envy angels their abode ;
I have a Heaven as bright and high
In the blest vision of my God !

ISAAC WATTS.

MAY 8.

FINITE AND INFINITE.

THE wind sounds only in opposing straits,
  The sea, beside the shore ; man's spirit rends
  Its quiet only up against the ends
Of wants and oppositions, loves and hates,
Where, worked and worn by passionate debates,
  And losing by the loss it apprehends,
  The flesh rocks round, and every breath it sends
Is ravelled to a sigh.   All tortured states

Suppose a straitened place.   Jehovah Lord,
  Make room for rest, around me ! out of sight
Now float me of the vexing land abhorred,
  Till in dark calms of space my soul may right
Her nature, shoot straight sail on lengthening cord,
  And rush exultant on the Infinite.

E. BARRETT BROWNING.

MAY 9.

Come, let us sound with melody the praises
Of the Kings' King, th' omnipotent Creator,
Author of number, that hath all the world in
                Harmonie framed.

Heav'n is His throne perpetually shining,
His devine power and glorie thence He thunders,
One in all, and all still in one abiding,
                Both Father and Sonne.

O sacred sprite invisible, eternall,
Ev'rywhere, yet unlimited, that all things
Canst in one moment penetrate, revive me,
                O holy Spirit!

Rescue, O rescue me from earthly darknes,
Banish hence all these elementall objects,
Guide my soule, that thirsts, to the lively Fountaine
                Of Thy devinenes!

Cleanse my soule, O God, Thy bespotted Image,
Altered with sinne so that heav'nly purenes
Cannot acknowledge me, but in Thy mercies,
                O Father of grace!

But when once Thy beames do remove my darknes,
O then Ile shine forth as an Angell of light,
And record, with more than an earthly voice, Thy
                Infinite honours.

Dr Thomas Campion.

MAY 10.

O VERREY light of eyen that ben blinde,
O verrey lust of labour and distresse,
O treasorer of bountee to mankinde,
Thee whom God chose to mother for humblesse !
From His ancille He maide thee maistresse
Of hevene and erthe, our bille up for to bede.[1]
This world awaiteth ever on thy goodnesse
For thou ne failest never wight at nede.

Virgine, that art so noble of apparaile
And ledest us into the high tower
Of Paradys, thou me wisse and counsaile,
How I may have thy grace and thy socour ;
Al have I been in filthe and in errour.
Lady, unto that court thou me ajourne
That cleped is thy bench, O fresshe flower !
Ther-as that mercy ever shal sojourne.

Xristus, thy Sone, that in this world alighte,
Upon the cros to suffre His passioun,
And eek that Longius His herte pighte,[2]
And made His herte blood to runne adoun ;
And al was this for my salvacioun ;
And I to Him am false and eek unkinde,
And yet He wol not my dampnacioun—
This thanke I you, socour of al mankinde.

Ysaac was figure of His death, certeyn,
That so fer-forth His father wolde obeye
That Him ne roughte[3] no-thing to be slayn ;
Right so thy Sone list, as a lamb, to deye.
Now lady, ful of mercy, I you preye
Sith He His mercy mesured so large,
Be ye not skant ; for alle we singe and seye
That ye ben from vengeaunce ay our targe.

[1] To proffer our petition.   [2] Should pierce.   [3] Recked.

Zacharie yon clepeth the open welle
To wasshe sinful soule out of his gilt.
Therfor this lessoun oughte I wel to telle
That, nere [1] thy tender herte, we weren spilt.[2]
Now lady brighte, sith thou canst and wilt
Ben to the seed of Adam merciable,
So bring us to that palais that is bilt
To penitents that ben to mercy able.

GEOFFREY CHAUCER.

MAY 11.

WHETHER amid the gloom of night I stray
Or my glad eyes enjoy revolving day,
Still Nature's various face informs my sense
Of an all-wise, all powerful Providence.
When the pure soul is from the body flown,
No more shall Night's alternate reign be known;
The Sun no more shall rolling light bestow,
But from th' Almighty streams of glory flow.
Oh, may some nobler thought my soul employ
Than empty, transient, sublunary joy!
The stars shall drop, the sun shall lose his flame,
But Thou, O God, forever shine the same.

JOHN GAY.

MAY 12.

DOMINE, NE IN FURORE.

O LORD! since in my mouthe Thy mightie name
Suffereth itselfe, my Lord, to name and call,
Here hath my harpe betaken by the same;
That the repentaunce, whiche I have and shall,

1 Were it not for.   2 Lost.

Maye at Thy hande seke mercy, as the thinge
Of onely comfort to wretched sinners all :
Whereby I dare with humble bemoaninge,
By Thy goodness, this thinge of Thee require ;
Chastice me not for my deservinge
According to Thy just conceaved ire.
O Lord, I dreade : and that I did not dreade
I me repente : and evermore desire
Thee, Thee to dreade.   I open here and spreade
My fault to Thee : But Thou, for Thy goodness,
Measure it not in largeness, nor in breade ;
Punish it not as asketh the greatness
Of Thy furor, provoked by myne offence.
Temper, O Lord, the harme of my excesse,
With mending will that I for recompence
Prepare againe : and rather pitye me :
For I am weake and cleane without defence :
More is the nede I have of remedye.
For of the whole the leche taketh no cure :
The shepe that strayeth, the sheparde seekes to see,
I, Lord, am strayed : and, sick without recure,
Fele all my limbs, that have rebelled, for feare
Shake in despaire, unless Thou me assure.

SIR THOMAS WYAT.

MAY 13.

RESIGNATION.

I HOPE for the salvation of the Lord,
   In Him I trust, when fears my being thrill,
Come life, come death, according to His word,
   He is my portion still.

Hence, doubting heart! I will the Lord extol
  With gladness, for in Him is my desire,
Which, as with fatness, satisfies my soul,
    That doth to heaven aspire.

All that is hidden shall mine eyes behold,
  And the great Lord of all be known to me,
Him will I serve, His am I as of old,
    I ask not to be free.

Sweet is e'en sorrow, coming in His name,
  Nor will I seek its purpose to explore,
His praise will continually proclaim,
    And bless Him evermore.

ABRAHAM IBN EZRA.
(Trs. Mrs Henry Lucas.)

MAY 14.

THOU that hast giv'n so much to me,
Give one thing more, a gratefull heart:
See now Thy beggar works on Thee
      By art:

He makes Thy gifts occasion more,
And sayes, if he in this be crost,
All Thou hast given him heretofore
      Is lost.

But Thou didst reckon, when at first
Thy word our hearts and hands did crave,
What it would come to at the worst
      To save.

Perpetuall knockings at Thy doore,
'Tears sullying Thy transparent rooms,
Gift upon gift ; much would have more,
     And comes.

'This notwithstanding, Thou went'st on,
And didst allow us all our noise ;
Nay, Thou hast made a sigh and grone
     Thy joyes.

Not that Thou hast not still above
Much better tunes than grones can make,
But that these countrey-aires Thy love
     Did take.

Wherefore I crie, and crie again,
And in no quiet canst Thou be,
Till I a thankfull heart obtain
     Of Thee.

Not thankfull when it pleaseth me,
As if Thy blessings had spare dayes ;
But such a heart whose pulse may be
     Thy praise.

       GEORGE HERBERT.

MAY 15.

AN EVENING PRAYER.

THE night is come, like to the day,
Depart not Thou, great God, away.
Let not my sins, black as the night,
Eclipse the lustre of Thy light.

Keep still in my horizon, for to me
The sun makes not the day, but Thee.
Thou whose nature cannot sleep,
On my temples sentry keep ;
Guard me 'gainst those watchful foes,
Whose eyes are open whilst mine close ;
Let no dreams my head infest,
But such as Jacob's temple blest.
While I do rest my soul advance ;
Make me to sleep a holy trance,
That I may, my rest being wrought,
Awake into some holy thought ;
And with as active vigour run
My course as doth the nimble sun.
Sleep is a death.   Oh, make me try
By sleeping, what it is to die !
And as gently lay my head
On my grave, as now my bed.
Howe'er I rest, great God, let me
Awake again at last with Thee !
And thus assured, behold I lie
Securely, or to wake or die.

SIR THOMAS BROWNE.

MAY 16.

THE CONTRITE HEART.

The Lord will happiness divine
    On contrite hearts bestow ;
Then tell me, gracious God, is mine
    A contrite heart or no?

I hear, but seem to hear in vain,
  Insensible as steel ;
If aught is felt, 'tis only pain,
  To find I cannot feel.

My best desires are faint and few,
  I fain would strive for more ;
But when I cry, " My strength renew ! "
  Seem weaker than before.

O make this heart rejoice or ache,
  Decide this doubt for me ;
And if it be not broken, break,—
  And heal it if it be.

WILLIAM COWPER.

MAY 17.

FRIENDSHIP.

MAY I through life's uncertain tide
  Be still from pain exempt ;
May all my wants be still supplied ;
My state too low to admit of pride,
  And yet above contempt.

But, should Thy Providence Divine
  A greater bliss intend,
May all these blessings you design,
If e'er those blessings shall be mine,
  Be centred in a friend !

JAMES MERRICK.

MAY 18.

A GENERAL SONG OF PRAISE TO ALMIGHTY GOD.

How shall I sing that Majesty
    Which angels do admire ?
Let dust in dust and silence lie ;
    Sing, sing, ye heavenly choir.
Thousands of thousands stand around
    Thy throne, O God most high ;
Ten thousand times ten thousand sound
    Thy praise ; but who am I ?

Thy brightness unto them appears
    Whilst I Thy footsteps trace ;
A sound of God comes to my ears ;
    But they behold Thy face.
They sing because Thou art their sun ;
    Lord, send a beam on me ;
For where heaven is but once begun,
    There hallelujahs be.

Enlighten with faith's light my heart,
    Enflame it with love's fire ;
Then shall I sing and bear a part
    With that celestial choir.
I shall, I fear, be dark and cold,
    With all my fire and light ;
Yet when Thou dost accept their gold,
    Lord, treasure up my mite.

How great a being, Lord, is Thine
    Which doth all being keep !
Thy knowledge is the only line
    To sound so vast a deep.

Thou art a sea without a shore,
  A sun without a sphere;
Thy time is now and evermore,
  Thy place is everywhere.

JOHN MASON.

MAY 19.

OUT of the night that covers me,
  Black as the Pit from pole to pole,
I thank whatever gods may be
  For my unconquerable soul.

In the fell clutch of circumstance
  I have not winced nor cried aloud.
Under the bludgeonings of chance
  My head is bloody but unbowed.

Beyond this place of wrath and tears
  Looms but the Horror of the shade,
And yet the menace of the years
  Finds, and shall find, me unafraid.

It matters not how strait the gate,
  How charged with punishments the scroll,
I am the master of my fate:
  I am the captain of my soul.

W. E. HENLEY.

MAY 20.

LIBERTY.

LORD, bind me up, and let me lie
A prisoner to my liberty,
If such a state at all can be
As an imprisonment serving Thee;

The wind, though gathered in Thy fist,
Yet doth it blow still where it list,
And yet shouldst Thou let go Thy hold,
Those gusts might quarrel and grow bold.
  As waters here, headlong and loose,
The lower grounds still chase and choose,
Where spreading all the way they seek
And search out every hole and creek ;
So my spilt thoughts, winding from Thee,
Take the down-road to vanity,
Where they all stray and strive, which shall
Find out the first and steepest fall.

HENRY VAUGHAN.

MAY 21.

THE FAITHFUL MEN.

THE faithful men have perished, one by one,
    And there remaineth none
  To stand, with words entreating Thee—
  Even as Abraham with his prayer,
  Saying—" Yet lacking still may be
  Five of the fifty righteous there."
    And God made answer then :
" Yea, I will spare the city even for ten ! "

The faithful men have perished, one by one,
    And there remaineth none
  Holy and strong Thy grace to win,
  Even as Amram's son did pray ;
  " Lord, if Thou pardon not their sin,
  Blot me from out Thy book this day."
    And answer made the Lord :
" Pardoned have I, according to thy word."

The faithful men have perished, one by one,
         And there remaineth none
    Help in the perilous hour to bring,
    Even as Aaron swiftly ran
    Forth with his incense offering,
    When that the pestilence began.
         The living and the dead
Between he stood, and lo ! the plague was stayed.

The faithful men have perished, one by one,
         And there remaineth none
    Thy mercy fitly to implore,
    As David did, when, sore distressed,
    Beside Araunah's threshing-floor
    He twice declared : " I have transgressed."
         Thus prayed he penitent,
And the Almighty ceased from chastisement.

The faithful men have perished, one by one,
         And there remaineth none
    To trust Thee with a perfect heart,
    Like to Elijah, when he stood,
    Praying in Carmel's mount, apart,
    And poured the water on the wood.
         And lo ! God's answer came,
Even at the Mincha [1] hour in heavenly flame.

The faithful men have perished, one by one,
         And there remaineth none
    With ceaseless prayer to seek Thine aid,
    Pleading for pardon, even as he,
    The faithful of Thy house, who prayed
    By night and day incessantly.
         Yet, as in days of old,
Have mercy on us, Lord, with mercies manifold.

ELIJAH BEN MORDECAI.
(Trs. Mrs Henry Lucas.)

---

[1] Concluding.

MAY 22.

On the edge of the world I lie, I lie,
Happy and dying and dazed and poor,
Looking up from the vast great floor
Of the infinite world that rises above
To God and to Faith and to Love, Love, Love!
What words have I to that world to speak,
Old and weary and dazed and weak,
From the very low to the very high?
Only this—and this is all:
From the fresh, green soil to the wide blue sky,
From the Greatness to Weariness, Life to Death,
One God have we on whom to call;
One great bond from which none can fall;
Love below, which is life and breath,
And Love above, which sustaineth all.

MRS OLIPHANT.

MAY 23.

I love! and love hath given me
    Sweet thoughts to God akin,
And oped a living paradise
    My heart of hearts within:
O from this Eden of my life,
    God keep the serpent sin!

I love! and into Angel-land
    With starry glimpses peer!
I drink in beauty like heaven-wine
    When One is smiling near!
And there's a rainbow round my soul
    For every rising tear.

K

Dear God in heaven, keep without stain
  My bosom's brooding Dove :
O clothe it meet for Angel-arms
  And give it place above !
For there is nothing from the world
  I yearn to take but Love.

GERALD MASSEY.

MAY 24.

[Queen Victoria born, 1819.]

A SONG OF LOVES.

My heart is inditing a good matter : I speak of the things which I have made touching the King; my tongue is the pen of a ready writer.

Thou art fairer than the children of men; grace is poured into thy lips : therefore God hath blessed thee for ever.

Gird thy sword upon thy thigh, O most Mighty, with thy glory and thy majesty.

And in thy majesty ride prosperously because of truth and meekness and righteousness; and thy right hand shall teach thee terrible things.

Thine arrows are sharp in the heart of the King's enemies; whereby the people fall under thee.

(Thy throne, O God, is for ever and ever : the sceptre of thy kingdom is a right sceptre.)

Thou lovest righteousness, and hatest wickedness : therefore God, thy God, hath anointed thee with the oil of gladness above thy fellows.

All thy garments smell of myrrh, and aloes, and cassia, out of the ivory palaces, whereby they have made thee glad.

King's daughters were among thy honourable women: upon thy right hand did stand the queen in gold of Ophir.

Hearken, O daughter, and consider, and incline thine ear; forget also thine own people, and thy father's house:

So shall the King greatly desire thy beauty; for he is thy Lord, and worship thou him.

And the daughter of Tyre shall be there with a gift; even the rich among the people shall entreat thy favour.

The King's daughter is all glorious within; her clothing is of wrought gold.

She shall be brought unto the King in raiment of needlework: the virgins her companions that follow her shall be brought unto thee.

With gladness and rejoicing shall they be brought: they shall enter into the King's palace.

Instead of thy fathers shall be thy children, whom thou mayest make princes in all the earth.[1]

I will make thy name to be remembered in all generations: therefore shall the people praise thee for ever and ever.

Psalm XLV.

May all love,

His love, unseen but felt, o'ershadow Thee,
The love of all Thy sons encompass Thee,
The love of all Thy daughters cherish Thee,
The love of all Thy people comfort Thee,
Till God's love set Thee at his side again!

Alfred, Lord Tennyson.

---

[1] *Mutatis mutandis*, compare this verse and the foregoing with Tennyson's Dedication to the Sovereign's Consort:

> Thou noble Father of her Kings to be,
> Laborious for her people and her poor, . . .
> Dear to thy land and ours.

MAY 25.

My Saviour, dare I come to Thee,
Who let the little children come?
But I? . . . My soul is faint in me!
I come from wandering to and fro
This weary world.   There still His round
The Accuser goes; but Thee I found
Not anywhere.   Both joy and woe
Have pass'd me by.   I am too weak.
I grieve or smile.   And yet I know
That tears lie deep in all I do.
The homeless that are sick for home
Are not so wretched.   Ere it break,
Receive my heart: and for the sake
Not of my sorrows, but of Thine,
Bend down Thy holy eyes on mine,
Which are too full of misery
To see Thee clearly, tho' they seek.
Yet, if I heard Thy voice say "Come,"
So might I, dying, die near Thee!

The EARL OF LYTTON
(OWEN MEREDITH).

MAY 26.

"WHERE NO SWEET SONG IS HEARD."

O NATURE! all thy seasons please the eye
Of him who sees a Deity in all.
It is His presence that diffuses charms
Unspeakable, o'er mountain, wood, and stream.
To think that He, who hears the heavenly choirs,
Hearkens complacent to the woodland song;--
To think that He, who rolls yon solar sphere,

Uplifts the warbling songster to the sky;
To mark His presence in the mighty bow
That spans the clouds, as in the tints minute
Of tiniest flower, to hear His awful voice
In thunder speak, and whisper in the gale;
To know, and feel His care for all that lives;—
'Tis this that makes the barren waste appear
A fruitful field, each grove a paradise.
Yes! place me 'mid far-stretching woodless wilds,
Where no sweet song is heard; the heath-bell there
Would soothe my weary sight, and tell of Thee!
There would my gratefully uplifted eye
Survey the heavenly vault, by day,—by night,
When glows the firmament from pole to pole;
There would my overflowing heart exclaim,
" The heavens declare the glory of the Lord,
The firmament shews forth His handiwork! "

JAMES GRAHAME.

MAY 27.

THANKSGIVING.

God who created me
    Nimble and light of limb,
In three elements free,
    To run, to ride, to swim:
    Not when the sense is dim,
But now from the heart of joy,
    I would remember Him:
Take the thanks of a boy.

Jesus, King and Lord,
    Whose are my foes to fight,
Gird me with Thy sword
    Swift and sharp and bright.

Thee would I serve if I might:
And conquer if I can,
From day-dawn till night,
Take the strength of a man.

Spirit of Love and Truth
Breathing in grosser clay,
The light and flame of youth,
Delight of men in the fray,
Wisdom in strength's decay;
From pain, strife, wrong to be free
This best gift I pray,
Take my spirit to Thee!

H. C. BEECHING.

MAY 28.

WHAT weight of ancient witness can prevail,
If private reason hold the public scale?
But, gracious God, how well dost Thou provide
For erring judgments an unerring guide!
Thy throne is darkness in the abyss of light,
A blaze of glory that forbids the sight.
O teach me to believe Thee thus conceal'd,
And search no farther than Thyself reveal'd;
But her alone for my director take
Whom Thou hast promised never to forsake!
My thoughtless youth was winged with vain desires;
My manhood, long misled by wandering fires,
Followed false lights; and, when their glimpse was
    gone,
My pride struck out new sparkles of her own.
Such was I, such by nature still I am;
Be Thine the glory, and be mine the shame!

JOHN DRYDEN.

MAY 29.

CHRIST, look upon us in this city,
And keep our sympathy and pity
Fresh, and our faces heavenward ;
        Lest we grow hard.

Had poor folk half they need, and pleasure
Of life in reasonable measure,—
But food and raiment—few of all
        Would sin or fall.

Life scarce can tread majestically
Foul court and fever-stricken alley ;
It is the rich, must be confessed,
        Are blamefullest.

THOMAS ASHE.

MAY 30.

"QUI SAIT AIMER, SAIT MOURIR."

" I BURN my soul away ! "
    So spake the Rose, and smiled : " Within my cup
All day the sunbeams fall in flame, all day
    They drink my sweetness up ! "

" I sigh my soul away ! "
    The Lily said : " All night the moonbeams pale
Steal round and round me, whispering in their play
    An all too tender tale ! "

" I give my soul away ! "
  The Violet said : " 'The West-wind wanders on,
The North-wind comes ; I know not what they say,
  And yet my soul is gone ! "

O Poet, burn away
  Thy fervent soul ! fond Lover, at the feet
Of her thou lovest, sigh ! dear Christian, pray
  And let the world be sweet.

DORA GREENWELL.

MAY 31.

PATER NOSTER.

ETERNAL Father, who didst all create,
In whom we live and to whose bosom move,
To all men be Thy name known, which is Love,
Till its loud praises sound at heaven's high gate.
Perfect Thy kingdom in our passing state,
That here on earth Thou mayest as well approve
Our service as Thou ownest theirs above,
Whose joy we echo and in pain await.

Grant body and soul each day their daily bread ;
And should, in spite of grace, fresh woe begin,
Even as our anger soon is past and dead,
Be Thy remembrance mortal of our sin ;
By Thee in paths of peace Thy sheep be led,
And in the vale of terror comforted.

ROBERT BRIDGES.

JUNE 1.

THE WILL AND THE DEED.

I believe it!   'Tis Thou, God, that givest, 'tis I that
    receive :
In the first is the last, in Thy will is my power to
    believe.
All's one gift : Thou canst grant it, moreover, as
    prompt to my prayer
As I breathe out this breath, as I open these arms to
    the air.
From Thy will stream the worlds, life and nature, Thy
    dread Sabaoth ;
I will ? the mere atoms despise me !   Why am I not
    loth
To look that, even that in the face too ?   Why is it
    I dare
Think but lightly of such impuissance ?   What stops
    my despair ?
This : 'tis not what man Does which exalts him, but
    what man Would do !

R. Browning.

JUNE 2.

" I wish that he were come to me,
    For he will come " she said.
" Have I not prayed in Heaven ? on Earth,
    Lord, Lord, has he not prayed ?
Are not two prayers a perfect strength ?
    And shall I feel afraid ?

When round his head the aureole clings,
    And he is clothed in white,
I'll take his hand and go with him
    To the deep wells of light;
As unto a stream we will step down,
    And bathe there in God's sight.

We too will stand beside that shrine,
    Occult, withheld, untrod,
Whose lamps are stirred continually,
    With prayer sent up to God;
And see our old prayers, granted, melt
    Each like a little cloud."

W. M. Rossetti.

JUNE 3.

THE PRIEST'S INTERCESSOR.

Yet, yet awhile, offended Saviour, pause;
        In act to break
        Thine outraged laws,
O spare Thy rebels for Thine own dear sake;
    Withdraw Thine hand, nor dash to earth
    The covenant of our second birth.

'Tis forfeit like the first—we own it all—
        Yet for love's sake,
        Let it not fall;
But at Thy touch let veilèd hearts awake,
    That nearest to Thine altar lie,
    Yet least of holy things descry.

Teacher of teachers! Priest of priests! from Thee
    The sweet strong prayer
    Must rise to free
First Levi, then all Israel, from the snare.
    Thou art our Moses out of sight—
    Speak for us, or we perish quite.

JOHN KEBLE.

JUNE 4.

"I LIFT UP MINE EYES UNTO THE HILLS."

SEEKE the Lord, and in His waies persever!
    O faint not, but, as Eagles, flye,
    For His steepe hill is high;
Then striving gaine the top, and triumph ever!

When with glory there thy browes are crowned,
    New joyes so shall abound in thee,
    Such sights thy soule shall see
That worldly thoughts shall by their beames be drowned.

Farewell, World, thou masse of meere confusion!
    False light, with many shadowes dimm'd!
    Old Witch, with new foyles trimm'd!
Thou deadly sleepe of soule, and charm'd illusion!

I the King will seeke, of Kings adored,
    Spring of light, tree of grace and bliss,
    Whose fruit so sov'raigne is,
That all who taste it are from death restored.

DR THOMAS CAMPION.

JUNE 5.

Ah! then my hungry Soule! which long hast fed
On idle fancies of thy foolish thought,
And, with false Beautie's flattering bait misled,
Hast after vaine decciptfull shadowes sought,
Which all are fled, and now have left thee nought
But late repentance through thy follies prief;
Ah! cease to gaze on matter of thy grief:

And looke at last up to that Soveraine Light,
From whose pure beams al perfect Beauty springs,
That kindleth love in every godly spright,
Even the love of God; which loathing brings
Of this vile world and these gay-seeming things;
With whose sweet pleasures being so possest,
Thy straying thoughts henceforth for ever rest.

EDMUND SPENSER.

JUNE 6.

Father of Heaven and Judge of Earth!
Whose word called out this universe to birth,
By whose kind power and influencing care
The various creatures move and live and are;
But, ceasing once that care, withdrawn that power,
They move, alas, and live and are no more:
Omniscient Master, omnipresent King,
To Thee, to Thee my last distress I bring.
Thou, that canst still the raging of the seas,
Chain up the winds and bid the tempests cease!
Redeem my shipwrecked soul from raging gusts
Of cruel passion and deceitful lusts:

From storms of rage and dangerous rocks of pride,
Let Thy strong hand this little vessel guide
(It was Thy hand that made it) through the tide
Impetuous of this life : let Thy command
Direct my course and bring me safe to land !
If, while this wearied flesh draws fleeting breath,
Not satisfied with life, afraid of death,
It haply be Thy will that I should know
Glimpse of delight or pause from anxious woe !
From Now, from instant Now, great Sire ! dispel
The clouds that press my soul : from Now reveal
A gracious beam of light ; from Now inspire
My tongue to sing, my hand to touch the lyre ;
My open thoughts to joyous prospects raise,
And for Thy mercy let me sing Thy praise.
Or, if Thy will ordains I still shall wait
Some new hereafter and a future state,
Permit me strength my weight of woe to bear,
And raise my mind superior to my care.
Let me, howe'er unable to explain
The secret labyrinths of Thy ways to man,
With humble zeal confess Thy awful power,
Still weeping hope, and wondering still adore.
So in my conquest be Thy might declared,
And for Thy justice be Thy name revered !

MATTHEW PRIOR.

JUNE 7.

HYMN.

Take me as a hermit lone
With a desert life and moan ;
Only Thou anear to mete,
Slow or quick, my pulse's beat ;

Only Thou, the night to chase,
With the sunlight in Thy face!
Pleasure to the eyes may come
    From a glory seen afar,
But if life concentre gloom
    Scattered by no little star,
    Then, how feeble, God, we are!
Nay, whatever bird there be
    (Aether by his flying stirred),
He, in this thing, must be free—
    And I, Saviour, am Thy bird,
Pricking with an open beak
At the words that Thou dost speak!
Leave a breath upon my wings,
That above these nether things
I may rise to where Thou art,
I may flutter next Thine heart!
For if a light within me burn,
It must be darkness in an urn,
Unless, within its crystalline,
That unbeginning light of Thine
Shine!—oh, Saviour, *let* it shine!

MAXIMUS MARGUNIUS of Crete.
(Trs. Eliz. Barrett Browning.)

JUNE 8.

To that sothfast Christ, that starf on rode,[1]
With al myn herte of mercy ever I preye;
And to the Lord right thus I speke and saye:
Thou oon and two and three, eterne on-lyve,[2]
That regnest ay in three and two and oon,
Uncircumscript, and al mayst circumscryve,

---

[1] Died on the Cross.   [2] Alive.

Us from visible and invisible foon [1]
Defende ; and to Thy mercy, everychoon,
So make us, Jesus, for Thy grace, digne,
For love of mayde and mother thine benigne !
Amen.

GEOFFREY CHAUCER.

JUNE 9.

PRAYER FOR DISSOLUTION.

COME, Lord, my head doth burn, my heart is sick,
   While Thou dost ever, ever stay ;
Thy long deferrings wound me to the quick,
   My spirit gaspeth night and day :
      O, show Thyself to me,
      Or take me up to Thee ! . . .

When man was lost, Thy pitie lookt about
   To see what help in th' earth or skie ;
But there was none, at least no help without ;
   The help did in Thy bosom lie :
      O, show Thyself to me,
      Or take me up to Thee !

There lay Thy Sonne ; and must He leave that nest,
   That hive of sweetnesse, to remove
Thraldom from those who would not at a feast
   Leave one poor apple for Thy love ?
      O, show Thyself to me,
      Or take me up to Thee ! . . .

---

[1] Foes.

Yet, if Thou stayest still, why must I stay?
  My God, what is this world to me,
This world of wo?   Hence, all ye clouds, away,
  Away! I must get up and see:
      O, show Thyself to me,
      Or take me up to Thee! . . .

Nothing but drought and dearth, but bush and brake,
  Which way soe'er I look, I see;
Some may dream merrily, but when they wake,
  They dresse themselves and come to Thee:
      O, show Thyself to me,
      Or take me up to Thee! . . .

O, loose this frame, this knot of man untie,
  That my free soul may use her wing,
Which now is pinion'd with mortalitie,
  As an intangled, hamper'd thing:
      O, show Thyself to me,
      Or take me up to Thee!

What have I left that I should stay and grone?
  The most of me to heav'n is fled;
My thoughts and joys are all packt up and gone,
  And for their old acquaintance plead:
      O, show Thyself to me,
      Or take me up to Thee!

Come, dearest Lord, passe not this holy season,
  My flesh and bones and joynts do pray;
And ev'n my verse, when by ryme and reason
  The word is "Stay," says ever "Come":
      O, show Thyself to me,
      Or take me up to Thee!

GEORGE HERBERT.

JUNE 10.

CHRIST WILL RETURN.

CROWNED with griefs Thou art,
Clad in rough rags, dishonoured or unknown ;
And so are these who love, they are Thine own.
Come, for they need Thee ! lay Thy bleeding heart
Against theirs broken ; make their love a part
Of Thy love—let them weep their tears with Thine :
Pour out to Thee the woe that makes divine,
Not of the world, their lives.   These who have given
And lost their love without a hope of heaven,
Will see Thee coming from the bitter ways
And deserts, from the life of wasted days,
Foot-weary, bearing within a burden wrought
Of every man's refusal.   God having sought
Love in each offered prayer : Christ having tried
The door of every heart for love, and cried
Sorely and waited ; Man having taken Thy stand
In each man's path and begged for love with hand
Out-held, begging for bread, now clothed withal
In shreds, the greatest beggar, yea, in all
The world, since only shreds Thy robes will be
Of love the world could give—these will see
Thee coming and run and fetch Thee to their home,
And Thou shalt rest at last.   When Thou art come,
These will bring water, greet Thee with a kiss,
Share the last crust with Thee ; Thou shalt not miss
The love Thou seekest in vain, for falling down,
Breaking the precious vessel of their own
Tear-laden hearts upon Thy weary feet,
So they will wash and ease them with the sweet
Weeping of all their lives : and it may be
That I, having shown men things they will not see,

Having spoken to the unreplying soul
Of man and woman, having poured out the whole
Vain-ruined heaven within me on the snows
And deathly ways of life, shall be of those
Sitting alone at last, to whom even Thou,
Before whose effigy men falsely bow,
Ever rejecting Thee, wilt come a-thirst,
A-hungered, greatest, saddest, most accurst
Of all the world, and have that hopeless last
Outpouring of our hearts; and as we cast
Our fallen, piteous look at Thy bent head,
Thou mayst be known in breaking of our last bread
To me and them! O keep that dying tryst!
Come unto those when Thou return'st, O Christ!
Having loved others, shall they not love Thee?
Come! Thou shalt save perchance that few and me.

ARTHUR O'SHAUGHNESSY.

JUNE 11.

Oh! Thou who taught my infant eye
To pierce the air and view the sky,
To see my God in earth and seas,
To hear Him in the vernal breeze,
To know Him midnight thoughts among,
O guide my soul and aid my song.
Spirit of Light, do Thou impart
Majestic truths and teach my heart:
Teach me to know how weak I am;
How vain my powers, how weak my frame;
Teach me celestial paths untrod—
The ways of glory and of God.
No more let me in vain surprise
To heathen art give up my eyes—

To piles laborious science reared
For heroes brave or tyrants feared ;
But quit Philosophy, and see
The Fountain of her works in Thee !

GEORGE CRABBE.

JUNE 12.

O LORD, be near when, clothed with conquering power,
The King of Terrors claims his own dread hour :
When, on the edge of that unknown abyss
Which darkly parts us from the realm of bliss,
Awe-struck alike the timid and the brave,
Alike subdued the monarch and the slave,
Must drink the cup of trembling—when we see
Nought in the Universe but Death and Thee,
Forsake us not—if still, when life was young,
Faith to Thy bosom, as her home, hath sprung ;
If Hope's retreat hath been, through all the past,
The shadow by the Rock of Ages cast,
Father, forsake us not !—when tortures urge
The shrinking soul to that mysterious verge,
When from Thy justice to Thy love we fly,
On Nature's conflict look with pitying eye,
Bid the strong wind, the fire, the earthquake cease,
Come in the small still voice and whisper " Peace ! "

MRS HEMANS.

JUNE 13.

VIEW me, Lord, a worke of Thine :
   Shall I then lye drown'd in night ?
Might Thy grace in me but shine,
   I should seeme made all of light.

But my soul still surfets so
  On the poysoned baytes of sinne,
That I strange and ugly growe,
  All is darke and foule within.

Cleanse me, Lord, that I may kneele
  At Thine altar, pure and white;
They that once Thy mercies feele,
  Gaze no more on earth's delight.

Worldly joyes, like shadowes, fade
  When the heav'nly light appeares;
But the cov'nants Thou hast made,
  Endlesse, know nor dayes nor yeares.

In Thy Word, Lord, is my trust,
  To Thy mercies fast I flie;
Though I am but clay and dust,
  Yet Thy grace can lift me high.

Dr Thomas Campion.

JUNE 14.

A BETTER RESURRECTION.

I have no wit, no words, no tears:
  My heart within me like a stone
Is numbed too much for hopes or fears.
  Look right, look left, I dwell alone;
I lift mine eyes, but dimmed with grief
  No everlasting hills I see;
My life is in the falling leaf:
  O Jesus, quicken me!

My life is like a faded leaf,
  My harvest dwindled to a husk ;
Truly my life is void and brief,
  And tedious in the barren dusk :
My life is like a frozen thing,
  No bud nor greenness can I see :
Yet rise it shall—the sap of Spring ;
  O Jesus, rise in me !

My life is like a broken bowl,
  A broken bowl that cannot hold
One drop of water for my soul,
  Or cordial in the searching cold ;
Cast in the fire the perished thing ;
  Melt and remould it till it be
A royal cup for Him, my King :
  O Jesus, drink of me !

CHRISTINA ROSSETTI.

JUNE 15.

[Magna Carta, 1215.]

PRAYER FOR THE LAND.

To-day, to-day, some great thing Zeus shall do :
I prophesy the triumph of the right.
Oh that I were a dove, that I might wing the wind
With pinion swift and strong,
And, from some airy pinnacle of cloud,
Content mine eyes with gazing on the fray !
Zeus, who beholdest all,
Whom all in earth and heaven obey,
Give ear unto my prayer,
That, with victorious might,

The guardians of this land
Upon the goodly prize may spring and make an end—
And hear me, Pallas Athene, Virgin dread:
And thou, Apollo, lover of the chase,
And Thou, his sister, huntress-maid, that followest up
The dappled fleet-foot stag—
Oh hear me both, and come, a double strength,
To help this land and people at their need.

SOPHOCLES.
(Trs. R. Whitelaw.)

JUNE 16.

EXAUDI, DEUS, ORATIONEM MEAM.

GIVE eare to my suit, Lord, fromward hide not Thy face,
Beholde, sinking in grief, lamenting, how I praye:
My fooes they bray so lowde and eke threpe on so fast,
Buckeled to do me scathe, so is their malice bent.
Care perceth my entrayles and traveyleth my sprite:
The greslye feare of death envyroneth my brest.
A tremblynge cold of dred clene overwhelmeth my
    hert:
O, thinke I, hadd I wings like to the symple dove,
This peryll might I flye and seke some place of rest
In wylder woods, where I might dwell far from these
    cares.
What speedy way of wing my playnts shold ther lay on,
To skape the stormye blast that threatned is to me:
Rayne those unbrydled tungs, breake that conjured
    league,
For I decyphred have amydd our toune the stryffe;
Gile and wrong do kepe the walles, they ward both
    day and night:

And mischief joynd with care doth kepe the market
    stede,
Whilst wickednesse with craft in heaps swarme thro'
    the streete.
Ne my declared foo wrought me all this reproche
By harme so looked for, yt wayeth halfe the lesse,
It was a friendly foo, by shadow of good will,
Myne old fere and dere frende, my guyde that trapped
    me,
Where I was wont to fetche the cure of all my care,
And in my bosome hyde my secret zeale to God.
Such soden surprys quicke may hym hell devoure,
Whilst I invoke the Lord, whose power shall me
    defende,
My prayer shall not cease from that the sunne descend
Till he his aulture wynn and hyde them in the sea,
With words of hott effect, that moveth from hert
    contryte,
Such humble suit, O Lord, doth perce my paycent
    care.

EARL OF SURREY.

JUNE 17.

THE GOD OF LOVE.

Heavy, O Lord, on me Thy judgments lie,
Accurst I am, while God rejects my cry:
O'erwhelmed in darkness and despair I groan,
And every place is hell: for God is gone.
O! Lord, and let Thy beam control
Those horrid clouds, that press my frighted soul:
Save the poor wanderer from eternal night,
    Thou that art the God of Light.

Downward I hasten to my destin'd place :
There none obtain Thy aid or sing Thy praise.
Soon I shall lie in Death's deep ocean drown'd :
Is mercy there or sweet forgiveness found ?
O save me yet, whilst on the brink I stand ;
Rebuke the storm and waft my soul to land.
O let her rest beneath Thy wing secure,
    Thou that art the God of Power.

Behold the prodigal !   To Thee I come,
To hail my Father and to seek my home.
Nor refuge could I find, nor friend abroad,
Straying in vice and destitute of God.
O let Thy terrours and my anguish end !
Be Thou my refuge and be Thou my friend :
Receive the son Thou didst so long reprove,
    Thou that art the God of Love !

MATTHEW PRIOR.

JUNE 18.

[Battle of Waterloo—1815.]

WHAT hallows ground where heroes sleep ?
'Tis not the sculptured piles you heap !
In dews that heavens far distant weep
    Their turf may bloom ;
Or Genii twine beneath the deep
    Their coral tomb.

But strew his ashes to the wind
Whose sword or voice has served mankind—
And is he dead whose glorious mind
    Lifts thine on high ?—
To live in hearts we leave behind
    Is not to die.

Is't death to fall for Freedom's right?
He's dead alone that lacks her light!
And murder sullies in Heaven's sight
    The sword he draws :—
What can alone ennoble fight?
    A noble cause!

Give that! and welcome War to brace
Her drums! and rend Heaven's reeking space!
The colours planted face to face,
    The charging cheer,
Though Death's pale horse lead on the chase,
    Shall still be dear.

And place our trophies where men kneel
To Heaven!—but Heaven rebukes my zeal!
The cause of Truth and human weal,
    O God above!
Transfer it from the sword's appeal
    To Peace and Love.

Peace, Love! the cherubim, that join
Their spread wings o'er Devotion's shrine—
Prayers sound in vain, and temples shine,
    Where they are not—
The heart alone can make divine
    Religion's spot. . . .

What's hallow'd ground?   'Tis what gives birth
To sacred thoughts in souls of worth!—
Peace! Independence! Truth! go forth
    Earth's compass round;
And your high priesthood shall make earth
    All hallow'd ground.

THOMAS CAMPBELL.

JUNE 19.

ALMIGHTY Maker, God!
How wondrous is Thy name!
Thy glories how diffus'd abroad
Through the Creation's frame!

Nature in every dress
Her humble homage pays,
And finds a thousand ways t'express
Thine undissembled praise.

In native white and red
The rose and lily stand,
And, free from pride, their beauties spread,
To show Thy skilful hand.

The lark mounts up the sky,
With unambitious song,
And bears her Maker's praise on high
Upon her artless tongue.

My soul would rise and sing
To her Creator too,
Fain would my tongue adore my King,
And pay the worship due.

But pride, that busy sin,
Spoils all that I perform;
Curs'd pride, that creeps securely in,
And swells a haughty worm.

Thy glories I abate,
Or praise Thee with design;
Some of the favours I forget,
Or think the merit mine.

The very songs I frame
Are faithless to Thy cause,
And steal the honours of Thy Name
To build their own applause.

Create my soul anew,
Else all my worship's vain;
This wretched heart will ne'er be true
Until 'tis formed again.

Descend, celestial fire,
And seize me from above;
Melt me in flames of pure desire,
A sacrifice to love.

Let joy and worship spend
The remnant of my days,
And to my God, my soul, ascend,
In sweet perfumes of praise.

ISAAC WATTS.

JUNE 20.

SUMMER.

Now the glories of the year
May be viewed at the best,
And the earth doth now appear
In her fairest garments drest;
  Sweetly smelling plants and flowers
  Do perfume the garden bowers;
  Hill and valley, wood and field,
  Mixed with pleasure, profits yield.

Much is found where nothing was :
Herds on every mountain go,
In the meadows flowery grass
Makes both milk and honey flow ;
    Now each orchard banquets giveth,
    Every hedge with fruit relieveth ;
    And on every shrub and tree
    Useful fruits or berries be.

Walks and ways which winter marr'd,
By the winds are swept and dried :
Moorish grounds are now so hard
That on them we safe may ride :
    Warmth enough the sun doth lend us :
    From his heat the shades defend us :
    And thereby we share in these,
    Safety, profit, pleasure, ease.

Other blessings, many more,
At this time enjoyed may be,
And in this my song therefore
Praise I give, O Lord, to Thee :
    Grant that this my free oblation
    May have gracious acceptation,
    And that I may well employ
    Everything which I enjoy.

GEORGE WITHER.

JUNE 21.

[Midsummer day.]

Πάντα ῥεῖ.

LET no man boast of cunning nor virtúe,
    Of treasure, riches, nor of sapience,
Of worldly support; for all com'th of Jesu,
    Counsel, comfórt, discretion, and prudence.
Provision for sight and Providence,
    Like as the Lord of Grace list dispose;
Some man hath wisdom, some man eloquence :—
    All stant in change like a midsummer rose.

JOHN LYDGATE.

JUNE 22.

THE THANKSGIVING OF CREATION.

GREAT are Thy works, Jehovah! infinite
Thy power! what thought can measure Thee, or tongue
Relate Thee—greater now in Thy return
Than from the giant-angels?   Thee that day
Thy thunders magnified; but to create
Is greater than created to destroy.
Who can impair Thee, mighty King, or bound
Thy Empire?   Easily the proud attempt
Of Spirits apostate, and their counsels vain,
Thou hast repelled, while impiously they thought
Thee to diminish, and from Thee withdraw
The number of Thy worshippers.   Who seeks
To lessen Thee, against his purpose, serves
To manifest the more Thy might; his evil
Thou usest, and from thence creat'st more good.

Witness this new-made World, another Heaven
From Heaven-gate not far, founded in view
On the clear hyaline, the glassy sea;
Of amplitude almost immense, with stars
Numerous, and every star perhaps a world
Of destined habitation—but Thou know'st
Their seasons; among these the seat of men,
Earth, with her nether ocean circumfused,
Their pleasant dwelling-place.   Thrice happy men,
And sons of men, whom God hath thus advanced,
Created in His image, there to dwell
And worship Him, and in reward to rule
Over His works, on earth, in sea, or air,
And multiply a race of worshippers
Holy and just !   Thrice happy, if they know
Their happiness, and persevere upright !

JOHN MILTON.

JUNE 23.

PRAYER FOR THE UNIVERSITIES.

PRAY for the nurses of our noble realm,
I mean the worthy Universities,
That they bring up their babes in decent wise :
That Philosophy smell no secret smoke
Which Magick makes in wicked mysteries ;
That Logick leap not over every stile
Before he comes a furlong near the hedge,
With curious quids to maintain argument ;
That Sophistry do not deceive itself,
That Cosmográphy keep his compass well,
And such as be Historiographers
Trust not too much in every tattling tongue
Nor blinded be by partiality.

That Physick thrive not overfast by murder;
That Numbering men, in all their evens and odds,
Do not forget that only Unity
Immeasurable, Infinite, and One.
That Geométry measure not so long
Till all their measures out of measure be;
That Musick with his heavenly harmony
Do not allure a heavenly mind from heaven,
Nor set men's thoughts in worldly melody
Till heavenly hierarchies be quite forgot;
That Rhetorick learn not to over-reach;
That Poetry presume not for to preach
And bite men's faults with Satire's córrosives,
Yet pamper up her own with poultices,
Or that she dote not upon Erato,
Which should invoke the good Calliope;
That Astrológy look not overhigh,
And 'light meanwhile in every puddled pit:
That Grammar grudge not at our English tongue
Because it stands by monysyllaba,
And cannot be declined as others are.
   Pray thus, my Priests, for Universities;
   And if I have forgotten any Art
   Which hath been taught or exercisèd there,
   Pray you to God the good be not abused
   With glorious show of overloading skill.
GEORGE GASCOIGNE.

JUNE 24.

THE SEVENTH DAY.

AGAIN the day returns of holy rest,
Which, when He made the world, Jehovah blest;
When, like His own, He bade our labours cease,
And all be piety and all be peace.

While impious men despise Thy sage decree
From vain deceit and false philosophy ;
Let us its wisdom own, its blessings feel,
Receive with gratitude, perform with zeal.

Let us devote this consecrated day
To learn His will, and all we learn obey ;
In pure religion's hallow'd duties share,
And join in penitence, and join in prayer.

So shall the God of mercy, pleas'd, receive
That only tribute man has power to give ;
So shall He hear, while fervently we raise
Our choral harmony in hymns of praise.

Father of Heaven ! in whom our hopes confide,
Whose pow'r defends us, and whose precepts guide :
In life our guardian, and in death our friend—
Glory supreme be Thine till time shalt end.

WILLIAM MASON.

JUNE 25.

AYE, do not go ! Thou know'st I'll die !
    My spring and fall are in Thy book !
Or, if Thou goest, do not deny
    To lend me, though from far, one look !

My sins long since have made Thee strange,
    A very stranger unto me ;
No morning meetings since this change,
    Nor evening walks have I with Thee.

Why is my God so slow and cold,
    When I am most, most sick and sad ?
Well fare those blessed days of old,
    When Thou didst hear the weeping lad !

O do not Thou do as I did,
    Do not despise a love-sick heart !
What though some clouds defiance bid,
    Thy sun must shine in every part.

Though I have spoiled, O spoil not Thou !
    Hate not Thine own dear gift and token !
Poor birds sing best and prettiest show
    When their nest is fallen and broken.

Dear Lord ! restore Thy ancient peace,
    Thy quickening friendship, man's bright wealth !
And if Thou wilt not give me ease
    From sickenesse, give my spirit health !

HENRY VAUGHAN.

JUNE 26.

THE POET'S PARADISE.

MOST sweet and pleasing are Thy wayes, O God,
    Like meadowes deckt with Christall streames and
        flowers :
Thy paths no foot prophane has ever trod,
    Nor hath the proud man rested in Thy bowers :
There lives no Vultur, no devouring Beare,
But onely doves and lambs are harbor'd there.

The Wolfe his young ones to their prey doth guide ;
    The foxe his Cubbes with false deceit endues ;
The Lyon's whelpe suckes from his Damme his pride ;
    In hers the Serpent malice doth infuse :
The darksome Desart all such beasts contains,
Not one of them in Paradice remaynes.

DR THOMAS CAMPION.

M

JUNE 27.

TO GOD.

Come to me, God; but do not come
To me as to the General Doom
In power; or come Thou in that state
When Thou Thy laws didst promulgate,
Whenas the mountain quaked for dread,
And sullen clouds bound up his head.
No; lay Thy stately terrors by
To talk to me familiarly;
For if Thy thunder-claps I hear,
I shall less swoon than die for fear.
Speak Thou of love, and Ile reply
By way of Epithalamy,
Or sing of mercy and Ile suit
To it my viol and my lute;
Thus let Thy lips but love distil,
Then come, my God, and hap what will.

R. Herrick.

JUNE 28.

THE DESPONDING SOUL'S WISH.

My spirit longeth for Thee
   Within my troubled breast,
Altho' I be unworthy
   Of so divine a Guest.

Of so divine a Guest,
   Unworthy tho' I be,
Yet has my heart no rest,
   Unless it come from Thee.

Unless it come from Thee,
  In vain I look around ;
In all that I can see,
  No rest is to be found

No rest is to be found
  But in Thy blessed love ;
O ! let my wish be crown'd,
  And send it from above !

JOHN BYROM.

JUNE 29.

"FAINT, YET PURSUING."

HEROIC Good, target for which the young
Dream in their dreams that every bow is strung,
And, missing, sigh
Unfruitful, or as disbelievers die,
Thee having miss'd, I will not so revolt,
But lowlier shoot my bolt,
And lowlier still, if still I may not reach,
And my proud stomach teach
That less than highest is good, and may be high.
An even walk in life's uneven way,
Though to have dreamt of flight and not to fly
Be strange and sad,
Is not a boon that's given to all who pray.
If this I had,
I'd envy none !
Nay, trod I straight for one
Year, month, or week,
Should Heaven withdraw, and Satan me amerce
Of power and joy, still would I seek
Another victory, with a like reverse ;

Because the good of victory does not die,
As dies the failure's curse,
And what we have to gain
Is, not one battle, but a weary life's campaign.
Yet meaner lot being sent
Should more than me content ;
Yea, if I lie
Among vile shards, though born for silver wings,
In the strong flight and feathers gold
Of whatsoever heavenward mounts and sings,
I must by admiration so comply
That there I should my own delight behold.
Yea, though I sin each day times seven,
And dare not lift the fearfullest eyes to Heaven,
Thanks must I give
Because that seven times are not eight or nine,
And that my darkness is all mine,
And that I live
Within this oak-shade one more minute even
Hearing the winds their Maker magnify.

COVENTRY PATMORE.

JUNE 30.

PRAYER FOR TRUE WISDOM.

WHOSO will be accounted wise, and truly claim the
    name,
By joining virtue to his deeds he must achieve the
    same.
But few there be that seek thereby true wisdom to
    attain :
O God, so rule our hearts therefore such fondness to
    refrain.

The wisdom which we most esteem, in this thing doth
    consist,
With glorious talk to show in words our wisdom when
    we list :
Yet not in talk but seemly deeds our wisdom we should
    place,
To speak so fair and do but ill doth wisdom quite
    disgrace.

To bargain well and shun the loss, a wisdom counted is,
And thereby through the greedy coin no hope of grace
    to miss.
To seek by honour to advance his name to brittle praise,
Is wisdom which we daily see increaseth in our days.

But heavenly wisdom sour seems, too hard for them to
    win,
But weary of the suit they seem, when they do once
    begin :
It teacheth us to frame our life while vital breath we
    have,
When it dissolveth earthly mass, the soul from death
    to save.

By fear of God to rule our steps from sliding into vice
A wisdom is, which we neglect, although of greater
    price :
A point of wisdom also this we commonly esteem,
That every man should Be indeed that he desires to
    Seem.

To bridle that desire of gain which forceth us to ill,
Our haughty stomachs, Lord, repress to tame presuming
    will :
This is the wisdom that we should above each thing
    desire,
O heavenly God, from sacred throne that grace in us
    inspire !

And print in our repugnant hearts the rules of wisdom
     true,
That all our deeds in worldly life may like thereof
     ensue :
Thou only art the living spring from whom this wisdom
     flows,
Oh, wash therewith our sinful hearts from vice that
     therein grows.

RICHARD EDWARDS
(Master of Queen Elizabeth's Chapel Royal).

JULY 1.

HYMN.

From my lips in their defilement,
From my heart in its beguilement,
From my tongue which speaks not fair,
From my soul, stained everywhere,
O my Jesus, take my prayer !

Spurn me not for all it says,
Not for words and not for ways,
Not for shamelessness endued !
Make me brave to speak my mood,
O my Jesus, as I would !
Or teach me, which I rather seek,
What to do and what to speak.

I have sinnèd more than she,
Who, learning where to meet with Thee,
    And bringing myrrh, the highest-priced,
Anointed bravely, from her knee,
Thy blessed feet accordingly.
    My God, my Lord, my Christ !
As Thou saidest not " Depart,"
To that suppliant from her heart,
Scorn me not, O Word, that art
The gentlest one of all words said !
But give Thy feet to me instead,
That tenderly I may them kiss
And clasp them close, and never miss

With over-dropping tears as free
And precious as that myrrh could be,
T''anoint them bravely from my knee !
Wash me with Thy tears : draw nigh me,
That their salt may purify me.
THOU remit my sins who knowest
All the sinning to the lowest—
Knowest all my wounds, and seest
All the stripes Thyself decreest ;
Yea, but knowest all my faith,
Seest all my force to death,
Hearest all my wailings low,
That mine evil should be so !
Nothing hidden but appears
In Thy knowledge, O Divine,
O Creator, Saviour mine—
Not a drop of falling tears,
Not a breath of inward moan,
Not a heart-beat—which is gone !

JOHN DAMASCENUS.
(Trs. Eliz. Barrett Browning.)

JULY 2.

THE LAW OF FAITH.

THE darts of anguish *fix* not where the seat
Of suffering hath been thoroughly fortified
By acquiescence in the will supreme
For time and for eternity ; by faith,
Faith absolute in God, including hope,
And the defence that lies in boundless love
Of His perfections ; with habitual dread
Of aught unworthily conceived, endured
Impatiently, ill done, or left undone,
To the dishonour of His holy name.

Soul of our souls, and safeguard of the world !
Sustain, Thou only canst, the sick of heart ;
Restore their languid spirits, and recall
Their lost affections unto Thee and Thine !

WILLIAM WORDSWORTH.

JULY 3.

TO HEAVEN.

GOOD and great God !   Can I not think of Thee,
But it must straight my melancholy be ?
Is it interpreted in me disease,
That, laden with my sins, I seek for ease ?
O be Thou witness, that the reins dost know
And hearts of all, if I be sad for show ;
And judge me after, if I dare pretend
To aught but grace or aim at other end.
As Thou art all, so be Thou all to me,
First, midst, and last, converted One and Three !
My faith, my hope, my love : and, in this state,
My judge, my witness, and my advocate !
Where have I been this while exiled from Thee,
And whither rapt, now Thou but stoop'st to me ?
Dwell, dwell here still !   O, being everywhere,
How can I doubt to find Thee ever here ?
I know my state, both full of shame and scorn,
Conceived in sin and unto labour born,
Standing with fear, and must with horror fall,
And destined unto judgment, after all.
I feel my griefs too, and there scarce is ground
Upon my flesh to inflict another wound ; —

Yet dare I not complain or wish for death,
With holy Paul, lest it be thought the breath
Of discontent : or that these prayers be
For weariness of life, not love of Thee.

BEN JONSON.

JULY 4.

THE PEOPLE'S ANTHEM.

WHEN wilt Thou save the people ?
  O God of mercy, when ?
Not kings and lords, but nations !
  Not thrones and crowns, but men !
Flowers of Thy heart, O God, are they ;
Let them not pass, like weeds away—
Their heritage a sunless day.
        God save the people !

Shall crime bring crime for ever,
  Strength aiding still the strong ?
Is it Thy will, O Father,
  That man shall toil for wrong ?
"No" say Thy mountains, "No" Thy skies !
Man's clouded sun shall brightly rise,
And songs be heard instead of sighs.
        God save the people !

When wilt Thou save the people ?
  O God of mercy, when ?
The people, Lord, the people,
  Not thrones and crowns, but men !
God save the people ; Thine they are,
Thy children, as Thy angels fair ;
Save them from bondage and despair !
        God save the people !

EBENEZER ELLIOT.

JULY 5.

WRITTEN IN THE ALARM OF INVASION.

Spare us yet awhile,
Father and God! Oh! spare us yet awhile!
Oh! let not English women drag their flight
Fainting beneath the burthen of their babes,
Of the sweet infants, that but yesterday
Laughed at the breast.   Sons, brothers, husbands, all
Who ever gazed with fondness on the forms
Which grew up with you round the same fireside,
And all who ever heard the Sabbath-bells
Without the infidel's scorn, make yourselves pure!
Stand forth! be men! repel an impious foe,
Impious and false, a light yet cruel race,
Who laugh away all virtue, mingling mirth
With deeds of murder; and still promising
Freedom, themselves too sensual to be free,
Poison life's amities and cheat the heart
Of faith and quiet hope and all that soothes
And all that lifts the spirit!   Stand we forth;
Render them back upon the unsalted ocean,
And let them toss as idly on its waves
As the vile sea-weed, which some mountain-blast
Swept from our shores!   And oh! may we return
Not with a drunken triumph, but with fear,
Repenting of the wrongs with which we stung
So fierce a foe to frenzy!
S. T. COLERIDGE.

JULY 6.

EVENING HYMN.

ALL praise to Thee, my God, this night,
For all the blessings of the light !
Keep me, O keep me, King of kings,
Beneath Thine own almighty wings.

Forgive me, Lord, for Thy dear Son,
The ill that I this day have done ;
That with the world, myself, and Thee,
I, ere I sleep, at peace may be.

Teach me to live, that I may dread
The grave as little as my bed ;
To die, that this vile body may
Rise glorious at the awful day.

O may my soul on Thee repose,
And may sweet sleep mine eyelids close—
Sleep that may me more vigorous make,
To serve my God when I awake.

When in the night I sleepless lie,
My soul with heavenly thoughts supply ;
Let no ill dreams disturb my rest,
No powers of darkness me molest.

Dull sleep !—of sense me to deprive ;
I am but half my time alive ;
Thy faithful lovers, Lord, are grieved
To lie so long of Thee bereaved.

But though sleep o'er my frailty reigns,
Let it not hold me long in chains;
But now and then let loose my heart,
Till it an Hallelujah dart.

The faster sleep the senses binds,
The more unfettered are our minds;
Oh, may my soul, from matter free,
Thy loveliness unclouded see.

Oh, when shall I, in endless day,
For ever chase dark sleep away;
And hymns with the supernal choir
Incessant sing, and never tire !

Oh, may my Guardian, while I sleep,
Close to my bed His vigils keep,
His love angelical distil,
Stop all the avenues of ill.

May He celestial joy rehearse,
And thought to thought with me converse;
Or in my stead, all the night long,
Sing to my God a grateful song.

Praise God, from whom all blessings flow,
Praise Him, all creatures here below,
Praise Him above, ye heavenly host,
Praise Father, Son, and Holy Ghost.

Bishop Thomas Ken.

JULY 7.

L'ENVOI.

My new-cut ashlar takes the light
  Where crimson-blank the windows flare;
By my own work, before the night,
  Great Overseer, I make my prayer.

If there be good in that I wrought,
  Thy hand compelled it, Master, Thine;
Where I have failed to meet Thy thought,
  I know, through Thee, the blame is mine.

One instant's toil to Thee denied
  Stands all Eternity's offence,
Of that I did with Thee to guide,
  To Thee, through Thee, be excellence.

Who, lest all thought of Eden fade,
  Bring'st Eden to the craftsman's brain,
Godlike to muse o'er his own trade,
  And Manlike stand with God again.

The depth and dream of my desire,
  The bitter paths wherein I stray,
Thou knowest Who hast made the fire,
  Thou knowest Who hast made the clay.

One stone the more swings to her place
  In that dread Temple of Thy Worth—
It is enough that through Thy grace
  I saw naught common on Thy earth.

Take not that vision from my ken;
  Oh, whatsoe'er may spoil or speed,
Help me to need no aid from men,
  That I may help such men as need!

RUDYARD KIPLING.

____

JULY 8.

PROMETHEUS APPEALS TO THE SYMPATHY OF NATURE.

Thou firmament of God and swift-winged winds,
Ye springs of rivers, and of ocean-waves
Thou smile innumerous! Mother of us all,
O Earth and Sun's all-seeing eye, behold,
I pray, what I a God from Gods endure.
    Behold in what foul case
    I for ten thousand years
    Shall struggle in my woe,
    In these unseemly chains.
Such doom the new-made Monarch of the Blest
    Hath now devised for me.
Woe! Woe!   The present and the oncoming pang
    I wail, as I search out
The place and hour when end of all these ills
    Shall dawn on me at last.
What say I?   All too clearly I foresee
The things that come, and nought of pain shall be
By me unlooked for; but I needs must bear
My destiny as best I may, knowing well
The might resistless of Necessity.
        Æschylus (*Trs.* E. H. Plumptre).

JULY 9.

WEARINESS.

I am! yet what I am who cares or knows?
My friends forsake me like a memory lost.
I am the self-consumer of my woes,
They rise and vanish, an oblivious host,
Shadows of life, whose very soul is lost.
And yet I am—I live—though I am tossed

Into the nothingness of scorn and noise,
Into the living sea of waking dream,
Where there is neither sense of life nor joys,
But the huge shipwreck of my own esteem
And all that's dear.   Even those I loved the best
Are strange,—nay, they are stranger than the rest.

I long for scenes where man has never trod,
For scenes where woman never smiled or wept,
There to abide with my Creator, God,
And sleep as I in childhood sweetly slept,
Full of high thoughts, unborn.   So let me lie,
The grass below; above, the vaulted sky.

JOHN CLARE.

JULY 10.

THE GOD OF PSALMODY.

THE radiant hope new-born
Expands like rising morn
In my life's life : and as a ripening rose
The crimson shadow of its glory throws,
More vivid, hour by hour, on some pure stream ;
So from that hope are spreading
Rich hues, o'er nature shedding
Each day a clearer, spiritual gleam.

Let not those rays fade from me !   Once enjoyed,
Father of Spirits ! let them not depart—
Leaving the chilled earth without form and void,
Darkened by mine own heart !
Lift, aid, sustain me ! Thou, by whom alone
All lovely gifts and pure
In the soul's grasp endure ;
Thou, to the steps of whose eternal throne
All knowledge flows—a sea for evermore
Breaking its crested waves on that sole shore—

Oh, consecrate my life ! that I may sing
Of Thee with joy that hath a living spring
In a full heart of music !   Let my lays
Through the resounding mountains waft Thy praise,
And with that theme the woods' green cloisters fill,
And make their quivering leafy dimness thrill
To the rich breeze of song !   Oh, let me wake
      The deep religion which hath dwelt from yore
Silently brooding by lone cliff and lake
      And wildest river-shore !
And let me summon all the voices dwelling
Where eagles build, and caverned rills are welling,
And where the cataracts' organ-peal is swelling,
      In that one spirit gathered to adore !

Forgive, O Father ! if presumptuous thought
      Too daringly in aspiration rise !
Let not Thy child all vainly have been taught
      By weakness and by wanderings and by sighs
Of sad confession ! lowly be my heart,
      And on its penitential altar spread
The offerings worthless, till Thy grace impart
      The fire from heaven, whose touch alone can shed
Life, radiance, virtue ! let that vital spark
Pierce my whole being, wildered else and dark !
Thine are all holy things—oh, make me Thine !
So shall I too be pure—a living shrine
Unto that Spirit which goes forth from Thee,
      Strong and divinely free,
Bearing Thy gifts of wisdom on its flight,
And brooding o'er them with a dove-like wing,
Till thought, word, song to Thee in worship spring,
      Immortally endowed for liberty and light.

MRS HEMANS.

N

JULY 11.

NEARER, my God, to Thee,
    Nearer to Thee !
Even though it be a cross
    That raiseth me,
Still all my song shall be,
Nearer, my God, to Thee,
    Nearer to Thee !

Though, like the wanderer,
    The sun gone down,
Darkness be over me,
    My rest a stone ;
Yet in my dreams I'd be
Nearer, my God, to Thee,
    Nearer to Thee !

Then let the way appear
    Steps unto heaven ;
All that Thou send'st to me,
    In mercy given ;
Angels to beckon me
Nearer, my God, to Thee,
    Nearer to Thee !

Then with my waking thoughts
    Bright with Thy praise,
Out of those stony griefs
    Bethel I'll raise ;
So by my woes to be
Nearer, my God, to Thee,
    Nearer to Thee !

Or if on joyful wing,
    Cleaving the sky,
Sun, moon, and stars forgot,
    Upward I fly;
Still all my song shall be,
Nearer, my God, to Thee,
    Nearer to Thee!

SARAH FLOWER ADAMS.

JULY 12.

"I REMEMBER, I REMEMBER."

THERE was a time when I was very small,
    When my whole frame was but an ell in height,
Sweetly, as I recall it, tears do fall,
    And therefore I recall it with delight.

Then seemed to me the world far less in size,
    Likewise it seemed to me less wicked far;
Like points in heaven I saw the stars arise,
    And longed for wings that I might catch a star.

I saw the moon behind the island fade,
    And thought, " O, were I on that island there,
I could find out of what the moon is made,
    Find out how large it is, how round, how fair ! "

Wondering, I saw God's sun, through western skies,
    Sink in the ocean's golden lap at night,
And yet upon the morrow early rise,
    And paint the eastern heaven with crimson light :

And thought of God, the gracious heavenly Father,
    Who made me and that lovely sun on high,
And all those pearls of heaven, thick-strung together,
    Dropped, clustering, from His hand o'er all the sky.

With childish reverence, my young lips did say
    The prayer my pious mother taught to me:
"O gentle God! O let me strive alway
    Still to be wise and good and follow Thee!"

So prayed I for my father and my mother,
    And for my sister and for all the town;
The king I knew not, or the beggar-brother
    Who, bent with age, went sighing up and down.

They perished, the blithe days of childhood perished,
    And all the gladness, all the peace I knew!
Now I have but their memory, fondly cherished—
    God! may I never, never lose that too.

H. W. LONGFELLOW.
—From the Danish of Baggesen.

JULY 13.

JESU CHRIST, Saint Mary's sonne,
Through whom this world was worthily wrought,
I pray Thee come and in me wonne,
And of all filthes clense my thought.

Jesu Christ, my Godde verray,
That of oure dere lady was borne,
Thou helpe now and ever and aye,
And let me never for sin be born.

Jesu Christ, Goddes son of heaven,
That for me died on the rood,
I pray Thee hear my simple steven,[1]
Through the virtue of Thy holy blood.

[1] Voice.

Jesu, Thy love me chafe within,
So that no thing but Thee I seke;
In Thy love make my soul to brynne,
Thy love me make both mild and meek!

Jesu, my joy and my loving,
Jesu, my comfort clear,
Jesu, my God, Jesu, my King,
Jesu withouten peer,

Jesu that all hast made of noughte,
Jesu, that bought me dear,
Jesu, joyne Thy love in my thoughte,
So that they never be sere!

Jesu, my dear and my drewrye,[1]
Delight Thou art to sing,
Jesu, my mirth and melodye,
Into Thy love me brynge!

Jesu, Jesu, my honey swete,
My heart, my comforting,
Jesu, all my bales Thou bete,[2]
And to Thy bliss me bring!

ANON. (Circa 1400.)

JULY 14.

CLEANSE THOU ME.

IF I could shut the gate against my thoughts,
  And keep out sorrow from this room within,
Or memory could cancel all the notes
  Of my misdeeds, and I unthink my sin:
How free, how clear, how clean my soul should lie,
Discharged of such a loathsome company!

---

[1] Affection.   [2] Assuage my sorrows.

Or were there other rooms without my heart
  That did not to my conscience join so near,
Where I might lodge the thoughts of sin apart,
  That I might not their clam'rous crying hear;
What peace, what joy, what ease should I possess,
Freed from their horrors that my soul oppress!

But, O my Saviour, who my refuge art,
  Let Thy dear mercies stand 'twixt them and me,
And be the wall to separate my heart,
  So that I may at length repose me free;
That peace and joy and rest may be within,
And I remain divided from my sin.

JOHN DANYEL.

JULY 15.

THE RESIGNATION.

O God, whose thunder shakes the sky,
  Whose eye this atom globe surveys,
To Thee, my only rock, I fly,
  Thy mercy in Thy justice praise.

The mystic mazes of Thy will,
  The shadows of celestial light,
Are past the power of human skill,—
  But what th' Eternal acts is right.

O teach me in the trying hour,
  When anguish swells the dewy tear,
To still my sorrows, own Thy power,
  Thy goodness love, Thy justice fear.

If in this bosom aught but Thee
    Encroaching found a boundless sway,
Omniscience could the danger see,
    And mercy look the cause away.

Then why, my soul, dost thou complain?
    Why, drooping, seek the dark recess?
Shake off the melancholy chain,
    For God created all to bless.

But, ah ! my heart is human still ;
    The rising sigh, the falling tear,
My languid vitals' feeble rill
    The sickness of my soul declare.

But yet, with fortitude resigned,
    I'll thank th' inflicter of the blow,
Forbid the sigh, compose my mind,
    Nor let the gush of mis'ry flow.

The gloomy mantle of the night,
    Which on my sinking spirit steals,
Will vanish at the morning light,
    Which God, my East, my Sun, reveals.

THOMAS CHATTERTON.

JULY 16.

TO HIS EVER-LOVING GOD.

Can I not come to Thee, my God, for these
So very many meeting hindrances,
That slack my pace, but yet not make me stay?
Who slowly goes, rids (in the end) his way ;
Cleere Thou my paths, or shorten Thou my miles,
Remove the barrs, or lift me o'er the stiles ;

Since rough the way is, help me when I call,
And take me up, or els prevent the fall.
I kenn my home ; and it affords some ease
To see far off the smoaking Villages.
Fain would I rest, yet covet not to die,
For feare of future-biting penurie ;
No, no (my God), Thou know'st my wishes be
To leave this life, not loving it, but Thee.

R. HERRICK.

JULY 17.

A PRAYER FOR PEACE.

DELIGHT of humankind and gods above,
Parent of Rome, propitious Queen of Love,
Whose vital power air, earth, and sea supplies,
And breeds whate'er is born beneath the rolling skies :
For every kind, by Thy prolific might,
Springs and beholds the regions of the light.
Thee, Goddess, Thee the clouds and tempests fear,
And at Thy pleasing presence disappear ;
For Thee the land in fragrant flowers is dress'd,
For Thee the Ocean smiles and smooths her wavy
    breast,
And heaven itself with more serene and purer light is
    blest.
For when the rising spring adorns the mead,
And a new scene of nature stands display'd,
When teeming buds and cheerful greens appear,
And western gales unlock the lazy year ;
The joyous birds their welcome first express,
Whose native songs Thy genial fire confess :
Then savage beasts bound o'er their slighted food,
Struck with Thy darts, and tempt the raging flood.

All nature is Thy gift : earth, air, and sea ;
Of all that breathes, the various progeny,
Stung with delight, is goaded on by Thee.
O'er barren mountains, o'er the flowery plain,
The leafy forest and the liquid main,
Extends Thy uncontroll'd and boundless reign.
Through all the living regions dost Thou move,
And scatter'st where Thou goest the kindly seeds of
    love.
Since, then, the race of every living thing
Obeys Thy power ; since nothing new can spring
Without Thy warmth, without Thy influence bear,
Or beautiful or lovesome can appear,—
Be Thou my aid, my tuneful song inspire,
And kindle with Thy own productive fire.
Meantime on land and sea let barbarous discord cease,
And lull the listening world in universal peace.
To Thee mankind their soft repose must owe,
For Thou alone that blessing canst bestow ;
Because the brutal business of the war
Is manag'd by Thy dreadful servant's care,
Who oft retires from fighting fields to prove
The pleasing pains of Thy eternal love,
And panting on Thy breast supinely lies,
While with Thy heavenly form he feeds his famish'd
    eyes,
Sucks in with open lips Thy balmy breath,
By turns restored to life and plunged in pleasing Death.
There, while Thy curling limbs about him move,
Involved and fetter'd in the links of love,
When wishing all, he nothing can deny
Thy charms in that auspicious moment try :
With winning eloquence our peace implore,
And quiet to the weary world restore !

LUCRETIUS.
(Trs. John Dryden.)

JULY 18.

DEATH ANSWERS PRAYER.

THE dew is on the summer's greenest grass,
　Through which the modest daisy blushing peeps;
The gentle wind, that like a ghost doth pass,
　A waving shadow on the corn-field keeps;
But I, who love them all, shall never be
Again among the woods, or on the moorland lea!

The sun shines sweetly—sweeter may it shine!—
　Blessed is the brightness of a summer day;
It cheers lone hearts, and why should I repine,
　Although among green fields I cannot stray?
Woods! I have grown, since last I heard you wave,
Familiar with death, and neighbour to the grave!

These words have shaken mighty human souls—
　Like a sepulchre's echo drear they sound—
E'en as the owl's wild whoop at midnight rolls
　The ivied remnants of old ruins round.
Yet wherefore tremble? Can the soul decay?
Or that which thinks and feels in aught e'er fade away?

Are there not aspirations in each heart
　After a better, brighter world than this?
Longings for beings nobler in each part—
　Things more exalted—steeped in deeper bliss?
Who gave us these? what are they? Soul, in thee
The bud is budding now for immortality.

Death comes to take me where I long to be;
　One pang, and bright blooms the immortal flower;
Death comes to lead me from mortality
　To lands which know not one unhappy hour;
I have a hope, a faith—from sorrow here
I'm led by Death away—why should I start and fear?

If I have loved the forest and the field,
  Can I not love them deeper, better there ?
If all that Power hath made to me doth yield
  Something of good and beauty—something fair—
Freed from the grossness of mortality,
May I not love them all, and better all enjoy ?

A change from woe to joy—from earth to heaven,
  Death gives me this—it leads me calmly where
The souls that long ago from mine were riven
  May meet again !   Death answers many a prayer.
Bright day, shine on ! be glad : days brighter far
Are stretched before my eyes than those of mortals are !

ROBERT NICOLL.

JULY 19.

Guide me, O Thou great Jehovah !
  Pilgrim through this barren land ;
I am weak, but Thou art mighty ;
  Hold me with Thy powerful hand.
    Bread of heaven !
Feed me till I want no more.

Open Thou the crystal fountain,
  Whence the healing streams do flow ;
Let the fiery, cloudy pillar
  Lead me all the journey through.
    Strong Deliverer !
Be Thou still my strength and shield.

When I tread the verge of Jordan,
  Bid my anxious fears subside ;
Death of death, and hell's destruction,
  Land me safe on Canaan's side ;
    Songs of praises,
I will ever give to Thee.

W. WILLIAMS.
(Originally written in Welsh.)

JULY 20.

JOHN THE PILGRIM.

BENEATH the sand-storm John the Pilgrim prays ;
  But when he rises, lo ! an Eden smiles,
  Green leafy slopes, meadows of camomiles,
Claspt in a silvery river's winding maze :
" Water, water ! blessed be God ! " he says,
  And totters, gasping, toward those happy isles.
  Then all is fled ! over the sandy piles
The bold-eyed vultures come and stand and gaze.
" God heard me not," says he, " blessed be God,"
  And dies.   But as he nears the pearly strand,
  Heav'n's outer coast, where waiting angels stand,
He looks below : " Farewell, thou hooded clod,
  Brown corpse the vultures tear on bloody sand,
God heard my prayer for life—blessèd be God ! "

THEODORE WATTS-DUNTON.

JULY 21.

[Robert Burns died, 1796.]

THROUGH busiest street and loneliest glen
Are felt the flashes of his pen ;
He rules 'mid winter snows, and when
    Bees fill their hives ;
Deep in the general heart of men
    His power survives.

What need of fields in some far clime
Where Heroes, Sages, Bards sublime,
And all that fetched the flowing rhyme
    From genuine springs,
Shall dwell together till old Time
    Folds up his wings ?

Sweet Mercy ! to the gates of heaven
This Minstrel lead, his sins forgiven ;
The rueful conflict, the heart riven
    With vain endeavour,
And memory of Earth's bitter leaven
    Effaced for ever.

But why to him confine the prayer,
When kindred thoughts and yearnings bear
On the frail heart the purest share
    With all that live ?—
The best of what we do and are,
    Just God, forgive !

WILLIAM WORDSWORTH.

JULY 22.

WESTWARD HO!

THERE lies the port : the vessel puffs her sail :
There gloom the dark broad seas.   My mariners,
Souls that have toil'd, and wrought, and thought with
     me—
That ever with a frolic welcome took
The thunder and the sunshine, and opposed
Free hearts, free foreheads—you and I are old ;
Old age hath yet his honour and his toil ;
Death closes all : but something ere the end,
Some work of noble note, may yet be done,
Not unbecoming men that strove with Gods.
The lights begin to twinkle from the rocks :
The long day wanes : the slow moon climbs : the deep
Moans round with many voices.   Come, my friends,
'Tis not too late to seek a newer world.
Push off, and sitting well in order smite
The sounding furrows ; for my purpose holds
To sail beyond the sunset, and the baths
Of all the western stars, until I die.
It may be that the gulfs will wash us down :
It may be we shall touch the Happy Isles,
And see the great Achilles, whom we knew.
Tho' much is taken, much abides ; and tho'
We are not now that strength which in old days
Moved earth and heaven ; that which we are, we are ;
One equal temper of heroic hearts,
Made weak by time and fate, but strong in will
To strive, to seek, to find, and not to yield.

ALFRED, LORD TENNYSON.

JULY 23.

THE LIGHT THAT IS FELT.

A TENDER child of summers three,
Seeking her little bed at night,
Paused on the dark stair timidly.
"O mother, take my hand," said she,
"And then the dark will all be light!"

We older children grope our way
From dark behind to dark before;
And only when our hands we lay,
Dear Lord, in Thine, the night is day,
And then is darkness nevermore.

Reach downward to the sunless days,
Wherein our guides are blind as we,
And faith is small and hope delays;
Take Thou the hands of prayer we raise,
And let us feel the light of Thee!

J. G. WHITTIER.

JULY 24.

"THERE REMAINETH A REST."

My Lord, my Love, was crucified;
    He all the pains did bear;
But in the sweetness of His rest
    He makes His servants share.
How sweetly rest Thy saints above
    Which in Thy bosom lie!
The Church below doth rest in hope
    Of that felicity.

Thou, Lord, who daily feed'st Thy sheep,
   Mak'st them a weekly feast;
Thy flocks meet in their several folds
   Upon this day of rest;
Welcome and dear unto my soul
   Are these sweet feasts of love;
But what a Sabbath shall I keep
   When I shall rest above!

I bless Thy wise and wondrous love,
   Which binds us to be free;
Which makes us leave our earthly snares,
   That we may come to Thee!
I come, I wait, I hear, I pray!
   Thy footsteps, Lord, I trace!
I sing to think this is the way
   Unto my Saviour's face!

JOHN MASON.

JULY 25.

LORD, many times I am aweary quite
   Of mine own self, my sin, my vanity—
Yet be not Thou, or I am lost outright,
     Weary of me.

And hate against myself I often bear,
   And enter with myself in fierce debate;
Take Thou my part against myself, nor share
     In that just hate.

Best friends might loathe us, if what things perverse
   We know of our own selves, they also knew;
Lord, Holy One! if Thou, who knowest worse,
     Should loathe us too!

RICHARD CHENEVIX TRENCH.

JULY 26.

*ETENIM RES CREATÆ EXERTO CAPITE OB-
SERVANTES EXPECTANT REVELATIONEM
FILIORUM DEI.*

I would I were a stone, or tree,
    Or flow'r by pedigree,
Or some poor highway herb, or spring
    To flow, or bird to sing!
Then should I, tied to one sure state,
    All day expect my date.
But I am sadly loose, and stray,
    A giddy blast each way;
    Oh let me not thus range!
        Thou canst not change.

Sometimes I sit with Thee, and tarry
    An hour or so, then vary.
Thy other creatures in this scene
    Thee only aim and mean;
Some rise to seek Thee, and with heads
    Erect peep from their beds;
Others, whose birth is in the tomb,
    And cannot quit the womb,
    Sigh there, and groan for Thee,
        Their liberty.

O let not me do less! shall they
    Watch, while I sleep or play?
Shall I Thy mercies still abuse
    With fancies, friends, or news?
O brook it not! Thy blood is mine,
    And my soul should be Thine;

O brook it not ! why wilt Thou stop
   After whole show'rs one drop ?
   Sure Thou wilt joy to see
     Thy sheep with Thee.

HENRY VAUGHAN.

JULY 27.

AT SEA.

ON those great waters now I am
   Of which I have been told,
That whosoever thither came
   Should wonders there behold.
In this unsteady place of fear,
   Be present, Lord, with me :
For in these depths of water here
   I depths of danger see.

A stirring courser now I sit,
   A headstrong steed I ride,
That champs and foams upon the bit
   Which curbs his lofty pride.
The softest whistling of the winds
   Doth make him gallop fast :
And as their breath increased, he finds
   The more he maketh haste.

Take Thou, O Lord, the reins in hand,
   Assume our Master's room :
Vouchsafe Thou at our helm to stand,
   And pilot to become.
Trim Thou the sails, and let good-speed
   Accompany our haste,
Send Thou the Channels at our need,
   And anchor for us cast.

A fit and favourable wind
  To further us provide,
And let it wait on us behind
  Or lackey by our side.
From sudden gusts, from storms, from sands,
  And from the raging wave,
From shallows, rocks, and pirates' hands
  Men, goods, and vessel save.

Preserve us from the wants, the fear,
  And sickness of the seas ;
But chiefly from our sins, which are
  A danger worse than these.
Lord ! let us also safe arrive
  Where we desire to be :
And for Thy mercies let us give
  Due thanks and praise to Thee.

GEORGE WITHER.

PRAYER OF ODYSSEUS, IN PERIL OF DROWNING.

KING of this River ! hear : whatever name
Makes Thee invoked, to Thee I humbly frame
My flight from Neptune's furies.   Reverend is
To all the ever-living Deities
What erring man soever seeks their aid,
To Thy both flood and knees a man dismay'd
With varied sufferance sues.   Yield then some rest
To him that is Thy suppliant professed !

HOMER.
(Trs. George Chapman.)

JULY 28.

READ AT HER MOTHER'S FEET.

Almighty Being, that dost dwell
  In the high Heavens apart,
Alone, and inaccessible
  Save to the seeing heart;
Shelter our herds, increase our folds,
  Ripen the swelling grain,
Breathe life into the barren rocks,
  And send the timely rain.

Grant to my father length of days,
  And to my mother give
A spirit meek, that in Thy gaze
  She humbly still may live!
Cause me to feel, through good, through ill,
  How poor a thing am I,
And, when I have fulfilled Thy will,
  Resignedly to die.

Alfred Austin.

JULY 29.

ADEQUACY.

Now, by the verdure on thy thousand hills,
  Beloved England, doth the earth appear
  Quite good enough for men to overbear
The will of God in, with rebellious wills!
We cannot say the morning sun fulfils
  Ingloriously its course, nor that the clear
  Strong stars without significance insphere
Our habitation: we, meantime, our ills

Heap up against this good, and lift a cry
  Against this work-day world, this ill-spread feast,
As if ourselves were better certainly
  Than what we come to.   Maker and High Priest,
I ask Thee not my joys to multiply,—
  Only to make me worthier of the least.

E. BARRETT BROWNING.

JULY 30.

IN THE VALE OF CHAMOUNI.

Awake! my soul! not only passive praise
Thou owest! not alone these swelling tears,
Mute thanks, and secret ecstasy!   Awake,
Voice of sweet song!   Awake, my heart, awake!
Green vales and icy cliffs, all join my hymn.
Thou, first and chief, sole sovereign of the Vale!
O struggling with the darkness all the night,
And visited all night by troops of stars,
Or when they climb the sky, or when they sink:
Companion of the morning star at dawn,
Thyself Earth's rosy star, and of the dawn
Co-herald: wake, O wake, and utter praise!
Who sank thy sunless pillars deep in Earth?
Who filled thy countenance with rosy light?
Who made thee parent of perpetual streams?
And you, ye five wild torrents fiercely glad!
Who called you forth from night and utter death,
From dark and icy caverns called you forth,
Down those precipitous, black, jagged rocks,
For ever shattered and the same for ever?
Who gave you your invulnerable life,
Your strength, your speed, your fury, and your joy,
Unceasing thunder and eternal foam?
And who commanded (and the silence came),
Here let the billows stiffen and have rest?
Ye Ice-falls! ye that from the mountain's brow

Adown enormous ravines slope amain—
Torrents, methinks, that heard a mighty voice,
And stopped at once amid their maddest plunge !
Motionless torrents ! silent cataracts !
Who made you glorious as the Gates of Heaven
Beneath the keen full moon ?   Who bade the sun
Clothe you with rainbows ?   Who, with living flowers
Of loveliest blue, spread garlands at your feet ?—
God ! let the torrents, like a shout of nations,
Answer ! and let the ice-plains echo, God !
God ! sing, ye meadow-streams, with gladsome voice !
Ye pine-groves, with your soft and soul-like sounds !
And they too have a voice, yon piles of snow,
And in their perilous fall shall thunder, God !
Ye living flowers that skirt the eternal frost !
Ye wild goats sporting round the eagle's nest !
Ye eagles, playmates of the mountain-storm !
Ye lightnings, the dread arrows of the clouds !
Ye signs and wonders of the element !
Utter forth God, and fill the hills with praise !
Thou too, hoar Mount ! with thy sky-pointing peaks,
Oft from whose feet the avalanche, unheard,
Shoots downward, glittering through the pure serene
Into the depth of clouds that veil thy breast—
Thou too again, stupendous Mountain !   Thou
That as I raise my head, awhile bowed low
In adoration, upward from thy base
Slow travelling with dim eyes suffused with tears,
Solemnly seemest, like a vapoury cloud,
To rise before me—Rise, O ever rise,
Rise like a cloud of incense from the Earth !
Thou kingly Spirit throned among the hills,
Thou dread ambassador from Earth to Heaven,
Great hierarch ! tell thou the silent sky,
And tell the stars, and tell yon rising sun,
Earth, with her thousand voices, praises God.

S. T. COLERIDGE.

JULY 31.

" Now more than ever seems it rich to die,
To cease upon the midnight with no pain."

THE last high upward slant of sun on the trees,
Like a dead soldier's sword upon his pall,
Seems to console earth for the glory gone.
O! I could weep to see the day die thus;
The death-bed of a day, how beautiful!
Linger, ye clouds, one moment longer there;
Fan it to slumber with your golden wings!
Like pious prayers, ye seem to soothe its end.
It will wake no more till the all-revealing day,
When, like a drop of water, greatened bright
Into a shadow, it shall show itself
With all its little tyrannous things and deeds
Unhomed and clear.   The day hath gone to God,—
Straight—like an infant's spirit, or a mocked
And mourning messenger of Grace to man.
    Would it had taken me too on its wing!
My end is nigh.   Would I might die outright,—
So o'er the sunset clouds of red mortality
The emerald hues of deathlessness diffuse
Their glory, heightening to the starry blue
Of all embosoming eternity.
Who that hath lain lonely on a high hill
In the imperious silence of full moon,
With nothing but the clear dark sky about him,
Like God's Hand laid upon the head of earth,
But has expected that some natural spirit
Should start out of the universal air,
And, gathering his cloudy robe about him,
As one in act to teach mysterious things,
Explain that he must die?

PHILIP JAMES BAILEY.

AUGUST I.

QUI LABORAT, ORAT.

O only source of all our light and life,
    Whom as our truth, our strength, we see and feel,
But whom the hours of mortal moral strife
    Alone aright reveal !

Mine inmost soul, before Thee inly brought,
    Thy presence owns ineffable, divine ;
Chastised each rebel self-encentered thought,
    My will adoreth Thine.

With eye down-dropt, if then this earthly mind
    Speechless remain, or speechless e'en depart,
Nor seek to see—for what of earthly kind
    Can see Thee as Thou art ?—

If well assured 'tis but profanely bold
    In thought's abstractest forms to seem to see,
It dare not dare the dread communion hold
    In ways unworthy Thee.

O not unowned, Thou shalt unnamed forgive,
    In worldly walks the prayerless heart prepare ;
And if in work its life it seem to live,
    Shalt make that work be prayer.

Nor times shall lack, when while the work it flies,
    Unsummoned powers the blinding film shall part,
And scarce by happy tears made dim, the eyes
    In recognition start.

But, as Thou willest, give, or e'en forbear,
  The beatific supersensual sight,
So with Thy blessing blest, that humbler prayer
  Approach Thee morn and night.

A. H. CLOUGH.

AUGUST 2.

CRUSH NOT MY MIND!

God! Thou art mind!   Unto the master-mind
Mind should be precious.   Spare my mind alone!
All else I will endure ; if, as I stand,
Here, with my gains, Thy thunder smite me down,
I bow me ; 'tis Thy will, Thy righteous will ;
I o'erpass life's restrictions, and I die ;
And if no trace of my career remain
Save a thin corpse at pleasure of the wind
In these bright chambers level with the air,
See Thou to it !   But if my spirit fail,
My once proud spirit forsake me at the last,
Hast Thou done well by me ?   So do not Thou !
Crush not my mind, dear God, though I be crushed !

ROBERT BROWNING.

AUGUST 3.

PRAYERS FOR REST.

O thou who art of Heav'n on high
And stillest ev'ry groan and sigh,
Who twice dost comfort and relieve
The sufferer who twice doth grieve,
I weary on my way and tire,
And vain are pain and long desire,—
O thou, sweet Peace,
Come thou to me, and bring surcease !

Peace on all the hills is sleeping,
See, in ev'ry folded dell,
Hardly is a vapour creeping;
Hush'd is all the woodland song;
Wait, and ere long
Thou'lt sleep as well.

J. W. VON GOETHE.
(*Trs.* Editors.)

AUGUST 4.

THANKSGIVING.

THE Lord is my shepherd; I shall not want.

He maketh me to lie down in green pastures: he leadeth me beside the still waters.

He restoreth my soul: he leadeth me in the paths of righteousness for his name's sake.

Yea, though I walk through the valley of the shadow of death, I will fear no evil: for thou art with me; thy rod and thy staff, they comfort me.

Thou preparest a table for me in the presence of mine enemies: thou anointest my head with oil; my cup runneth over.

Surely goodness and mercy shall follow me all the days of my life; and I will dwell in the house of the Lord for ever.

PSALM XXIII.

AUGUST 5.

ON SOLITUDE.

HAPPY the man whose wish and care
A few paternal acres bound,
Content to breathe his native air
In his own ground.

Whose herds with milk, whose fields with bread,
  Whose flocks supply him with attire,
Whose trees in summer yield him shade,
          In winter fire.

Blest, who can unconcern'dly find
  Hours, days, and years glide soft away,
In health of body, peace of mind,
          Quiet by day,

Sound sleep by night; study and ease,
  Together mixt; sweet recreation:
And innocence, which most doth please
          With meditation.

Thus let me live, unseen, unknown,
  Thus unlamented, let me die,
Steal from the world, and not a stone
          Tell where I lie.

ALEXANDER POPE.

AUGUST 6.

My soul, there is a country
    Afar beyond the stars,
Where stands a wingèd sentry
    All skilful in the wars.

There, above noise and danger,
    Sweet Peace sits, crowned with smiles,
And One born in a manger
    Commands the beauteous files.

He is thy gracious Friend,
    And (O my soul, awake!)
Did in pure love descend,
    To die here for thy sake.

If thou canst get but thither,
  There grows the flower of peace,
The rose that cannot wither,
  Thy fortress, and thy ease.

Leave then thy foolish ranges ;
  For none can thee secure,
But One, who never changes,
  Thy God, thy Life, thy Cure.

HENRY VAUGHAN.

AUGUST 7.

ANGELUS.

AVE MARIA ! o'er earth and sea,
That heavenliest hour of Heaven is worthiest thee !

Ave Maria ! blessed be the hour,
  The time, the clime, the spot where I so oft
Have felt that moment in its fullest power
  Sink o'er the earth so beautiful and soft,
While swung the deep bell in the distant tower,
  Or the faint dying day-hymn stole aloft,
And not a breath crept through the rosy air,
And yet the forest leaves seem'd stirred with prayer.

Ave Maria ! 'tis the hour of prayer.
  Ave Maria ! 'tis the hour of love !
Ave Maria ! may our spirits dare
  Look up to thine and to thy Son's above !
Ave Maria ! oh that face so fair !
  Those downcast eyes beneath the Almighty dove—
What though 'tis but a pictured image ? strike—
That painting is no idol—'tis too like.

LORD BYRON.

AUGUST 8.

"*ANIMULA, VAGULA, BLANDULA.*"

God, God!
With a child's voice I cry,
Weak, sad, confidingly—
God, God!

Thou knowest, eyelids, raised not always up
Unto Thy love (as none of ours are) droop
        As ours, o'er many a tear ;
Thou knowest, though Thy Universe is broad,
Two little tears suffice to cover all :
Thou knowest, Thou who art so prodigal
Of beauty, we are oft but stricken deer
Expiring in the woods, that care for none
Of those delightsome flowers they die upon.

O blissful Mouth which breathed the mournful breath,
We name our souls, self-spoilt !—by that strong passion
Which paled Thee once with sighs, by that strong death
Which made Thee once unbreathing—from the wrack
Themselves have called about them, call them back,
Back to Thee in continuous aspiration !
        For here, O Lord,
For here they travel vainly, vainly pass
From city pavement to untrodden sward,
Where the lark finds her deep nest in the grass,
Cold with the earth's last dew.   Yea, very vain
The greatest speed of all these souls of men,

Unless they travel upward to the throne
Where sittest Thou, the satisfying One,
With help for sins and holy perfectings
For all requirements: while the archangel, raising
Unto Thy face his full ecstatic gazing,
Forgets the rush and rapture of his wings.

E. BARRETT BROWNING.

AUGUST 9.

THE PILLAR OF THE CLOUD.

LEAD, kindly Light, amid the encircling gloom,
      Lead Thou me on!
The night is dark, and I am far from home—
      Lead Thou me on!
Keep Thou my feet; I do not ask to see
The distant scene,—one step enough for me.

I was not ever thus, nor pray'd that Thou
      Shouldst lead me on.
I loved to choose and see my path, but now
      Lead Thou me on!
I loved the garish day, and, spite of fears,
Pride ruled my will: remember not past years.

So long Thy power hath blest me, sure it still
      Will lead me on,
O'er moor and fen, o'er crag and torrent, till
      The night is gone;
And with the morn those angel-faces smile
Which I have loved long since, and lost awhile.

CARDINAL NEWMAN.

AUGUST 10.

" To humbleness of heart descends
This prescience from on high."

     . . . WHAT hand unseen
Impels me onward through the glowing orbs
Of habitable nature, far remote,
To the dread confines of eternal night,
To solitudes of waste, unpeopled space,
To deserts of creation, wide and wild;
Where embryo systems and unkindled suns
Sleep in the womb of Chaos?   Fancy droops,
And Thought, astonish'd, stops her bold career.
But O thou mighty Mind! whose powerful word
Said, Thus let all things be, and thus they were,
Where shall I seek Thy presence? how unblamed
Invoke Thy dread perfection?
Have the broad eyelids of the morn beheld Thee?
Or does the beamy shoulder of Orion
Support Thy throne?   Oh, look with pity down
On erring, guilty man; not in Thy names
Of terror clad; not with those thunders arm'd
That conscious Sinai felt, when fear appall'd
The scatter'd tribes; Thou hast a gentler voice,
That whispers comfort to the swelling heart,
Abash'd, yet longing to behold her Maker!
    But now my soul, unused to stretch her powers
In flight so daring, drops her weary wing,
And seeks again the known accustom'd spot,
Drest up with sun, and shade, and lawns, and streams,
A mansion fair and spacious for its guests,
And all replete with wonders.   Let me here,

Content and grateful, wait th' appointed time,
And ripen for the skies; the hour will come
When all these splendours, bursting on my sight,
Shall stand unveil'd, and to my ravish'd sense
Unlock the glories of the world unknown.

ANNA LÆTITIA BARBAULD.

AUGUST 11.

COMPLAINE we may, much is amisse,
Hope is nie gone to have redresse,
These daies ben ill, nothing sure is,
Kinde harte is wrapte in heavinesse.

The sterne is broke, the saile is rent,
The ship is given to winde and wave,
All helpe is gone, the rocke present,
That will be lost, what man can save?

Thinges hard, therefore, are now refused;
Labour in youth is thought but vaine:
Duty by will-not is excused,
Remove the stop, the way is plaine.

Wyly is witty, brainsick is wise,
Trouth is folly, and might is right,
Wordes are reason, and reason is lies,
The bad is good, darknesse is light.

Folly and falshood prateth apace,
Trouth under bushel is faine to crepe,
Flattery is treble, pride sings the base,
The meane, the best part, scant doth pepe.

This fiery playe the world infects,
To vertue and trouth it geves no rest,
Men's harts are burnde with sundry sects,
And to eche man his way is best.

With flodes and storms thus we be tost ;
Awake, good Lord, to Thee we crye :
Our ship is almost sunk and lost,
Thy mercy help our misery.

Man's strength is weake : man's wit is dull,
Man's reason is blinde, these things to amend,
Thy hand (O Lord) of might is full,
Awake betyme, and helpe us send.

In Thee we trust and in no wight,
Save us, as chickens under the hen ;
Our crokedness Thou canst make right,
Glory to Thee for aye.   Amen.

ANON.   (Circa 1500.)

AUGUST 12.

No coward soul is mine,
No trembler in the world's storm-troubled sphere :
I see Heaven's glories shine,
And faith shines equal, arming me from fear.

O God within my breast,
Almighty, ever-present Deity !
Life,—that in me has rest,
As I—undying Life—have power in Thee !

Vain are the thousand creeds
That move men's hearts : unutterably vain :
Worthless as withered weeds
Or idlest froth amid the boundless main,

To waken doubt in one
Holding so fast by Thine infinity :
    So surely anchored on
The stedfast rock of immortality.

With wide embracing love
Thy spirit animates eternal years,
    Pervades and broods above,
Changes, sustains, dissolves, creates, and rears.

Though earth and man were gone,
And suns and universes ceased to be,
    And Thou wert left alone,
Every existence would exist in Thee.

There is not room for Death,
Nor atom that his might could render void ;
    Thou—Thou art Being and Breath,
And what Thou art may never be destroyed.

EMILY BRONTË.

AUGUST 13.

REGENERATION.

SURELY if each one saw another's heart,
    There would be no commerce,
No sale or bargain pass : all would disperse
    And live apart.

Lord, mend, or rather make us : one creation
    Will not suffice our turn :
Except Thou make us daily, we shall spurn
    Our own salvation.

GEORGE HERBERT.

AUGUST 14.

THE AGONY.

My God ! my God ! and can it be
That I should sin so lightly now,
And think no more of evil thoughts
Than of the wind that waves the bough ?

I sin—and heaven and earth go round,
As if no dreadful deed were done,
As if Christ's blood had never flowed
To hinder sin, or to atone.

I walk the earth with lightsome step,
Smile at the sunshine, breathe the air,
Do my own will, nor ever heed
Gethsemane and Thy long prayer.

Shall it be always thus, O Lord ?
Wilt Thou not work this hour in me
The grace Thy passion merited—
Hatred of self and love of Thee ?

Ever when tempted, make me see,
Beneath the olive's moon-pierced shade,
My God, alone, outstretched, and bruised,
And bleeding, on the earth He made.

And make me feel it was my sin,
As though no other sins there were,
That was to Him who bears the world
A load that He could scarcely bear !

FREDERICK WILLIAM FABER.

AUGUST 15.

THE SUN-DIAL.

'Tis true, of old the unchanging sun
His daily course refused to run ;
   The pale moon, hurrying to the west,
Paused at a mortal's call, to aid
The avenging storm of war, that laid
Seven guilty realms at once on earth's defilèd breast.

But can it be, one suppliant tear
Should stay the ever-moving sphere ?
   A sick man's lowly-breathèd sigh,
When from the world he turns away
And hides his weary eyes to pray,
Should change your mystic dance, ye wanderers of the
   sky ?

We, too, O Lord, would fain command,
As then, Thy wonder-working hand,
   And backward force the waves of Time,
That now so swift and silent bear
Our restless bark from year to year ;
Help us to pause and mourn to Thee our tale of crime.

Bright hopes, that erst the bosom warmed,
And vows, too pure to be performed,
   And prayers, blown wide by gales of care,—
These, and such faint half-waking dreams,
Like stormy lights on mountain streams,
Wavering and broken all, athwart the conscience glare.

How shall we escape the o'erwhelming Past?
Can spirits broken, joys o'ercast,
    And eyes that nevermore may smile,—
Can these the avenging bolt delay,
Or win us back one little day
The bitterness of death to soften and beguile?

Father and Lover of our souls!
Though darkly round Thine anger rolls,
    Thy sunshine smiles beneath the gloom,
Thou seek'st to warn us, not confound,
Thy showers would pierce the hardened ground,
And win it to give out its brightness and perfume.

Thou smil'st on us in wrath, and we,
E'en in remorse, would smile on Thee;
    The tears that bathe our offered hearts,
We would not have them stained and dim,
But dropped from wings of seraphim,
All glowing with the light accepted love imparts.

Time's waters will not ebb nor stay,
Power cannot change them, but Love may;
    What cannot be, Love counts it done.
Deep in the heart, her searching view
Can read where Faith is fixed and true,
Through shades of setting life can see Heaven's work
    begun.

O Thou who keep'st the Key of Love,
Open Thy fount, eternal Dove,
    And overflow this heart of mine
Enlarging as it fills with Thee,
Till in one blaze of Charity
Care and remorse are lost, like motes, in light divine;

Till, as each moment wafts us higher,
By every gush of pure desire
    And high-breathed hope of joys above,
By every secret sigh we heave,
Whole years of folly we outlive
In His unerring sight, who measures Life by Love.

JOHN KEBLE.

AUGUST 16.

DO NOT DELAY.

Never weather-beaten Saile more willing bent to shore,
Never tired Pilgrim's limbs affected slumber more,
Than my weary spright now longs to flye out of my
    troubled brest.
O come quickly, sweetest Lord, and take my soule to
    rest !

Ever blooming are the joyes of Heav'n's high paradice,
Cold age deafes not there our eares, nor vapour dims
    our eyes :
Glory there the sun outshines, whose beames the
    blessed onely see.
O come quickly, glorious Lord, and raise my spright to
    Thee !

DR THOMAS CAMPION.

AUGUST 17.

LONG BARREN.

Thou didst hang upon a barren tree,
    My God, for me :
Though I till now be barren, now at length,
    Lord, give me strength,
To bring forth fruit to Thee.

Thou didst bear for me the crown of thorn,
    Spitting and scorn :
Though I till now have put forth thorns, yet now
    Strengthen me Thou,
That better fruit be borne.

Thou Rose of Sharon, Cedar of broad roots,
    Vine of sweet fruits,
Thou Lily of the Vale with fadeless leaf,
    Of thousands Chief,
Feed Thou my feeble shoots.

CHRISTINA ROSSETTI.

AUGUST 18.

USQUE QUO, DOMINE?

How long, O Lord, shall I forgotten be ?
        What ? ever ?
How long wilt thou Thy hidden face from me
        Dissever ?
How long shall I consult with carefull spright
        In anguish ?
How long shall I with foes' triumphant might
        Thus languish ?
Behold me, Lord ; let to Thy hearing creep
        My crying :
Nay, give me eyes and light, lest that I sleep
        In dying :
Lest my foe brag, that in my ruyne he
        Prevailed ;
And at my fall they joy that troublous me
        Assailed.
No ! No ! I trust on Thee, and joy in Thy
        Great pity :
Still, therefore, of Thy graces shall be my
        Song's ditty.

SIR PHILIP SIDNEY.

AUGUST 19.

DE PROFUNDIS.

O Father, in that hour
When Earth all succouring power
    Shall·disavow;
When spear and shield and crown
In faintness are cast down,
    Sustain us Thou!

By Him who bowed to take
The death cup for our sake,
    The thorn, the rod;
From whom the last dismay
Was not to pass away,
    Aid us, O God!

MRS HEMANS.

AUGUST 20.

INVOCATION.

Such grateful haunts forgoing, if I oft
Must turn elsewhere—to travel near the tribes
And fellowships of men, and see ill sights
Of madding passions mutually inflamed;
Must hear Humanity in fields and groves
Pipe solitary anguish; or must hang
Brooding above the fierce confederate storm
Of sorrow, barricadoed evermore
Within the walls of cities,—may these sounds
Have their authentic comment, that even these
Hearing, I be not downcast or forlorn!—

Descend, prophetic Spirit! that inspir'st
The human Soul of universal earth,
Dreaming on things to come, and dost possess
A metropolitan temple in the hearts
Of mighty Poets; upon me bestow
A gift of genuine insight, that my Song
With star-like virtue in its place may shine,
Shedding benignant influence, and secure
Itself from all malevolent effect
Of those mutations that extend their sway
Throughout the nether sphere!—And if with this
I mix more lowly matter; with the thing
Contemplated describe the Mind and Man
Contemplating, and who and what he was—
Be not this labour useless! If such theme
May sort with highest objects, then, dread Power!
Whose gracious favour is the primal source
Of all illumination, may my Life
Express the image of a better time,
More wise desires, and simpler manners;—nurse
My Heart in genuine freedom:—all pure thoughts
Be with me;—so shall Thy unfailing love
Guide, and support, and cheer me to the end!

WILLIAM WORDSWORTH.

AUGUST 21.

FIAT VOLUNTAS TUA.

He sendeth sun, He sendeth shower,
Alike they're needful to the flower,
And joys and tears alike are sent
To give the soul fit nourishment:
As comes to me or cloud or sun,
Father, Thy will, not mine, be done.

Can loving children e'er reprove
With murmurs, whom they trust and love ?
Creator, I would ever be
A trusting, loving child to Thee ;
As comes to me or cloud or sun,
Father, Thy will, not mine, be done.

O ne'er will I at life repine,
Enough that Thou hast made it mine,
When falls the shadow cold of death,
I yet will sing with parting breath :
As comes to me or cloud or sun,
Father, Thy will, not mine, be done.

SARAH FLOWER ADAMS.

AUGUST 22.

Thee, God, I come from, to Thee go,
All day long I like fountain flow
From Thy hand out, swayed about
Mote-like in Thy mighty glow.

What I know of Thee, I bless,
As acknowledging Thy stress
On my being, and as seeing
Something of Thy holiness.

Once I turned from Thee and hid,
Bound on what Thou hadst forbid ;
Sow the wind I would : I sinned,
I repent of what I did.

Bad I am, but yet Thy child,
Father, be Thou reconciled.
Spare Thou me, since I see
With Thy might that Thou art mild.

I have life left with me still,
And Thy purpose to fulfil;
Yes, a debt to pay Thee yet:
Help me, Sir, and so I will.

GERALD HOPKINS.

AUGUST 23.

A POET'S PRAYER.

ALMIGHTY Father! let Thy lowly child,
Strong in his love of truth, be wisely bold,—
A patriot bard, by sycophants reviled,
Let him live usefully and not die old!
Let poor men's children, pleased to read his lays,
Love, for his sake, the scenes where he hath been;
And, when he ends his pilgrimage of days,
Let him be buried where the grass is green;
Where daisies, blooming earliest, linger late
To hear the bee his busy note prolong :—
There let him slumber and in peace await
The dawning morn, far from the sensual throng,
Who scorn the wind-flower's blush, the redbreast's
    lonely song.

EBENEZER ELLIOT.

AUGUST 24.

LITANY TO THE HOLY SPIRIT.

In the hour of my distress,
When temptations me oppress,
And when I my sins confess,
    Sweet Spirit, comfort me!

When I lie within my bed,
Sick in heart, and sick in head,
And with doubts discomforted,
     Sweet Spirit, comfort me!

When the house doth sigh and weep,
And the world is drowned in sleep,
Yet mine eyes the watch do keep,
     Sweet Spirit, comfort me!

When the artless doctor sees
No one hope but of his fees,
And his skill runs on the lees,
     Sweet Spirit, comfort me!

When his potion and his pill
Has or none or little skill,
Meet for nothing but to kill,
     Sweet Spirit, comfort me!

When the passing-bell doth toll,
And the furies in a shoal
Come to fright a parting soul,
     Sweet Spirit, comfort me!

When the tapers now burn blue,
And the comforters are few,
And that number more than true,
     Sweet Spirit, comfort me!

When the priest his last hath prayed,
And I nod to what is said,
'Cause my speech is now decayed,
     Sweet Spirit, comfort me!

When (God knows) I'm tossed about,
Either with despair or doubt;
Yet, before the glass be out,
        Sweet Spirit, comfort me!

When the tempter me pursu'th
With the sins of all my youth,
And half damns me with untruth,
        Sweet Spirit, comfort me!

When the flames and hellish cries
Fright mine ears, and fright mine eyes,
And all terrors me surprise,
        Sweet Spirit, comfort me!

When the Judgment is reveal'd,
And that open'd which was sealed;
When to Thee I have appeal'd,
        Sweet Spirit, comfort me!

ROBERT HERRICK.

AUGUST 25.

THE CHEERFUL LIFE.

O God, my Father and my Friend,
Ever Thy blessings to me send!
Let me have virtue for my guide,
And wisdom always at my side;
Thus cheerfully through life I'll go,
Nor ever feel the sting of woe:
Contented with the humblest lot,
Happy, though in the meanest cot.

MRS HEMANS.

AUGUST 26.

A PRAYER OF AGE.

They do their Maker wrong
Who in the pride of age
Cry down youth's heritage
And all the eager throng
Of thoughts and plans and schemes
With which the young brain teems. . . .
The joy of toil, the thrill of pleasure,
The gladness without measure :
All the struggle for the right,
The combats with the banded might
Of selfishness and wrong and greed,
The ringing glory of the victor's meed :
The faring of adventurous thought
O'er seas of doubt with danger fraught ;
The search beyond the seeming and the show
Of outward shapes, in hope to know
The open secret of the cosmic plan ;
The bitter gladness of the heart's deep riving,
All the yearning and the passion and the striving,
All that speaks the prisoned God in man.
    Ah, no ! the fair full days of youth,
I cannot do them wrong
In memory or in song :
Indeed, I hold it for a truth
That age alone is well and fair
When youth's ideal, boyhood's prayer,
Lives ever in the heart of age,
And, spite of manhood's pilgrimage
Thro' wildering ways and doubts and fears,
'Mid friendless failure's bitter tears,
Rests high hope yet and wisdom mild,
" Ordained strength " of sage and child.

Be such age mine, dear God, I pray,
A second childhood's trust alway :
And for the deed of Death, to 'Thee
I trust it, for, indeed, I know that he
Who thro' his life's appointed days
Has stood not idle in the market-place,
He dies not, no ! there is no death for him,
No death, but only change,
Beyond this earthly range,
New life, new work, with servant seraphim.
    O Lord of Service ! Lord of Life !
Grant me that guerdon in the other life,
New service there—that, with my latest breath,
Be my one prayer, O Living Lord of Death.

DEAN STUBBS.

AUGUST 27.

SONNET.

At the round earth's imagin'd corners blow
Your trumpets, angels ; and arise, arise
From death, you numberless infinities
Of souls, and to your scattered bodies go,
All whom th' flood did, and fire overthrow :
All whom war, death, age, ague's tyrannies,
Despair, law, chance, hath slain ; and you whose eyes
Shall behold God and never taste death's woe.
But let them sleep, Lord, and me mourn a space ;
For if above all these my sins abound,
'Tis late to ask abundance of Thy grace
When we are there.   Here on this holy ground
Teach me how to repent, for that's as good
As if Thou hadst sealed my pardon with Thy blood.

JOHN DONNE.

AUGUST 28.

THE LOADSTONE.

Like to the arctic needle, that doth guide
 The wand'ring shade by his magnetic power,
And leaves his silken gnomon to decide
 The question of the controverted hour,
First frantics up and down from side to side,
 And restless beats his crystal'd iv'ry case,
 With vain impatience jets from place to place,
And seeks the bosom of his frozen bride;
 At length he slacks his motion, and doth rest
His trembling point at his bright pole's beloved breast.

E'en so my soul, being hurried here and there
 By ev'ry object that presents delight,
Fain would be settled, but she knows not where;
 She likes at morning what she loathes at night;
She bows to honour; then she lends an ear
 To that sweet swan-like voice of dying pleasure,
 Then tumbles in the scatter'd heaps of treasure;
Now flatter'd with false hope; now foil'd with fear;
 Thus finding all the world's delight to be
But empty toys, good God, she points alone to Thee.

But hath the virtued steel a power to move?
 Or can the untouch'd needle point aright?
Or can my wand'ring thoughts forbear to rove,
 Unguided by the virtue of Thy Spirit?
O hath my leaden soul the art t'improve
 Her wasted talent, and unrais'd, aspire
 In this sad moulting time of her desire?
Not first belov'd, have I the power to love?
 I cannot stir, but as Thou please to move me,
Nor can my heart return Thee love, until Thou love me.

The still commandress of the silent night
  Borrows her beams from her bright brother's eye :
His fair aspect fills her sharp horns with light ;
  If he withdraw, her flames are quench'd and die :
E'en so the beams of Thy enlight'ning Sp'rit,
  Infus'd and shot into my dark desire,
  Inflame my thoughts, and fill my soul with fire,
That I am ravish'd with a new delight ;
  But if Thou shroud Thy face, my glory fades,
And I remain a nothing, all composed of shades.

Eternal God ! O Thou that only art
  The sacred fountain of eternal light
And blessed loadstone of my better part,
  O Thou, my heart's desire, my soul's delight !
Reflect upon my soul, and touch my heart,
  And then my heart shall prize no good above Thee ;
And then my trembling thoughts shall never start
  From Thy commands, or swerve the least degree,
Or once presume to move, but as they move in Thee.

FRANCIS QUARLES.

AUGUST 29.

A SONG OF DIVINE LOVE.

Lord ! when the sense of Thy sweet grace
Sends up my soul to seek Thy face,
Thy blessed eyes breed such desire,
I die in love's delicious fire.
O love ! I am thy sacrifice ;
Be still triumphant, blessed eyes.
Still shine on me, fair sun, that I
Still may behold, though still I die.

Q

Though still I die, I live again,
Still longing so to be still slain,
So gainful is such loss of breath,
I die even in desire of death.
Still live in me this longing strife
Of living death and dying life,
For, while Thou sweetly slayest me,
Dead to myself, I live in Thee.

R. CRASHAW.

AUGUST 30.

THAT THY WAY MAY BE KNOWN UPON EARTH.

Alas! long-suffering and most patient God,
Thou needst be surelier God to bear with us
Than even to have made us! Thou aspire, aspire
From henceforth for me! Thou who hast Thyself
Endured this fleshhood, knowing how as a soaked
And sucking vesture it can drag us down
And choke us in the melancholy Deep,
Sustain me, that with Thee I walk these waves,
Resisting!—breathe me upward, Thou in me
Aspiring, who art the way, the truth, the life,—
That no truth henceforth seem indifferent,
No way to truth laborious, and no life,
Not even this life I live, intolerable!

E. BARRETT BROWNING.

AUGUST 31.

TO THE FATHER OF HEAVEN.

O RADIANT luminary of light interminable,
Celestiall Father, potenciall God of might,
Of heaven and earth.   O Lord incomperable,
Of al perfections the essenciall most perfighte,
O Maker of Mankind, that formed day and night,
Whose power imperial comprehendeth every place,
Mine hart, my mind, my thought, my whole delighte
Is, after this lyfe, to see Thy glorious face.

Whose magnificence is incomprehensible,
Al arguments of reason which far doth excede
Whose deite doutles is indivisible,
From whom al goodness and vertue doth procede,
Of Thy support al creatures have nede.
Assist me, good Lord, and graunt me of Thy grace
To live to Thy pleasure, in word, thought, and dede ;
And after this lyfe to see Thy glorious face.

JOHN SKELTON.

SEPTEMBER 1.

THE AUTUMN OF LIFE.

These hairs of age are messengers
Which bid me fast repent and pray;
They be of death the harbingers
That doth prepare and dress the way,
Wherefore I joy that you may see
Upon my head such hairs to be.

They be the lines that lead the length
How far my race was for to run;
They say my youth is fled with strength,
And how old age is well begun;
The which I feel and you may see
Such lines upon my head to be.

They be the strings of sober sound,
Whose music is harmonical;
Their tunes declare a time from ground
I came, and how thereto I shall;
Wherefore I love that you may see
Upon my head such hairs to be.

God grant to those that white hairs have,
No worse them take than I have meant,
That after they be laid in grave,
Their souls may joy their lives well spent;
God grant, likewise, that you may see
Upon my head such hairs to be.

Lord Vaux.

SEPTEMBER 2.

THE FOUNTAIN OF TEARS.

If you go over desert and mountain,
 Far into the country of sorrow,
 To-day and to-night and to-morrow,
And maybe for months and for years,
 You shall come with a heart that is bursting
 For trouble and toiling and thirsting,
You shall certainly come to the Fountain
At length,—to the Fountain of Tears. . . .

And it flows and it flows with a motion
 So gentle and lovely and listless,
 And murmurs a tune so resistless
To him who hath suffered and hears,—
 You shall surely, without a word spoken,
 Kneel down there and know your heart broken,
And yield to the long-curbed emotion,
That day by the Fountain of Tears. . . .

And the tears shall flow faster and faster,
 Brim over and battle resistance,
 And roll'd down bleared roads to each distance
Of past desolation and years;
 Till they cover the place of each sorrow,
 And leave you no Past and no Morrow;
For what man is able to master
And stem the great Fountain of Tears?

But the floods of the tears meet and gather,
 The sound of them all grows like thunder:
 O, into what bosom, I wonder,
Is poured the whole sorrow of years?

For Eternity only seems keeping
  Account of the great human weeping :
May God, then, the Maker and Father,
May He find a place for the tears !

ARTHUR O'SHAUGHNESSY.

SEPTEMBER 3.

PATER NOSTER.

OUR Father, Thou who dwellest in the heavens,
  Not circumscribed, but from the greater love
  Thou bearest to the first effects on high,
Praised be Thy name and Thine omnipotence
  By every creature, as befitting is
  To render thanks to Thy sweet effluence.
Come unto us the peace of Thy dominion,
  For unto it we cannot of ourselves,
  If it come not, with all our intellect.
Even as Thine own Angels of their will
  Make sacrifice to Thee, Hosanna singing,
  So may all men make sacrifice of theirs.
Give unto us this day our daily manna,
  Withouten which in this rough wilderness
  Backward goes he who toils most to advance.
And even as we the trespass we have suffered
  Pardon in one another, pardon Thou
  Benignly and regard not our desert.
Our virtue, which is easily o'ercome,
  Put not to proof with the old adversary,
  But Thou from him who spurs it so, deliver.
This last petition verily, dear Lord,
  Not for ourselves is made, who need it not,
  But for their sake who have remained behind us.

DANTE.

(*Trs.* H. W. Longfellow.)

SEPTEMBER 4.

ALL service ranks the same with God:
If now, as formerly He trod
Paradise, His presence fills
Our earth, each only as God wills
Can work—God's puppets, best and worst,
Are we; there is no last nor first.

Say not "a small event!"   Why "small"?
Costs it more pain that this, ye call
A "great event," should come to pass
Than that?   Untwine me from the mass
Of deeds which make up life, one deed
Power shall fall short in or exceed!

ROBERT BROWNING.

SEPTEMBER 5.

THE POET'S REBUKE.

YE stately wights that live in quiet rest
  Through worldly wealth which God hath given to
      you,
Lament with tears and sighs from doleful breast
  The shame and power that vice obtaineth now.
    Behold how God doth daily proffer grace,
    Yet we disdain repentance to embrace.

The suds of sin do suck into the mind,
  And cankered vice doth virtue quite expel.
No change to good, alas! can resting find,
  Our wicked hearts so stoutly do rebel.
    Not one there is that hasteth to amend,
    Though God from heaven His daily threats do send.

We are so slow to change our blameful life,
  We are so pressed to match alluring vice,
Such greedy hearts on every side be rife,
    So few that guide their will by counsel wise
      To let our tears lament the wretched case,
      And call to God for undeserved grace.

You worldly wights that have your fancies fixt
  On slipper joy of terrain pleasure here,
Let some remorse in all your deeds be mixt,
    Whiles you have time let some redress appear :
      Of sudden death the hour you shall not know,
      And look for death, although it seemeth slow.

Oh, be no judge in other men's offence,
  But purge thyself, and seek to make thee free,
Let everyone apply his diligence,
    A change to good within himself to see.
      O God, direct our feet in such a stay,
      From cankered vice to shame the hateful way !
           RICHARD HILL.

SEPTEMBER 6.

ERE on my bed my limbs I lay,
It hath not been my use to pray
With moving lips or bended knees,
But silently, by slow degrees,
My spirit I to Love compose,
In humble trust mine eyelids close
With reverential resignation,
No wish conceived, no thought exprest,
Only a sense of supplication ;
A sense all o'er my soul imprest
That I am weak, yet not unblest,
Since in me, round me, everywhere,
Eternal strength and wisdom are.
           S. T. COLERIDGE.

SEPTEMBER 7.

VOLUNTARY.

How beautiful this dome of sky;
And the vast hills, in fluctuation fixed
At Thy command, how awful!   Shall the Soul,
Human and rational, report of Thee
Even less than these ?—Be mute who will, who can,
Yet I will praise Thee with impassioned voice :
My lips, that may forget Thee in the crowd,
Cannot forget Thee here, where Thou hast built,
For Thy own glory, in the wilderness !

    . . . By Thy grace
The particle divine remained unquenched ;
And, 'mid the wild weeds of a rugged soil,
Thy bounty caused to flourish deathless flowers,
From paradise transplanted : wintry age
Impends ; the frost will gather round my heart ;
If the flowers wither, I am worse than dead !
Come, labour, when the worn-out frame requires
Perpetual Sabbath ; come, disease and want ;
And sad exclusion through decay of sense ;
But leave me unabated trust in Thee—
And let Thy favour, to the end of life,
Inspire me with ability to seek
Repose and hope among eternal things—
Father of heaven and earth ! and I am rich,
And will possess my portion in content.

WILLIAM WORDSWORTH.

SEPTEMBER 8.

PRAYER IN PROSPERITY.

Son of Eternity, fettered in time, and an exile, the
    spirit
Tugs at his chains evermore and struggles, like flame,
    ever upward.
Still he recalls, with emotion, his Father's manifold
    mansions,
Thinks of the lands of his fathers, where blossomed
    more freshly the flowerets,
Shone a more beautiful sun and he played with the
    wingèd angels.
Then grows the earth too narrow, too close: and
    homesick for heaven
Longs the wanderer again; and the spirit's longings
    are worship!
Worship is called his most beautiful hour and its tongue
    is entreaty.
Ah! when the infinite burden of life descendeth upon
    us,
Crushes to earth our hope, and, under the earth, in the
    graveyard,
Then it is good to pray unto God; for His sorrowing
    children
Turns He ne'er from His door, but He heals and helps
    and consoles them.
Yet it is better to pray when all things are fortunate
    with us—
Pray in fortunate days; for life's most beautiful Fortune
Kneels before the Eternal's throne and, with hands
    interfolded,
Praises, thankful and moved, the only Giver of blessings.

H. W. Longfellow.
(*From the Swedish of* Bishop Tegner.)

SEPTEMBER 9.

" ' Tis, by comparison, an easy task
Earth to despise, but to converse with heaven—
This is not easy."

O MAY I join the choir invisible
Of those immortal dead who live again
In minds made better by their presence : live
In pulses stirred to generosity,
In deeds of daring rectitude, in scorn
For miserable aims that end with self,
In thoughts sublime that pierce the night like stars,
And with their mild persistence urge man's search
To vaster issues.   So to live is heaven :
To make undying music in the world,
Breathing as beauteous order that controls
With growing sway the growing life of man.
So we inherit that sweet purity
For which we struggled, failed, and agonised
With widening retrospect that bred despair.
Rebellious flesh that would not be subdued,
A vicious parent shaming still its child,
Poor anxious penitence, is quick dissolved ;
The discords, quenched by meeting harmonies,
Die in the large and charitable air.
And all our rarer, better, truer self,
That sobbed religiously in yearning song,
That watched to ease the burthen of the world,
Laboriously tracing what must be,
And what may yet be better—saw within
A worthier image for the sanctuary,
And shaped it forth before the multitude
Divinely human, raising worship so
To higher reverence more mixed with love—
That better self shall live till human Time
Shall fold its eyelids and the human sky

Be gathered like a scroll within the tomb
Unread for ever.   This is life to come,
Which martyred men have made more glorious
For us who strive to follow.   May I reach
That purest heaven, be to other souls
The cup of strength in some great agony,
Enkindle generous ardour, feed pure love,
Beget the smiles that have no cruelty—
Be the sweet presence of a good diffused,
As in diffusion ever more intense.
So shall I join the choir invisible
Whose music is the gladness of the world.

GEORGE ELIOT.

SEPTEMBER 10.

WITH kind compassion hear me cry,
O Jesu, Lord of life on high !
As, when the summer's seasons beat
With scorching flame and parching heat,
The trees are burn'd, the flowers fade,
And thirsty gaps in earth are made :
My thoughts of comfort languish so,
And so my soul is broke by woe.
Then on Thy servant's drooping head
Thy dews of blessing sweetly shed ;
Let those a quick refreshment give,
And raise my mind, and bid me live.
My fears of danger, while I breathe
My dread of endless hell beneath,
My sense of sorrow for my sin,
To springing comfort change within ;
Change all my sad complaints for ease
To cheerful notes of endless praise,
Nor let a tear mine eyes employ
But such as owe their birth to joy. . . .

O, tender mercy's art divine!
Thy sorrow proves the cure of mine!
Thy dropping wounds, thy woeful smart
Allay the bleedings of my heart;
Thy death, in death's extreme of pain,
Restores my soul to life again.
Guide me then, for here I burn
To make my Saviour some return.
I'll rise—if that will please Him still,
And sure I've heard Him own it will,—
I'll trace His steps, and bear my Cross,
Despising every grief and loss;
Since He, despising pain and shame,
First took up His, and did the same.

THOMAS PARNELL.

SEPTEMBER 11.

AUTHOR of light, revive my dying sprite!
Redeem it from the snares of all-confounding night!
    Lord, light me to Thy blessed way!
For blinde with worldly vaine desires, I wander as a
       stray,
  Sunne and Moone, Starres and underlights I see;
But all their glorious beames are mists and darknes,
      being compared to Thee.

Fountaine of health, my soule's deepe wounds recure!
Sweet showres of pitty raine, wash my uncleannesse
      pure!
    One drop of Thy desired grace
The faint and fading heart can raise, and in joye's
      bosome place.
  Sinne and Death, Hell and tempting Fiends may rage,
But God His owne will guard, and their sharp paines
      and griefe in time asswage.

DR THOMAS CAMPION.

SEPTEMBER 12.

ODE.

How are Thy servants blest, O Lord,
  How sure is their defence !
Eternal wisdom is their guide,
  Their help Omnipotence.

In foreign realms, and lands remote,
  Supported by Thy care,
Thro' burning climes I pass'd unhurt,
  And breath'd in tainted air.

Thy mercy sweeten'd every soil,
  Made every region please ;
The hoary Alpine hills it warm'd,
  And smooth'd the Tyrrhene seas.

Think, O my soul, devoutly think,
  How, with affrighted eyes,
Thou saw'st the wide-extended deep
  In all its horrors rise.

Confusion dwelt on every face,
  And fear in every heart,
When waves on waves, and gulfs on gulfs
  O'ercame the pilot's art.

Yet then from all my griefs, O Lord !
  Thy mercy set me free ;
Whilst in the confidence of prayer
  My soul took hold on Thee.

For though in dreadful whirls we hung
  High on the broken wave,
I knew Thou wert not slow to hear,
  Nor impotent to save.

The storm was laid, the winds retired
 Obedient to Thy will;
The sea, that roar'd at Thy command,
 At Thy command was still.

In midst of dangers, fears, and death,
 Thy goodness I'll adore;
And praise Thee for Thy mercies past,
 And humbly hope for more.

My life, if Thou preserv'st my life,
 Thy sacrifice shall be;
And death, if death must be my doom,
 Shall join my soul to Thee.

JOSEPH ADDISON.

SEPTEMBER 13.

HOSHANA.

O God! like lost sheep we have gone astray:
From out Thy book wipe not our name away.
    Save! O save!

O God! sustain the sheep for slaughter; see
These dealt with wrathfully and slain for Thee,
    Save! O save!

O God! Thy sheep! the sheep whom Thou didst tend
In pasture; Thy creation and Thy friend
    Save! O save!

O God! the poor among the sheep! Take heed:
Answer in time of favour to their need.
    Save! O save!

O God ! they lift their eyes to Thee, long sought ;
Let those that rise against Thee count as nought.
                              Save ! O save !

O God ! they pouring water,[1] worshipping,
Let them be drawing from salvation's spring.
                              Save ! O save !

O God ! let saviours come to Zion at length,
Endowed of Thee, and saved by Thy name's strength.
                              Save ! O save !

O God ! in garb of vengeance clad about,
In mighty wrath cast all deceivers out.
                              Save ! O save !

O God ! and Thou wilt surely not forget
Her, by love-tokens bought, that hopeth yet.[2]
                              Save ! O save !

O God ! they seeking Thee with willow bough ![3]
Regard their crying from Thine Heaven now.
                              Save ! O save !

O God ! as with a crown bless Thou the year ;
Yea, Lord, my singing, I beseech Thee, hear.
                              Save ! O save !

                    ANON.   (*Trs. from the
              medieval Hebrew by* Nina Davis.)

[1] A ritual ceremony at the Temple in Tabernacles.
[2] Hosea iii. 2.
[3] Levit. xxiii. 40.

SEPTEMBER 14.

HOSHANA.

Thou, who dost dwell alone—
Thou, who dost know Thine own—
Thou, to whom all are known
From the cradle to the grave—
    Save, oh! save.
From the world's temptations,
  From tribulations,
From that fierce anguish
Wherein we languish,
From that torpor deep
Wherein we lie asleep,
Heavy as death, cold as the grave,
    Save, oh! save. . . .

O let the false dream fly
Where our sick souls do lie
Tossing continually!
O where Thy voice doth come,
Let all doubts be dumb,
Let all words be mild,
All strifes be reconciled,
All pains beguiled!
Light bring no blindness,
Love no unkindness,
Knowledge no ruin,
Fear no undoing!
From the cradle to the grave,
    Save, oh! save.

MATTHEW ARNOLD.

K

SEPTEMBER 15.

LITANY.

FATHER of Heav'n, and Him by whom
It, and us for it, and all else for us,
Thou mad'st and govern'st ever; come,
And recreate me, now grown ruinous;
My heart is by dejection clay,
And by self-murder red.
From this red earth, O Father, purge away
All vicious tinctures, that new-fashioned
I may rise up from death before I'm dead.

O Son of God, who seeing two things,
Sin and death, crept in which were never made;
By bearing one, tri'dst with what stings
The other could Thine heritage invade;
O be Thou nail'd unto my heart,
And crucified again.
Part not from it, though it from Thee would part,
But let it be, by applying so Thy pain,
Drown'd in Thy blood, and in Thy passion slain.

O Holy Ghost, whose temple I
Am, but of mud walls and condensed dust,
And being sacrilegiously
Half-wasted with youth's fires of pride and lust,
Must with new storms be weather-beat;
Double in my heart Thy flame,
Which let devout sad tears intend, and let
(Though this glass lanthorn flesh do suffer maim)
Fire, sacrifice, priest, altar, be the same.

JOHN DONNE.

SEPTEMBER 16.

EMPLOYMENT.

IF, as a flower doth spread and die,
  Thou wouldst extend me to some good
Before I were by frost's extremity
    Nipt in the bud,

The sweetness and the praise were Thine;
  But the extension and the room
Which in Thy garland I should fill were mine
    At Thy great doom.

For as Thou dost impart Thy grace,
  The greater shall our glory be.
The measure of our joys is in this place,
    The stuff with Thee.

Let me not languish then, and spend
  A life as barren to Thy praise
As is the dust to which that life doth tend
    But with delays.

All things are busy; only I
  Neither bring honey with the bees,
Nor flowers to make that, nor the husbandry
    To water these.

I am no link of Thy great chain,
  But all my company is a weed.
Lord, place me in Thy concert; give one strain
    To my poor reed.

GEORGE HERBERT.

SEPTEMBER 17.

"ALL I BELIEVED IS TRUE."

FIRST I will pray.   Do Thou
  That ownest the soul,
  Yet wilt grant control
To another, nor disallow
For a time, restrain me now !

I admonish me while I may,
  Not to squander guilt,
  Since require Thou wilt
At my hand its price one day !
What the price is, who can say ?

ROBERT BROWNING.

SEPTEMBER 18.

GREAT God ! at whose creative word
Arising, Nature owned her Lord :
At whose behest, from gloomy night
The earth arose in order bright !
To whom the poet swells the song,
And cherubs' loftier notes belong :
To Thee be glory, honour, praise :
Great God, who canst depress or raise.
Say, all ye learned, all ye wise,
What towering pillars prop the skies ?
What massy chain suspends the earth ?
'Tis His high power who gave it birth.

'Tis He who sends the grateful shower ;
'Tis He who paints the glowing flower.
Let the loud anthem raise the strain,
While echo murmurs it again.
And ye who wander o'er the sheaf-crowned fields,
Praise Him for all the plenty harvest yields ;
Let harp and voice their swelling notes combine,
To praise all Nature's God, the Architect divine.

MRS HEMANS.

SEPTEMBER 19.

MORNING HYMN.

As for some dear familiar strain
Untired we ask, and ask again,
Ever, in its melodious store,
Finding a spell unheard before ;

Such is the bliss of souls serene,
When they have sworn, and steadfast mean,
Counting the cost, in all to espy
Their God, in all themselves deny.

O, could we learn that sacrifice,
What lights would all around us rise !
How would our hearts with wisdom talk
Along Life's dullest, dreariest walk !

We need not bid, for cloistered cell,
Our neighbour and our work farewell,
Nor strive to wind ourselves too high
For sinful man beneath the sky :

The trivial round, the common task,
Would furnish all we ought to ask ;
Room to deny ourselves ; a road
To bring us, daily, nearer God.

Seek we no more ; content with these,
Let present Rapture, Comfort, Ease,
As Heaven shall bid them, come and go :—
The secret this of Rest below.

Only, O Lord, in Thy dear love,
Fit us for perfect Rest above ;
And help us, this and every day,
To live more nearly as we pray.

JOHN KEBLE.

SEPTEMBER 20.

A HYMN TO MY GOD.

O THOU Great Power ! in whom I move,
For whom I live, to whom I die,
Behold me through Thy beams of love
Whilst on this couch of tears I lie ;
And cleanse my sordid soul within
By Thy Christ's blood, the bath of sin !

No hallowed oils, no grains I need,
No rags of saints, no purging fire ;
One rosy drop from David's seed
Was worlds of seas to quench Thine ire.
O precious ransom ! which once paid,
That *consummatum est* was said ;

And said by Him that said no more,
But sealed it with His sacred breath ;
Thou, then, that hast dispunged my score,
And dying wast the death of Death,
Be to me now, on Thee I call,
My life, my strength, my joy, my all !

Sir Henry Wotton.

THE DEAR BARGAIN.

O my Saviour, make me see,
How dearly Thou hast paid for me,
That lost again, my life may prove,
As then in death, so now in love.

R. Crashaw.

SEPTEMBER 21.

HIPPOLYTUS PRAYS TO ARTEMIS.

Fairest of the goddesses,
Dwelling in Olympian bliss,
Hail to thee, fair Artemis !
Thine, Lady, is the garland that I bear,
Fresh-woven, from a maiden meadow-land,
Where never herdman deems to feed his flock,
Nor sickle ever came,—a maiden mead,
Tended by Innocence with running dews,
And haunt of murmurous bees on April eves.
That man alone whose equal temperance
Is rooted, and not grafted, in his mind,
May pluck its blossoms, but the base may not.

'Thou, dearest Lady, for thy golden hair
Take from a pious hand the binding spray :
Mine only is this honour among men,
To be with thee, and join in thy discourse,
Hearing thy voice, yet seeing not thy face,—
And, Lady, may I end as I began life's race !

EURIPIDES (Trs. Editors).

SEPTEMBER 22.

As, down in the sunless retreats of the ocean
  Sweet flowers are springing no mortals can see,
So, deep in my soul the still prayer of devotion,
  Unheard by the world, rises silent to Thee ;
    My God ! silent to Thee ;
    Pure, warm, silent to Thee !
So, deep in my soul the still prayer of devotion,
  Unheard by the world, rises silent to Thee.

As still, to the star of its worship, though clouded,
  The needle points faithfully o'er the dim sea,
So, dark as I roam, in this wintry world shrouded,
  The hope of my spirit turns trembling to Thee ;
    My God, trembling to Thee ;
    True, fond, trembling to Thee !
So, dark as I roam, in this wintry world shrouded,
  The hope of my spirit turns trembling to Thee !

THOMAS MOORE.

SEPTEMBER 23.

BENEDICTION.

FATHER of Spirits ! Thine all secrets be.
  I bless Thee for the light Thou hast revealed
And that Thou hidest.   Part of me I see,
  And part of me Thy wisdom hath concealed,

Till the new life divulge it.   Lord, imbue me
  With will to work in this diurnal sphere,
  Knowing myself my life's day-labourer here,
Where evening brings the day's-work's wages to me.

I work my work.   All its results are Thine.
  I know the loyal deed becomes a fact
Which Thou wilt deal with : nor will I repine
  Altho' I miss the value of the act.
Thou carest for the creatures : and the end
  Thou seest.   The world unto Thy hands I leave :
  And to Thy hands my life.   I will not grieve
Because I know not all Thou dost intend.

But teach me, O Omnipotent, since strife,
  Sorrow, and pain are but occurrences
Of that condition thro' which flows my life,
  Not part of me, the immortal, whom distress
Cannot retain, to vex not thought for these :
  But to be patient, bear, forbear, restrain
  And hold my spirit pure above my pain.
No star, that looks thro' life's dark lattices,

But what gives token of a world elsewhere.
  I bless Thee for the loss of all things here
Which proves the gain to be : the hand of Care
  That shades the eyes from Earth and beckons near
The rest which sweetens all : the shade Time throws
  On Love's pale countenance, that he may gaze
  Across Eternity for better days
Unblinded, and the wisdom of all woes.

The Earl of Lytton
(Owen Meredith).

SEPTEMBER 24.

O FATHER, we approach Thy Throne,
  Who biddest the glorious sun arise,
  All-good, Almighty and All-wise,
Great source of all things, God alone !

We see Thee ! Brighter than the rays
  Of the bright sun, we see Thee shine !
  As in a fountain's face, divine,
We see Thee, endless Fount of days !

We see Thee, who our frames hast wrought,
  With one swift word, from senseless clay,
  Waked, with one glance of heavenly ray,
Our never-dying souls from nought !

Those souls Thou lightedst with the spark
  At Thy pure fire : and gracious still
  Gavest immortality, free-will,
And language, not involved or dark !

Trs. from the Danish by
SIR J. BOWRING.

SEPTEMBER 25.

NON NOBIS, DOMINE.

No marble statue, nor high
Aspiring pyramid be rais'd,
To lose its head within the sky !
What claim have I to memory ?
  God, be Thou only prais'd !

Thou in a moment canst defeat
The mighty conquests of the proud,
And blast the laurels of the great.
Thou canst make brightest glory set
  O' th' sudden in a cloud.

How can the feeble works of art
Hold out against th' assault of storms?
Or how can brass to him impart
Sense of surviving fame, whose heart
   Is now resolv'd to worms?

Blinde folly of triumphing pride!
Eternity, why build'st Thou here?
Dost Thou not see the highest tide
Its humbled stream i' th' ocean hide,
   And ne'er the same appear?

That tide which did its banks o'erflow,
As sent abroad by th' angry sea
To level vastest buildings low,
And all our trophies overthrow,
   Ebbs like a thief away.

And thou, who to preserve thy name
Leav'st statues in some conquer'd land!
How will posterity scorn fame,
When th' idol shall receive a maim,
   And lose a foot or hand!

How wilt thou hate thy wars, when he,
Who only for his hire did raise
Thy counterfeit in stone, with thee
Shall stand competitor, and be
   Perhaps thought worthier praise!

No laurel wreath about my brow!
To Thee, my God, all praise, whose law
The conquer'd doth and conqueror bow!
For both dissolve to air, if Thou
   Thy influence but withdraw.

SIR WILLIAM HABINGTON.

SEPTEMBER 26.

THE PASTOR'S PRAYER.

WHENCE but from Thee, the true and only God,
And from the faith derived through Him who bled
Upon the cross, this marvellous advance
Of good from evil? as if one extreme
Were left, the other gained.—O ye, who come
To kneel devoutly in yon reverend pile,
Called to such office by the peaceful sound
Of Sabbath-bells; and ye, who sleep in earth,
All cares forgotten, round its hallowed walls!
For you, in presence of this little band
Gathered together on the green hillside,
Your Pastor is emboldened to prefer
Vocal thanksgiving to the Eternal King;
Whose love, whose counsel, whose commands, have
    made
Your very poorest rich in peace of thought
And in good works; and him, who is endowed
With scantiest knowledge, master of all truth
Which the salvation of his soul requires. . . .
These barren rocks, your stern inheritance,
These fertile fields, that recompense your pains;
The shadowy vale, the sunny mountain-top;
Woods waving in the wind their lofty heads,
Or hushed; the roaring waters, and the still—
They see the offering of my lifted hands,
They hear my lips present their sacrifice,
They know if I be silent, morn or even:
For, though in whispers speaking, the full heart
Will find a vent; and thought is praise to Him,
Audible praise to Thee, omniscient Mind,
From whom all gifts descend, all blessings flow!

WILLIAM WORDSWORTH.

SEPTEMBER 27.

PROSTRATE, O Lord, I lie,
Behold me, Lord, with pity,
Stop not Thine ears against my cry,
My sad and mourning ditty,
Breath'd from an inward soul,
From heart heartily contrite,
An offering sweet, a sacrifice,
In Thy high heav'nly sight.

Observe not sins, O Lord,
For who may then abide it,
But let Thy mercy cancel them,
Thou hast not man denied it,
Man melting with remorse and thoughts,
Thought past repenting,
O lighten, Lord, and hear our songs,
Our sins full sore lamenting.

The wonders of Thy works
Above all reason reacheth,
And yet Thy mercy above all
This, us Thy spirit teacheth.
Then let no sinner fall
In depth of soul's despair,
Since never soul so foul there was
But mercy made it fair.

WILLIAM BYRD.

SEPTEMBER 28.

Life of the world, Immortal Mind,
Father of all the human kind !
Whose boundless eye, that knows no rest,
Intent on Nature's ample breast,
Explores the space of earth and skies,
And sees eternal incense rise,—
    To Thee my humble voice I raise ;
    Forgive, while I presume to praise !

Though Thou this transient being gave,
That shortly sinks into the grave,
Yet 'twas Thy goodness still to give
A being that can think and live ;
In all Thy works Thy wisdom see,
And stretch its tow'ring mind to Thee.
    To Thee my humble voice I raise ;
    Forgive, while I presume to praise !

And still this poor contracted span,
This life, that bears the name of Man,
From Thee derives its vital ray,
Eternal Source of life and day !
Thy bounty still the sunshine pours,
That gilds its morn and evening hours.
    To Thee my humble voice I raise ;
    Forgive, while I presume to praise !

Thro' Error's maze, thro' Folly's night,
The lamp of Reason lends me light.
When stern affliction waves her rod,
My heart confides in Thee, my God !
When Nature shrinks, oppressed with woes,
E'en then she finds in Thee repose.
    To Thee my humble voice I raise ;
    Forgive, while I presume to praise !

Affliction flies, and Hope returns;
Her lamp with brighter splendour burns;
Gay Love, with all his smiling train,
And Peace and Joy are here again.
These, these I know 'twas Thine to give;
I trusted, and, behold! I live.
    To Thee my humble voice I raise;
    Forgive, while I presume to praise!

O may I still Thy favour prove,
Still grant me gratitude and love!
Let truth and virtue guide my heart,
Nor peace, nor hope, nor joy depart;
But yet, whate'er my life may be,
My heart shall still repose in Thee.
    To Thee my humble voice I raise;
    Forgive, while I presume to praise!

JOHN LANGHORNE.

SEPTEMBER 29.

PRAYER TO THE PENATES.

        HEARKEN your hymn of praise,
Penates! to your shrines I come for rest,
There only to be found.   Often at eve,
As in my wanderings I have seen far off
Some lonely light that spake of comfort there,
It told my heart of many a joy of home,
When I was homeless.   Often as I gazed
From some high eminence on goodly vales
And cots and villages embower'd below,
The thought would rise that all to me was strange,
Amid the scene so fair, not one small spot
Where my tired mind might rest, and call it *Home*.

There is a magic in that little word :
It is a mystic circle that surrounds
Comforts and virtues never known beyond
The hallowed limit.   Often has my heart
Ached for that quiet haven !   Haven'd now,
I think of those in this world's wilderness
Who wander on, and find no home of rest
Till to the grave they go.   Them Poverty,
Hollow-eyed fiend, the child of Wealth and Power,
Bad offspring of worse parents, age afflicts,
Cankering with her foul mildews the chill'd heart ;
Them Want with scorpion scourge drives to the den
Of Guilt ; them Slaughter for the price of Death
Throws to her raven brood.   Oh, not on them,
God of eternal Justice, not on them
·Let fall Thy thunder.

                          Household Deities !
Then only shall be Happiness on earth
When man shall feel your sacred power and love,
Your tranquil joys ; then shall the city stand
A huge void sepulchre, and on the site
Where fortresses and palaces have stood
The olive grow ; there shall the Tree of Peace
Strike its roots deep, and flourish.   This the state
Shall bless the race redeem'd of Man, when Wealth,
And Power, and all their hideous progeny
Shall sink annihilate, and all mankind
Live in the equal brotherhood of love.
Heart-calming hope and sure !   For hitherward
Tend all the tumults of the troubled world,
Its woes, its wisdom, and its wickedness
Alike ; . . . So He hath will'd, whose will is just.
    Meantime, all hoping and expecting all,
In patient faith, to you, Domestic Gods !
Studious of other lore than song, I come.

ROBERT SOUTHEY.

SEPTEMBER 30.

THE LAST VICTORY.

I HAVE consider'd it, and finde
There is no dealing with Thy mighty Passion;
For though I die for Thee, I am behinde;
My sinnes deserve the condemnation.

O, make me innocent, that I
May give a disentangled state and free;
And yet Thy wounds still my attempts defie,
For by Thy death I die for Thee.

Ah, was it not enough that Thou
By Thy eternall glorie didst outgo me?
Couldst Thou not Grief's sad conquests me allow,
But in all vict'ries overthrow me?

Yet by confession will I come
Into Thy conquest.   Though I can do nought
Against Thee, in Thee I will overcome
The man who once against Thee fought.

GEORGE HERBERT.

OCTOBER 1.

"A HARMONY IN AUTUMN."

I vowed that I would dedicate my powers
  To thee and thine—have I not kept the vow?
  With beating heart and streaming eyes, even now
I call the phantoms of a thousand hours
Each from his voiceless grave: they have in visioned
      bowers
  Of studious zeal of love's delight
  Outwatched with me the envious night—
They know that never joy illumined my brow
  Unlinked with hope that thou wouldst free
  This world from its dark slavery,
  That thou, O awful Loveliness,
Wouldst give whate'er these words cannot express.

The day becomes more solemn and serene
  When noon is past—there is a harmony
  In autumn and a lustre in its sky
Which through the summer is not heard or seen,
As if it could not be, as if it had not been!
  Thus let thy power, which like the truth
  Of Nature on my passive youth
Descended, to my onward life supply
  Its calm—to one who worships thee,
  And every form containing thee,
  Whom, Spirit fair, thy spells did bind
To fear himself and love all humankind.

PERCY BYSSHE SHELLEY.

OCTOBER 2.

A PRAYER IN BATTLE.

FATHER, I cry to Thee !
Cannon with thunder-clouds compass me round ;
Flashes of lightning are sped from the sound ;
  Lord of the battle-line, I cry to Thee,
    O Father, lead Thou me !

O Father, lead Thou me !
Lead me to victory, lead me to death.
Lo ! I acknowledge the source of my breath ;
  Lord, as Thou willest, so lead Thou me,
    God, I acknowledge Thee !

God, I acknowledge Thee !
There, where the West-wind is blown thro' the pines ;
Here, in the storm and the crash of the lines ;
  Father of mercies, I acknowledge Thee,
    O Father, bless Thou me !

O Father, bless Thou me !
Into Thy hand do I render my day ;
Thou, who hast given, canst take it away ;
  Living or dying, Lord, bless Thou me,
    O Father, I praise Thee !

O Father, I praise Thee !
Not for the goods of the world do we fight ;
With the sword we're defending our holiest right ;
  Falling or conquering, praise I Thee,
    God, I surrender me !

God, I surrender me !
In the moment when thunderous Death cometh near,
And my new-opened veins flow with life-blood dear,
    Into Thy hands I surrender me,
        Father, I cry to Thee !

THEODOR KÖRNER.
(Trs. Editors.)

OCTOBER 3.

HYMN.

WAKE, O my soul ! awake, and raise
Up every part to sing His praise
Who from His sphere of glory fell
To raise thee up from death and Hell :
See how His soul, vext for thy sin,
Weeps blood without, feels Hell within ;
        See where He hangs :
            Hark how He cries :
        Oh, bitter pangs !
            Now, now He dies.

Wake, O mine eyes ! awake, and view
Those two twin lights, whence Heavens drew
Their glorious beams, whose gracious sight
Fills you with joy, with life, and light ;
See how with clouds of sorrow drown'd,
They wash with tears thy sinful wound :
        See, how with streams
            Of spit th' are drench'd ;
        See, how their beams
            With death are quench'd.

Wake, O mine ear ! awake, and hear
That powerful voice, which stills thy fear,
And brings from Heaven those joyful news,
Which Heav'n commands, which Hell subdues ;
Hark how His ears (Heav'n's mercy-seat)
Foul slanders with reproaches beat :
    Hark, how the knocks
      Our ears resound ;
    Hark, how their mocks
      His hearing wound.

Wake, O my heart ! tune every string :
Wake, O my tongue ! awake, and sing :
Think not a thought in all thy lays,
Speak not a word but of His praise :
Tell how His sweetest tongue they drown'd
With gall : think how His heart they wound :
    That bloody spout,
      Gagg'd for thy sin ;
    His life lets out,
      Thy death lets in.

PHINEAS FLETCHER.

OCTOBER 4.

"HUMILITY IS CROWN'D, AND FAITH RECEIVES THE PRIZE."

SINCE the dear hour that brought me to Thy foot,
And cut up all my follies by the root,
I never trusted in an arm but Thine,
Nor hoped, but in Thy righteousness divine :
My pray'rs and alms, imperfect and defil'd,
Were but the feeble efforts of a child.

Howe'er perform'd, it was their brightest part
That they proceeded from a grateful heart
Cleans'd in Thine own all-purifying blood,—
Forgive their evil, and accept their good ;
I cast them at Thy feet—my only plea
Is what it was, dependence upon Thee,
While struggling in the vale of tears below,
That never fail'd, nor shall it fail me now.

WILLIAM COWPER.

OCTOBER 5.

THEN give Thy saints
That faithful zeal which neither faints
Nor wildly burns, but meekly still
Dares own the truth and shew the ill.
Frustrate those cancerous, close arts
Which cause solution in all parts,
And strike them dumb, who, for mere words
Wound Thy beloved more than swords.
Dear Lord, do thus ! and then let grace
Descend and hallow all the place ;
Incline each hard heart to do good,
And cement us with Thy Son's blood ;
That like true sheep, all in one fold,
We may be fed and one mind hold.
Give watchful spirits to our guides :
For sin—like water—hourly glides
By each man's door, and quickly will
Turn in, if not obstructed still.
Therefore write in their hearts Thy law,
And let these long, sharp judgments awe
Their very thoughts, that by their clear
And holy lives Mercy may here

Sit regent yet, and blessings flow
As fast as persecutions now.
So shall we know, in war and peace,
Thy service to be our sole ease,
With prostrate souls adoring Thee,
Who turned our sad captivity.

HENRY VAUGHAN.

OCTOBER 6.

THE PRAYER OF THE LIBATION-POURERS.

OH! hear me, hear my prayer, Thou mighty Lord!
  Sire of all gods that on Olympus dwell,
Hear Thou, and grant my longing heart's desire,
  That those who wise of heart would fain do well
    May see each prayer for right
    Fulfilled in holiest might:
  That prayer, O Zeus, I pray.

Do Thou protect him, yea, O Zeus, and bring
  Before his foes on yonder secret way;
For if Thou raise him high, then Thou, O King,
  Shalt to Thy heart's content
Receive a twofold, threefold recompense,
    For that Thine anger bent
    Against each old offence.

Look on the son of one whom Thou didst love,
  Like orphan colt fast bound to car of woes;
Set Thou a mark that may as limit prove;
  Ah! might one watch his footsteps as he goes,
    In measured course and true
    This his own country through!

And ye who in our home
Stand in the shrine with plenteous wealth full stored,
   Hear, O ye Gods, and come,
   Yea, come with one accord,
   Lead him on, wash away
With vengeance new the blood of crime of old ;
   Let not the old guilt stay
To breed fresh offspring where our home we hold.

   But grant him good success,
O Thou who dost within the great Cave dwell !
With upward glance of joy our chief's house bless,
   And that he too, full well,
Freely and brightly with the dear, loved eyes,
May look from out the veil of cloudy skies.

   And then may Maia's son
Assist him, as is meet, in this his task !
   Through Him success is won,
   The boon that now we ask :
And many secret things will He make clear,
   If that should be His will ;
But should He choose the truth should not appear,
   Before men's eyes He still
Brings darkness and the blackness of the night ;
Nor is He clearer in the day's full light.

   And then will we pour forth
All that our house contains of costliest worth,
   Past evil to redeem,
And through the city we will raise the strain
Shrill-voiced of women's chant yet once again.
   All this is good, I deem ;
This, this my gain increaseth more and more,
And far from those I love is sorrow's bitter stour.

ÆSCHYLUS (Trs. E. H. Plumptre).

OCTOBER 7.

" He that would make a real progress in knowledge must dedicate his age as well as youth, the latter growth as well as the first fruits, at the altar of Truth."—BERKELEY.

THE ABOVE IMITATED.

BEFORE thy mystic altar, heavenly Truth,
I kneel in manhood as I knelt in youth :
Thus let me kneel, till this dull form decay,
And life's last shade be brightened by thy ray :
Then shall my soul, now lost in clouds below,
Soar without bound, without consuming glow.

SIR WILLIAM JONES.

SUN of the soul ! whose cheerful ray
    Darts o'er this gloom of life a smile,
Sweet Hope ! yet further gild my way,
    Yet light my weary steps awhile,
Till Thy fair lamp dissolve in endless day.

JOHN LANGHORNE.

OCTOBER 8.

THE LIFE OF THE BLESSED.

REGION of life and light !
Land of the good whose earthly toils are o'er !
    Nor frost nor heat may blight
    Thy vernal beauty, fertile shore,
Yielding thy blessed fruits for evermore !

There, without crook or sling,
Walks the good Shepherd, blossoms white and red
Round His meek temples cling :
And to sweet pastures led
His own loved flock beneath His eye is fed.

He guides, and near Him they
Follow delighted, for He makes them go
Where dwells eternal May,
And heavenly roses blow
Deathless, and gathered but again grow.

He leads them to the height
Named of the infinite and long-sought Good,
And fountains of delight :
And where His feet have stood
Springs up, along the way, their tender food.

And when, in the mid skies,
The climbing sun has reached his highest bound,
Reposing as He lies,
With all His flock around,
He witches the still air with numerous sound.

From His sweet lute flow forth
Immortal harmonies, of power to still
All passions born of earth,
And draw the ardent will
Its destiny of goodness to fulfil.

Might but a little part,
A wandering breath, of that high melody
Descend into my heart,
And change it till it be
Transformed and swallowed up, oh love ! in Thee.

Ah, then my soul should know
Beloved ! where Thou liest at noon of day,
And from this place of woe
Released, should take its way
To mingle with Thy flock and never stray.

LUIS PONCE DE LEON.
(*Trs.* William Cullen Bryant.)

OCTOBER 9.

O THOU who sweetly bend'st my stubborn will,
Who send'st Thy stripes to teach, and not to kill :
Thy cheerful face from me no longer hide,
Withdraw these clouds, the scourges of my pride ;
I sink to Hell, if I be lower thrown ;
I see what man is, being left alone.
My substance, which from nothing did begin,
Is worse than nothing by the weight of sin ;
I see myself in such a wretched state
As neither thoughts conceive, or words relate—
How great a distance parts us ! for in Thee
Is endless good, and boundless ill in me.
All creatures prove me abject, but how low,
Thou only know'st, and teachest me to know.
To paint this baseness, nature is too base ;
This darkness yields not but to beams of grace.
Where shall I then this piercing splendour find ?
Or found, how shall it guide me, being blind ? . . .
Grace comes as oft, clad in the dusky robe
Of desolation, as in white attire,
Which better fits the bright celestial choir.
Some in foul seasons perish through despair,
But more through boldness when the days are fair.
This then must be the medicine for my woes,
To yield to what my Saviour shall dispose :

To glory in my baseness, to rejoice
In mine afflictions, to obey His voice
As well when threat'nings my defects reprove,
As when I cherish'd am with words of love,
To say to Him in every time and place,
" Withdraw Thy comforts, so Thou leave Thy grace ! "

SIR JOHN BEAUMONT.

OCTOBER 10.

THE PRAYER OF IPHIGENIA IN TAURIS.

I WOULD not judge the gods—but sure the lot
Of womankind is worthy to be pitied.
At home, at war, man lords it as he lists ;
In foreign provinces he is not helpless ;
Possession gladdens him ; him conquest crowns ;
E'en death to him extends a wreath of honour.
Confined and narrow is the woman's bliss :
Obedience to a rude imperious husband
Her duty and her comfort ; and, if fate
On foreign shores have cast her, how unhappy !
So Thoas (yet I prize his noble soul)
Detains me here in hated hallow'd bondage.
For, tho' with shame I feel it, I acknowledge
It is with secret loathness that I serve thee,
My great Protectress ! thee, to whom my life
"Twere fitting I in gratitude devoted ;
But I have ever hoped, and still I hope,
That thou, Diana, wilt not quite forsake
The banisht daughter of the first of kings.
O born of Jove ! if him, the mighty man
Whose soul thou woundedst with unhealing pangs
When thou didst ask his child in sacrifice—

If godlike Agamemnon, to thy altar
Who led his darling, from the fallen Troy
Thy hand hath to his country reconducted,
And on the hero hath bestow'd the bliss
To clasp his wife, Electra, and his son—
Restore me also to my happy home ;
And save me, whom thou hast from death preserv'd,
From worse than death, from banishment in Tauris.

J. W. von GOETHE.
(*Trs.* William Taylor of Norwich.)

OCTOBER 11.

"*It is good for us to be here : if Thou wilt, let us make here three tabernacles ; one for Thee, and one for Moses, and one or Elias.*"—MATTHEW XVII. 4.

METHINKS it is good to be here,
If Thou wilt, let us build—but for whom ?
Nor Elias nor Moses appear ;
But the shadows of eve that encompass with gloom
The abode of the dead and the place of the tomb.

Shall we build to Ambition ?   Ah, no !
Affrighted, he shrinketh away ;
For see, they would pin him below
In a small narrow cave, and, begirt with cold clay,
To the meanest of reptiles a peer and a prey.

To Beauty ?   Ah, no ! she forgets
The charms which she wielded before ;
Nor knows the foul worm that he frets
The skin which but yesterday fools could adore
For the smoothness it held or the tint which it wore.

Shall we build to the purple of Pride,
  The trappings which dizen the proud?
    Alas! they are all laid aside,
And here's neither dress nor adornment allowed,
But the long winding-sheet and the fringe of the shroud.

    To Riches?   Alas! 'tis in vain;
  Who hide in their turns have been hid;
    The treasures are squandered again;
And here in the grave are all metals forbid
But the tinsel that shines on the dark coffin-lid.

    To the pleasures which Mirth can afford,
  The revel, the laugh, and the jeer?
    Ah, here is a plentiful board!
But the guests are all mute as their pitiful cheer,
And none but the worm is a reveller here.

    Shall we build to Affection and Love?
  Ah, no! they have withered and died,
    Or fled with the spirit above.
Friends, brothers, and sisters are laid side by side,
Yet none have saluted, and none have replied.

    Unto Sorrow?—the Dead cannot grieve;
  Not a sob, not a sigh meets mine ear,
    Which Compassion itself could relieve.
Ah, sweetly they slumber, nor love, hope, or fear;
Peace! peace is the watchword, the only one here.

    Unto Death, to whom monarchs must bow?
  Ah, no! for his empire is known,
    And here there are trophies enow!
Beneath the cold dead, and around the dark stone,
Are the signs of a sceptre that none may disown.

The first tabernacle to Hope we will build,
And look for the sleepers around us to rise !
The second to Faith, which insures it fulfilled ;
And the third to the Lamb of the great sacrifice,
Who bequeathed us them both when He rose to the skies.

HERBERT KNOWLES.
(*Written in the churchyard of
Richmond, Yorkshire.*)

OCTOBER 12.

TO HIS ANGRIE GOD.

THROUGH all the night
Thou dost me fright
And hold'st mine eyes from sleeping ;
And day by day
My cup can say,
My wine is mixt with weeping.

Thou dost my bread
With ashes knead
Each evening and each morrow :
Mine eye and eare
Do see and heare
The coming in of sorrow.

The scourge of steele,
(Ay me !) I feele,
Upon me beating ever ;
While my sick heart
With dismall smart
Is disacquainted never.

Long, long, I'm sure,
This can't endure ;
But in short time 'twill please Thee,
My gentle God,
To burn the rod,
Or strike so as to ease me.

ROBERT HERRICK.

OCTOBER 13.

METHOUGHT (it was the midnight of my soul,
  Dead midnight) that I stood on Calvary :
I found the Cross but not the Christ.   The whole
  Of Heaven was dark : and I went bitterly,
Weeping because I found Him not.   Methought
  (It was the twilight of the dawn and mist)
  I stood before the sepulchre of Christ :
The sepulchre was vacant : void of aught

Saving the cere-clothes of the grave, which were
  Upfolden straight and empty : bitterly
Weeping I stood, because not even there
  I found Him.   Then a voice spake unto me,
"Whom seekest thou ?   Why is thy heart dismayed ?
  Jesus of Nazareth ; He is not here :
  Behold the Lord is risen.   Be of good cheer :
Approach, behold the place where He was laid."

And while He spoke, the sunrise smote the world.
  " Go forth and tell thy brethren," spake the voice :
" The Lord is risen."   Suddenly unfurled,
  The whole unclouded Orient did rejoice
In glory.   Wherefore should I mourn that here
  My heart feels vacant of what most it needs ?
  Christ is arisen ! . . . the cere-clothes and the weeds
That wrapped Him, lying in this sepulchre

Of earth He hath abandoned : being gone
    Back into Heaven, where we too must turn
Our gaze to find Him.   Pour, O risen Sun
    Of Righteousness, the light for which I yearn
Upon the darkness of this mortal hour,
    This tract of night in which I walk forlorn :
    Behold the night is now far spent.   The morn
Breaks, breaking from afar through a night shower !

The Earl of Lytton
(Owen Meredith).

OCTOBER 14.

THE PRAYER OF ELIJAH,

When he rebuked the worshippers of Baal.

        . . . Then at the long day's close,
Even at the Mincha [1] hour, Elijah's prayer arose :

        "O Lord of all !
God of my fathers, hear me when I call.
        Let it be known
For evermore that Thou art Lord alone ;
        That I, even I,
Thy servant am, who still unceasingly
        To serve Thee run,
And at Thy bidding all these things have done.
        Hear, when I pray,
And make Thy people know Thy power this day,
        And turn once more
Their hearts to Thee, as in the days of yore."

[1] Concluding.

T

Then fell there fire from heaven at his word,
And all the people cried with one accord :
" The Lord is God—He only—God and Lord ! "

Jehuda ibn Giat.
(Trs. Mrs Henry Lucas.)

OCTOBER 15.

Blessed light of saints on high,
Who fill the mansions of the sky ;
Sure defence, whose mercy still
Preserves Thy subjects here from ill ;
Oh, my Jesus, make me know
How to pay the thanks I owe.
 As the fond sheep that idly strays,
With wanton play, through winding ways,
Which never hits the road of home,
O'er wilds of danger learns to roam,
Till, wearied out with idle fear,
And, passing there, and turning here,
He will, for rest, to covert run,
And meet the wolf he wish'd to shun ;
Thus wretched I, through wanton will,
Run blind and headlong on in ill :
'Twas thus from sin to sin I flew,
And thus I might have perish'd too :
But mercy dropp'd the likeness here,
And show'd, and sav'd me from my fear.
While o'er the darkness of my mind
The sacred spirit purely shin'd,
And mark'd and brighten'd all the way
Which leads to everlasting day,
And broke the thickening clouds of sin,
And fix'd the light of love within.

From hence my ravish'd soul aspires,
And dates the rise of its desires.
From hence to Thee, my God! I turn,
And fervent wishes say I burn,
I burn, Thy glorious face to see,
And live in endless joy with Thee. . . .

Oh, my flame, my pleasing pain,
Burn and purify my stain,
Warm me, burn me, day by day,
Till you purge my earth away;
Till at the last I throughly shine,
And turn a torch of love divine.

THOMAS PARNELL.

OCTOBER 16.

HE HEALETH THE BROKEN HEART.

O THOU who dry'st the mourner's tear!
  How dark this world would be
If, when deceived and wounded here,
  We could not fly to Thee.
The friends, who in our sunshine live,
  When winter comes, are flown:
And he who has but tears to give
  Must weep those tears alone.
But Thou wilt heal that broken heart,
  Which, like the plants that throw
Their fragrance from the wounded part,
  Breathes sweetness out of woe.

When joy no longer soothes or cheers,
  And e'en the hope that threw
A moment's sparkle o'er our tears,
  Is dimmed and vanished too,

Oh! who would bear life's stormy doom,
  Did not Thy wing of love
Come, brightly wafting through the gloom
  Our peace-branch from above?
Then sorrow, touched by Thee, grows bright
  With more than rapture's ray;
As darkness shows us worlds of light
  We never saw by day.

THOMAS MOORE.

OCTOBER 17.

THE TEARS OF PENITENCE.

I LIVE again my youth of godless merriment
  With bitter tears and groaning and repentant sighs;
This is the fruit I gather from those days misspent,
  Tears and burning shame and hateful memories.

These sighs and tears before Thee are my sole defence,
  Through them the sinner hopes Thine anger to
    appease,
Hast Thou not streams to quench the thirst of penitence?
  Merciful God, 'tis time their waters to release.

Where, wretched sinner, shall I hide, or whither fly,
  If Thou in anger come to reckon, Lord, with me?
What can I say? It comforts me, O Lord Most High,
  My reckoning must be made with Thee, and only
    Thee!

Thou never wilt despise a humble, contrite heart
  (Out of Thy mouth, O Lord, that promise has been
    spoken),
Look then on mine, O Man of Sorrows that Thou art,
  Worthy 'tis of Thee, for with sorrow it is broken.

Bruise and burn this body, but spare my soul, O Lord!
　Chastise me and exact to the uttermost my debt!
O visit me, in this life, with fire and with sword,
　But, in the life to come, pity and spare me yet!

Louis Racine (Trs. Editors).

OCTOBER 18.

LORD OF THE UNIVERSE.

What art Thou, Mighty One! and where Thy seat?
　Thou broodest on the calm that cheers the lands,
　And Thou dost bear within Thine awful hands
The rolling thunders and the lightnings fleet;

Stern on Thy dark-wrought car of cloud and wind,
　Thou guid'st the northern storm at night's dead noon,
　Or, on the red wing of the fierce monsoon,
Disturb'st the sleeping giant of the Ind.

In the drear silence of the polar span
　Dost Thou repose? or in the solitude
Of sultry tracts, where the lone caravan
　Hears nightly howl the tiger's hungry brood?
Vain thought! the confines of His throne to trace,
Who glows through all the field of boundless space.

Henry Kirke White.

Oh God! let me breathe, and look up at the sky!
　Good is as hundreds, evil as one;
　Round about goeth the golden sun.

Leigh Hunt.

OCTOBER 19.

[Imitated from the Persian.]

Lord! who art merciful as well as just,
Incline Thine ear to me, a child of dust!
Not what I would, O Lord! I offer Thee,
          Alas! but what I can.
Father Almighty, who hast made me man,
And bade me look to Heav'n, for Thou art there,
Accept my sacrifice and humble prayer;
Four things which are not in Thy treasury,
I lay before Thee, Lord, with this petition,—
My nothingness, my wants, my sin, and my contrition.

                              Robert Southey.

OCTOBER 20.

SAILORS' PRAYER BEFORE AN ENGAGEMENT.

Hear us, O hear, Almighty Power!
Our guide in counsel and our strength in fight!
    Now war's important die is thrown,
    If left the day to man alone,
How blind is wisdom and how weak is might!

    Let prostrate hearts and awful fear
    And deep remorse and sighs sincere
For Britain's guilt, the wrath divine appease;
    A wrath, more formidable far
    Than angry Nature's wasteful war,
The whirl of tempests and the roar of seas.

From out the deep, to Thee we cry,
To Thee, at Nature's helm on high !
Steer Thou our conduct, dread Omnipotence !
To Thee for succour we resort,
Thy favour is our only port,
Our only rock of safety, Thy defence.

Britain in vain extends her care
To climes remote for aids in war,
Still farther must it stretch to crush the foe ;
There's one alliance, one alone,
Can crown her arms or fix her throne ;
And that alliance is not found below.

Ally Supreme, we turn to Thee :
We learn obedience from the sea,
With seas and winds, henceforth, Thy laws fulfil :
'Tis Thine our blood to freeze or warm,
To rouse or hush the martial storm,
And turn the tide of conquest, at Thy will.

'Tis Thine to beam sublime renown,
Or quench the glories of a crown,
'Tis Thine to doom, 'tis Thine from death to free ;
To turn aside his levelled dart,
Or pluck it from the bleeding heart :—
There we cast anchor, we confide in Thee.

EDWARD YOUNG.

OCTOBER 21.

[Trafalgar Day, 1805.]

JOHN OF GAUNT'S PRAYER FOR ENGLAND.

This Royal throne of kings, this sceptred isle,
This earth of majesty, this seat of Mars,
This other Eden, demi-Paradise ;
This fortress, built by nature for herself
Against infection and the hand of war ;
This happy breed of men, this little world,
This precious stone set in the silver sea,
Which serves it in the office of a wall,
Or as a moat defensive to a house,
Against the envy of less happier lands ;
This blessed plot, this realm, this earth, this England,
This nurse, this teeming womb of Royal kings,
Feared for their breed, and famous for their birth ;
Renownèd for their deeds as far from home
(For Christian service and true chivalry)
As is the Sepulchre in stubborn Jewry
Of the world's Ransom, Blessed Mary's Son ;
This land of such dear souls, this dear, dear land,
Dear for her reputation through the world,
Is now leased out (I die pronouncing it)
Like to a tenement or pelting farm :
England, bound in with the triumphant sea,
Whose rocky shore beats back the envious siege
Of watery Neptune, is now bound in with shame,
With inky blots and rotten parchment bonds ;
That England, which was wont to conquer others,
Hath made a shameful conquest of itself ;
Ah, would the scandal vanish with my life,
How happy then were my ensuing death !

WILLIAM SHAKESPEARE.

OCTOBER 22.

MATTENS.

I cannot ope mine eyes,
But Thou art ready there to catch
My morning-soul and sacrifice ;
Then we must needs for that day make a match.

My God, what is a heart ?
Silver, or gold, or precious stone,
Or star, or rainbow, or a part
Of all these things, or all of them in one ?

My God, what is a heart,
That Thou shouldst it so eye, and woo,
Pouring upon it all Thy art,
As if that Thou hadst nothing else to do ?

Indeed man's whole estate
Amounts (and richly) to serve Thee ;
He did not heav'n and earth create,
Yet studies them, not Him by whom they be.

Teach me Thy love to know ;
That this new light, which now I see,
May both the work and Workman show ;
Then by a sunbeam I will climb to Thee.

GEORGE HERBERT.

OCTOBER 23.

TO THE SECONDE PERSON.

O benigne Jesu, my soverain lorde and kynge,
The only Sonne of God, by filiacion
The second person, without beginning,
Both God and Man, our faith maketh plain relacion,

Mary the Mother, by way of incarnacion,
Whose glorious passion our soules doth revive,
Against al bodely and ghostly tribulacion,
Defend me with Thy piteous woundes five.

O pereles prynce, paynted to the death,
Rufully rent, Thy body wan and blo
For my redemption gave up Thy vytal breathe,
Was never sorow lyke to Thy deadly wo.
Graunt me, out of this world when I shal go,
Thine endles mercy, for my preservative.
Against the world, the flesh, the devill also
Defend me with Thy piteous woundes five.

JOHN SKELTON.

OCTOBER 24.

TO HIS MERCIFUL GOD.

COME not, O Lord ! in the dread robe of splendour
  Thou worest on the Mount, in the day of Thine ire :
Come, veiled in those shadows, deep, awful, but tender,
  Which Mercy flings over Thy features of fire.

Lord ! Thou rememberest the night when Thy nation
  Stood fronting her foe by the red-rolling stream,
On Egypt Thy pillar frowned dark desolation,
  While Israel basked all the night in its beam.

So, when the dread clouds of anger enfold Thee,
  From us, in Thy mercy, the dark side remove,
While shrouded in terrors the guilty behold Thee,
  Oh ! turn upon us the mild light of Thy love !

THOMAS MOORE.

OCTOBER 25.

IF it must be; if it must be, O God!
    That I die young and make no further moans;
That underneath the unrespective sod,
    In unescutcheoned privacy, my bones
Shall crumble soon,—then give me strength to bear
    The last convulsive throe of too sweet breath!
I tremble from the edge of life, to dare
    The dark and fatal leap, having no faith,
No glorious yearning for the Apocalypse;
    But, like a child that in the night-time cries
For light, I cry: forgetting the eclipse
    Of knowledge and our human destinies.
O peevish and uncertain soul! obey
The law of life in patience till the Day.

DAVID GRAY.

OCTOBER 26.

A FOREST HYMN.

THERE have been holy men who hid themselves
Deep in the woody wilderness and gave
Their lives to thought and prayer, till they outlived
The generation born with them, nor seemed
Less aged than the hoary trees and rocks
Around them: and there have been holy men
Who deemed it were not well to pass life thus.
But let me often to these solitudes
Retire: and in Thy presence reassure
My feeble virtue. Here its enemies,
The passions, at Thy plainer footsteps shrink
And tremble, and are still. Oh God! when Thou

Dost scare the world with tempests, set on fire
The heavens with falling thunderbolts, or fill
With all the waters of the firmament
The swift dark whirlwind that uproots the woods
And drowns the villages : when, at Thy call,
Uprises the great deep and throws himself
Upon the continent and overwhelms
Its cities—who forgets not, at the sight
Of these tremendous tokens of Thy power,
His pride and lays his strife and follies by ?
Oh, from these sterner aspects of Thy face
Spare me and mine, nor let us need the wrath
Of the mad, unchained elements to teach
Who rules them.   Be it ours to meditate
In these calm shades Thy milder majesty,
And to the beautiful order of Thy works
Learn to conform the order of our lives.

WILLIAM CULLEN BRYANT.

OCTOBER 27.

LIFE IN DEATH.

If I were a dead leaf thou mightest bear ;
If I were a swift cloud to fly with thee ;
A wave to pant beneath thy power, and share
The impulse of thy strength, only less free
Than thou, O uncontroulable !   If even
I were as in my boyhood, and could be
The comrade of thy wanderings over heaven,
As then, when to outstrip thy skiey speed
Scarce seemed a vision ; I would ne'er have striven
As thus with thee in prayer in my sore need.
Oh ! lift me as a wave, a leaf, a cloud !
I fall upon the thorns of life !   I bleed !

A heavy weight of hours has chained and bowed
One too like thee : tameless and swift and proud.

Make me thy lyre, even as the forest is :
What if my leaves are falling like its own !
The tumult of thy mighty harmonies
Will take from both a deep autumnal tone,
Sweet though in sadness.   Be thou, spirit fierce,
My spirit.   Be thou me, impetuous one !
Drive my dead thoughts over the universe
Like withered leaves, to quicken a new birth !
And, by the incantation of this verse,
Scatter, as from an unextinguished hearth
Ashes and sparks, my words among mankind !
Be through my lips to unawakened earth
The trumpet of a prophecy !   O, wind,
If Winter comes, can Spring be far behind ?

PERCY BYSSHE SHELLEY.

OCTOBER 28.

PRAYER FOR HELP.

LORD, I pray with hands uplifted,
And my tears flow fast,
For my manifold transgressions
And my sinful past.
Heal my inward wound and straighten
All my ways at last.
Merciful, O Father, be,
Even when Thou judgest me,
Answer when I call on Thee,
God of my salvation !

Glad, yet fearful, I am seeking
Pardon 'midst the throng
Of Thy chosen congregation
With sweet sound of song,
Hymns and praise and patient striving,
To amend the wrong.
Lord, Thy power I will proclaim,
And exalt Thy glorious name,
Yea, my love for Thee, like flame,
Burns, Thou my salvation !
Well-spring Thou of strength and gladness,
Lord, I hope in Thee,
And declare the power eternal
Of Thy sovereignty.
O ! command Thou Thy salvation
To abide with me.
Let it guide me on my way,
Evermore my help and stay,
Bringing me from day to day
Still my daily portion.
    Thou wilt save me, Thou wilt guard me,
Mine exalted King.
Have regard to my entreaty,
And good tidings bring.
Unto us Thy needy people
Let Thine answer ring :
" Fear thou not, for I behold thee,
I will strengthen and enfold thee,
Yea, my right hand shall uphold thee !
I am thy salvation ! "

ABRAHAM IBN EZRA.
(Trs. Mrs Henry Lucas.)

OCTOBER 29.

THE PRODIGAL.

Unto the living God for pardon do I pray,
From whom, I grant, e'en from the shell, I have run
    still astray ;
  And other lives there none (my death shall well
    declare)
On whom I ought to grate for grace, as faulty folks
    do fare :
  But Thee, O Lord, alone I have offended so,
That this small scourge is much too scant for mine
    offence, I know.
  I ran without return the way the world liked best,
And what I ought most to regard, that I respected least.
  The throng wherein I thrust hath thrown me in
    such case
That, Lord, my soul is sore beset without Thy greater
    grace.
  My guilts are grown so great, my power doth so
    appear,
That with great force they argue oft, and mercy much
    despair.
  But then with faith I flee to Thy prepared store,
Where there lieth help for every hurt and salve for
    every sore.
  My lost time to lament, my vain ways to bewail,
No day, no night, no place, no hour, no moment I
    shall fail ;
  My soul shall never cease, with an assured faith,
To knock, to crave, to call, to cry to Thee for help,
    which saith,
  " Knock, and it shall be heard ; but ask, and giv'n
    it is,"
And all that like to keep this course of mercy shall
    not miss.

For when I call to mind how the one wand'ring
        sheep
Did bring more joy with his return than all the flock
        did keep,
    It yields full hope and trust, my stray'd and wand'ring
        ghost
Shall be received and held more dear than those were
        never lost.
        O Lord, my hope behold, and for my help make
        haste
To pardon the forepassed race that, careless, I have
        past. . . .
        Not my will, Lord, but Thine, fulfill'd be in each
        case,
To whose great will and mighty power all powers shall
        once give place.
        My faith, my hope, my trust, my God, and eke my
        guide,
Stretch forth Thy hand to save the soul, what so the
        body bide :
    Refuse not to receive that Thou so dear hast bought,
For but by Thee alone, I know, all safety in vain is
        sought.
    I know and acknowledge eke, albeit very late,
That Thou it is I ought to love and dread in each
        estate,
        And with repentant heart to laud Thee, Lord on
        high,
That hast so gently set me straight that erst walk'd so
        awry.
        Now grant me grace, my God, to stand Thine strong
        in sprete,
And let the world then work such ways as to the
        world seems meet.

ANON.   (Circa 1550.)

OCTOBER 30.

King of Mercy, King of Love,
In whom I live, in whom I move,
Perfect what Thou hast begun,
Let no night put out this sun.
Grant I may, my chief desire,
Long for Thee, to Thee aspire!
Let my youth, my bloom of dayes,
Be my comfort and Thy praise;
That hereafter, when I look
O'er the sullied, sinful book,
I may find Thy hand therein
Wiping out my shame and sin!
O, it is Thy only art,
To reduce a stubborn heart,
And, since Thine is victorie,
Strongholds should belong to Thee:
Lord, then take it, leave it not
Unto my dispose or lot:
But since I would not have it mine,
O my God, let it be Thine!

Henry Vaughan.

OCTOBER 31.

PARAPHRASE FROM ISAIAH.

My soul hath longed for Thee, O Lord, by night,
  And in the morn my spirit for Thee hath sought:
Thy judgments to the earth give such a light
  As all the world by them Thy truth is taught.

U

But show Thy mercy to the wicked man,
  He will not learn Thy righteousness to know :
His chief delight is still to curse and ban,
  And unto Thee himself he will not bow.

They do not once at all regard Thy power :
  Thy people's zeal shall let them see their shame ;
But with a fire Thou shalt Thy foes devour,
  And clean consume them with a burning flame.

With peace Thou wilt preserve us, Lord, alone,
  For Thou hast wrought great wonders for our sake;
And other gods beside Thee we have none,
  Only in Thee we all our comforts take.

MICHAEL DRAYTON.

NOVEMBER 1.

LADY of Heaven and Earth and therewithal
    Crowned Empress of the nether clefts of Hell,—
I, thy poor Christian, on thy name do call,
    Commending me to thee, with thee to dwell,
    Albeit in nought I be commendable.
But all mine undeserving may not mar
Such mercies as thy sovereign mercies are:
    Without the which (as true words testify)
No soul can reach thy Heaven so fair and far.
    Even in this faith I choose to live and die.

Unto thy Son say thou that I am His,
    And to me graceless make Him gracious,
Sad May of Egypt lacked not of that bliss,
    Nor yet the sorrowful clerk Theophilus,
Whose bitter sins were set aside even thus,
Though to the Fiend his bounden service was.
Oh help me, lest in vain for me should pass
    (Sweet Virgin, that shalt have no loss thereby!)
The blessed Host and sacring of the Mass.
    Even in this faith I choose to live and die.

FRANÇOIS VILLON.
(Trs. W. M. Rossetti.)

NOVEMBER 2.

How should I praise Thee, Lord? how should my
    rymes
Gladly engrave Thy love in steel,
If, what my soul doth feel sometimes,
My soul might ever feel!

Although there were some fourtie heav'ns or more,
Sometimes I peere above them all ;
Sometimes I hardly reach a score,
Sometimes to hell I fall.

O, rack me not to such a vast extent,
Those distances belong to Thee ;
The world's too little for Thy tent,
A grave too big for me.

Wilt Thou meet arms with man, that Thou dost stretch
A crumme of dust from heav'n to hell ?
Will great God measure with a wretch ?
Shall he Thy stature spell ?

O, let me, when Thy roof my soul hath hid,
O, let me roost and nestle there ;
Then of a sinner Thou art rid,
And I of hope and fear.

Yet take Thy way ; for sure Thy way is best ;
Stretch or contract me, Thy poore debtor ;
This is but tuning of my breast,
To make the musick better.

Whether I fly with angels, fall with dust,
Thy hands made both, and I am there ;
Thy power and love, my love and trust,
Make our place ev'rywhere.

GEORGE HERBERT.

NOVEMBER 3.

A PRAYER TO AVERT WRATH.

THOU mighty formidable King,
Thou mercy's unexhausted spring !
Some comfortable pity bring.

Forget not what my ransom cost,
Nor let my dear-bought soul be lost,
In storms of guilty terror tost.

Thou who for me didst feel such pain,
Whose precious blood the Cross did stain,
Let not those agonies be vain.

Thou whom avenging Pow'rs obey,
Cancel my debt—too great to pay—
Before the sad accounting-day.

Surrounded with amazing fears,
Whose load my soul with anguish bears,
I sigh, I weep; accept my tears. . . .

Prostrate, my contrite heart I rend,
My God! my Father! and my Friend!
Do not forsake me in my end.

Well may they curse their second breath
Who rise to a reviving death;
Thou, great Creator of mankind!
Let guilty man compassion find.

WENTWORTH DILLON
(LORD ROSCOMMON).

NOVEMBER 4.

ALMIGHTY Framer of the skies,
O let our pure devotion rise
  Like incense in Thy sight!
Wrapt in impenetrable shade,
The texture of our souls was made,
  Till Thy command gave light.

The sun of glory gleamed, the ray
Refined the darkness into day,
  And bid the vapours fly :
Impelled by His eternal love,
He left His palaces above
  To cheer our gloomy sky.

How shall we celebrate the day
When God appeared in mortal clay,
  The mark of worldly scorn ?
When the archangel's heavenly lays
Attempted the Redeemer's praise,
  And hailed Salvation's morn ?

A humble form the Godhead wore,
The pains of poverty He bore,
  To gaudy pomp unknown :
Though in a humble walk He trod,
Still was the man Almighty God,
  In glory all His own.

Despised, oppressed, the Godhead bears
The torments of this vale of tears,
  Nor bids His vengeance rise ;
He saw the creatures He had made
Revile His power, His peace invade,
  He saw with Mercy's eyes.

THOMAS CHATTERTON.
(Written at the age of eleven years.)

NOVEMBER 5.

RESURGAM.

'Tis night, and the landscape is lovely no more ;
I mourn, but, ye woodlands, I mourn not for you ;
For morn is approaching your charms to restore,
Perfumed with fresh fragrance, and glittering with dew :

Nor yet for the ravage of winter I mourn;
Kind Nature the embryo blossom will save.
But when shall spring visit the mouldering urn—
O when shall it dawn on the night of the grave?

'Twas thus, by the glare of false science betrayed,
That leads, to bewilder; and dazzles, to blind;
My thoughts want to roam, from shade onward to
    shade,
Destruction before me, and sorrow behind.
"O pity, great Father of Light," then I cried,
"Thy creature, who fain would not wander from Thee;
Lo, humbled in dust, I relinquish my pride:
From doubt and from darkness Thou only canst free."

And darkness and doubt are now flying away,
No longer I roam in conjecture forlorn.
So breaks on the traveller, faint and astray,
The bright and the balmy effulgence of morn.
See Truth, Love, and Mercy, in triumph descending,
And Nature all glowing in Eden's first bloom!
On the cold cheek of death smiles and roses are blend-
    ing,
And beauty immortal awakes from the tomb.

JAMES BEATTIE.

NOVEMBER 6.

That last best effort of Thy skill,
To form the life and rule the will,
    Propitious Power! impart;
Teach me to cool my passion's fires,
Make me the judge of my desires,
    The master of my heart.

Raise me above the vulgar's breath,
Pursuit of fortune, fear of death,
   And all in life that's mean ;
Still true to reason be my plan,
Still let my actions speak the man
   Through every various scene.

MARK AKENSIDE.

NOVEMBER 7.

O God, who sitt'st in glory crowned
Where heavenly light is poured around,
   Who on the wings of the wind dost ride,
O God, Thy throne the angels bear,
Yet Thou Thy praise from children's lips to hear
   Art surely satisfied.

Thou seest the soreness of our need,
   Give to Thy Name the victory,
   Endure not that Thy might should be
Claimed by gods of an alien creed.

Arm Thee, Thy people to defend !
Descend as on the ocean once Thou didst descend !
   Let the wicked and ungodly learn at last
Thy potent wrath to dread !
Let them like dust and chaff be scattered,
   Driven before the blast !

JEAN RACINE (Trs. Editors).

NOVEMBER 8.

A PRAYER

*Left by the author at a reverend friend's house in the
room where he slept.*

O THOU dread Pow'r who reign'st above!
  I know Thou wilt me hear
When for this scene of peace and love
  I make my prayer sincere.

The hoary sire—the mortal stroke,
  Long, long be pleased to spare!
To bless his filial little flock,
  And show what good men are.

She who her lovely offspring eyes
  With tender hopes and fears,
Oh, bless her with a mother's joys,
  And spare a mother's tears!

Their hope—their stay—their darling youth
  In manhood's dawning blush—
Bless him, Thou God of love and truth,
  Up to a parent's wish!

The beauteous, seraph-sister band,
  With earnest tears I pray,
Thou know'st the snares on ev'ry hand—
  Guide Thou their steps alway!

When soon or late they reach that coast,
  O'er life's rough ocean driven,
May they rejoice, no wand'rer lost,
  A family in Heaven!

ROBERT BURNS.

NOVEMBER 9.

[Prince of Wales born, 1841.]

A PSALM FOR SOLOMON.

GIVE the king thy judgments, O God, and thy righteousness unto the king's son.

He shall judge thy people with righteousness, and thy poor with judgment.

The mountains shall bring peace to the people, and the little hills, by righteousness.

He shall judge the poor of the people, he shall save the children of the needy, and shall break in pieces the oppressor.

They shall fear thee as long as the sun and moon endure, throughout all generations.

He shall come down like rain upon the mown grass; as showers that water the earth.

In his days shall the righteous flourish; and abundance of peace so long as the moon endureth.

He shall have dominion also from sea to sea, and from the river unto the ends of the earth.

They that dwell in the wilderness shall bow before him; and his enemies shall lick the dust.

The kings of Tarshish and of the isles shall bring presents: the kings of Sheba and Seba shall offer gifts.

Yea, all kings shall fall down before him; all nations shall serve him.

For he shall deliver the needy when he crieth; the poor also, and him that hath no helper.

He shall spare the poor and needy, and shall save the souls of the needy.

He shall redeem their soul from deceit and violence: and precious shall their blood be in his sight.

And he shall live, and to him shall be given of the gold of Sheba: prayer also shall be made for him continually; and daily shall he be praised.

There shall be an handful of corn in the earth upon the top of the mountains ; the fruit thereof shall shake like Lebanon : and they of the city shall flourish like grass of the earth.

His name shall endure for ever : his name shall be continued as long as the sun : and men shall be blessed in him : all nations shall call him blessed.

Blessed be the Lord God, the God of Israel, who only doeth wondrous things.

And blessed be his glorious name for ever : and let the whole earth be filled with his glory.   Amen, and Amen.

PSALM LXXII.

NOVEMBER 10.

THE DAWNING.

O AT what time soever Thou,
Unknown to us, the heavens wilt bow,
And, with Thy angels in the van,
Descend to judge poor careless man,
Grant I may not like puddle lie
In a corrupt security,
Where if a traveller water crave,
He finds it dead, and in a grave.
But as this restless, vocal spring
All day and night doth run, and sing,
And though here born, yet is acquainted
Elsewhere, and flowing keeps untainted ;
So let me all my busy age
In Thy free services engage ;
And though (while here) of force I must
Have commerce sometimes with poor dust,

And in my flesh, though vile and low,
As this doth in her channel flow,
Yet let my course, my aim, my love,
And chief acquaintance be above;
So when that day and hour shall come,
In which Thyself will be the sun,
Thou'lt find me drest and on my way,
Watching the break of Thy great day.

HENRY VAUGHAN.

NOVEMBER 11.

"FOR A DAY IN THY COURTS IS BETTER THAN A THOUSAND."

The golden palace of my God
  Towering above the clouds I see,
Beyond the cherubs' bright abode,
  Higher than angels' thoughts can be;
How can I in those courts appear
  Without a wedding-garment on?
Conduct me, Thou life-giver, there,
  Conduct me to Thy glorious throne!
And clothe me with Thy robes of light,
And lead me through sin's darksome night,
  My Saviour and my God!

Trs. from the Sclavonic by
SIR JOHN BOWRING.

NOVEMBER 12.

NEC SINE TE.

I LOVE—and have some cause to love—the earth :
She is my Maker's creature ; therefore good :
She is my mother, for she gave me birth ;
She is my tender nurse—she gives me food ;
    But what's a creature, Lord, compared with Thee ?
    Or what's my mother or my nurse to me ?

I love the air : her dainty sweets refresh
My drooping soul, and to new sweets invite me ;
Her shrill-mouthed quire sustains me with their flesh,
And with their polyphonian notes delight me :
    But what's the air or all the sweets that she
    Can bless my soul withal, compared to Thee ?

I love the sea : she is my fellow-creature,
My careful purveyor ; she provides me store :
She walls me round ; she makes my diet greater ;
She wafts my treasure from a foreign shore :
    But, Lord of oceans, when compared with Thee,
    What is the ocean or her wealth to me ?

To heaven's high city I direct my journey,
Where spangled suburbs entertain mine eye ;
Mine eye, by contemplation's great attorney,
Transcends the crystal pavement of the sky :
    But what is heaven, great God, compared to Thee ?
    Without Thy presence heaven's no heaven to me.

Without Thy presence earth gives no refection :
Without Thy presence sea affords no treasure ;
Without Thy presence air's a rank infection ;
Without Thy presence heaven itself no pleasure :
    If not possessed, if not enjoyed in Thee,
    What's earth, or sea, or air, or heaven to me ?

The highest honours that the world can boast
Are subjects far too low for my desire ;
The brightest beams of glory are—at most—
But dying sparkles of Thy living fire :
   The loudest flames that earth can kindle be
   But nightly glow-worms, if compared to Thee.

Without Thy presence wealth is bags of cares ;
Wisdom but folly ; joy disquiet—sadness :
Friendship is treason, and delights are snares ;
Pleasures but pain, and mirth but pleasing madness ;
   Without Thee, Lord, things be not what they be,
   Nor have they being, when compared with Thee.

In having all things, and not Thee, what have I ?
Not having Thee, what have my labours got ?
Let me enjoy but Thee, what further crave I ?
And having Thee alone, what have I not ?
   I wish nor sea, nor land ; nor would I be
   Possessed of heaven, heaven unpossessed of Thee.

FRANCIS QUARLES.

NOVEMBER 13.

PATIENCE TAUGHT BY NATURE.

" O DREARY life," we cry, " O dreary life ! "
   And still the generations of the birds
   Sing through our sighing, and the flocks and herds
Serenely live while we are keeping strife

With Heaven's true purpose in us, as a knife
   Against which we may struggle !   Ocean girds
   Unslackened the dry land, savannah-swards
Unweary sweep, hills watch unworn, and rife

Meek leaves drop yearly from the forest-trees
  To show, above, the unwasted stars that pass
    In their old glory: O Thou God of old,
Grant me some smaller grace than comes to these!—
  By so much patience as a blade of grass
    Grows by, contented through the heat and cold.

E. BARRETT BROWNING.

NOVEMBER 14.

THE TOYS.

My little son, who look'd from thoughtful eyes,
And moved and spoke in quiet grown-up wise,
Having my law the seventh time disobey'd,
I struck him, and dismiss'd
With hard words and unkiss'd;
His mother, who was patient, being dead.
Then fearing lest his grief should hinder sleep,
I visited his bed,
But found him slumbering deep,
With darken'd eyelids, and their lashes yet
From his late sobbing wet.
And I with moan,
Kissing away his tears, left others of my own;
For, on a table drawn beside his head,
He had put, within his reach,
A box of counters, and a red-vein'd stone,
A piece of glass abraded by the beach,
And six or seven shells,
A bottle of bluebells,
And two French copper coins, ranged there with
    careful art,
To comfort his sad heart.
So when that night I pray'd
To God, I wept, and said:—

Ah, when at last we lie with trancèd breath,
Not vexing Thee in death,
And Thou rememberest of what toys
We made our joys,
How weakly understood
Thy great commanded good,
Then Fatherly not less
Than I whom Thou hast moulded from the clay,
Thou'lt leave Thy wrath and say,
" I will be sorry for their childishness."

COVENTRY PATMORE.

NOVEMBER 15.

FROM THE DESERT.

THOU hast visited me with Thy storms,
And the vials of Thy sore displeasure
Thou hast poured on my head, like a bitter draught
Poured forth without stint or measure ;
Thou hast bruised me as flax is bruised ;
Made me clay in the potter's wheel ;
Thou hast hardened Thy face like steel,
And cast down my soul to the ground ;
Burnt my life in the furnace of fire, like dross,
And left in prison where souls are bound :
Yet my gain is more than my loss.

What if Thou hadst led my soul
To the pastures where dull souls feed ;
And set my steps in smooth paths, far away
From the feet of those that bleed ;
Penned me in low, fat plains,
Where the air is as still as death,
And Thy great winds are sunk to a breath,

And Thy torrents a crawling stream,
And the thick steam of wealth goes up day and night,
Till Thy sun gives a veilèd light,
And heaven shows like a vanished dream !

What if Thou hadst set my feet
With the rich in a gilded room ;
And made me to sit where the scorners sit,
Scoffing at death and doom !
What if I had hardened my heart
With dark counsels line upon line ;
And blunted my soul with meat and wine,
Till my ears had grown deaf to the bitter cry
Of the halt and the weak and the impotent ;
Nor hearkened, lapt in a dull content,
To the groanings of those who die !

My being had waked dull and dead
With the lusts of a gross desire ;
But now Thou hast purged me throughly, and burnt
My shame with a living fire.
So burn me, and purge my will
Till no vestige of self remain,
And I stand out white without spot or stain.
Then let Thy flaming angel at last
Smite from me all that has been before ;
And sink me, freed from the load of the past,
In Thy dark depths evermore.

Sir Lewis Morris.

NOVEMBER 16.

How can I deem that Thou hast heard me, Lord !
Lord of the Highest Heaven ! when the frail prayer
Which sought an utterance in a trembling word
Is so unworthy of Thy sacred ear.

x

But nought is veiled from Thee,—and Thou wilt hear
The voice that from the heart, whose cells are stored
With reverence and humility and fear,
Mounts upward.   Grant, Thou Source of Good adored,
That this my contrite heart, submissive, may
Be led by Thee, for it has lost its way,
And none but Thou may guide it.   Lord ! untie
The knot which binds it to earth's vanities :
And Thou mayest save it, for Thou canst devise
Salvation even where doubts despairing lie.

FELIPE MEY.
(Trs. from the Spanish by Sir John Bowring.)

NOVEMBER 17.

THUS far have I pursued my solemn theme,
    With self-rewarding toil ; thus far have sung
Of godlike deeds, far loftier than beseem
    The lyre which I in early days have strung ;
    And now my spirits faint, and I have hung
        The shell that solaced me in saddest hour
On the dark cypress ; and the strings which rung
    With Jesus' praise, their harpings now are o'er,
Or, when the breeze comes by, moan, and are heard no
        more.

And must the harp of Judah sleep again ?
    Shall I no more reanimate the lay ?
Oh ! Thou who visitest the sons of men,
    Thou who dost listen when the humble pray,
    One little space prolong my mournful day ;
        One little lapse suspend Thy last decree !
I am a youthful traveller in the way,
        And this slight boon would consecrate to Thee
Ere I with Death shake hands, and smile that I am
        free.   HENRY KIRKE WHITE.

NOVEMBER 18.

THE ELIXIR.

Teach me, my God and King,
In all things Thee to see,
And what I do in anything,
To do it as for Thee;

Not rudely, as a beast,
To run into an action;
But still to make Thee prepossest,
And give it his perfection.

A man that looks on glass,
On it may stay his eye;
Or if he pleaseth, through it pass,
And then the heav'n espy.

All may of Thee partake;
Nothing can be so mean
Which with his tincture, for Thy sake,
Will not grow bright and clean.

A servant with this clause
Makes drudgery divine;
Who sweeps a room, as for Thy laws,
Makes that and th' action fine.

This is the famous stone
That turneth all to gold;
For that which God doth touch and own
Cannot for less be told.

George Herbert.

NOVEMBER 19.

TO THE ANGELS.

IT is the cruel God of Death
Who on his pale horse approacheth,
I hear the thud of hooves, the stir
Of th' Horseman dark, the Ravisher.
He drags me forth !   My loved one I am leaving !
The thought afflicts my heart beyond conceiving.

She was my wife and child in one.
When to the Land of Shades I'm gone,
Widow and orphan she will be.
And here I leave, bereft of me,
The wife, the child, who in my valour trusting,
Secure and faithful on my heart was resting.

Angels of Heaven, hear, O hear,
Hearken my complaint and prayer !
O guard my wife, my love, when I
Within the lonely grave do lie.
Keep watch and ward o'er her, your Angel-sister,
Guard my poor child, and with your grace assist her !

By all the tears that e'er did flow
From your sad eyes for human woe,
By that dread Name the Priest alone
May know, and scarce his lips dare own,
By your own Beauty, Grace, and Mercy movèd,
O Angels, hear my prayer, guard my belovèd !

HEINE (Trs. Editors).

NOVEMBER 20.

Lord of all beings,
Verily strong art Thou
Mortals to save.
Thy Name is Wonderful,
Beauteous, and Glorious
Through all Creation.
Thy decrees ever
Are true and potent,
Yea, and triumphant
    Even as Thou art.
Surely Thy fiats
Govern the universe
Mightily, rightly,
    Ruler of Heavens !
Turn now and save us,
Maker of Spirits !
Graciously help us,
Holiest Lord !
    Fulfil Thy promise now,
Manifest Thy saying
And Thy might in us.
Show to the nations Thy
    Wisdom and Power,
Which the Chaldeans
And many peoples,
Who under heaven
Live yet in darkness,
Know but by rumour ;
Show that Thou only art
Lord everlasting,
Ruler of Hosts,
Ruler of worldly things,
Giver of victories,
Most just Creator !
              Cædmon (*Trs.* Editors).

NOVEMBER 21.

LAVATER'S PRAYER.

O Jesus, let all else depart,
  But Thou, dwell Thou within,
Be daily nearer Thee my heart,
  And further off from sin !
Daily Thine innocence and might
  Make pure and strong my breath,
And let Thy sunshine pierce my might,
  Thy life dissolve my death !
O, in that shining light refined
  Let all desires grow less,
Do Thou fulfil me when I find
  My daily nothingness !
Be near me, Christ, when at Thy feet
  I weep, contrite and still,
And let Thy God-sent reason sweet
  Be master of my will !
O, let Thy beauty grow in me
  With wisdom, joy, and grace ;
Thy living likeness let me be,
  Tho' sad or glad my face !
Make all within me gay and good,
  And purge me, fault by fault ;
Thy loving-kindness unwithstood
  Shall all my soul exalt !
Let pride and langour disappear,
  And every fancy flee,
As I with pains and toil draw near
  Thy Kingdom, Lord, and Thee !
This little idle self and vain
  Daily let smaller be,
Ah, daily thro' Thee would I fain
  Be worthier of Thee !

More full of Thee from day to day,
  Thine Image let me wear;
Do Thou, to whom all creatures pray,
  Give ear unto my prayer!
Let faith in Thee and in Thy power
  All motions else remove,
Be Thou my strength in Passion's hour,
  Be Thou my joy and love!

JOHANN CASPAR LAVATER.
(Trs. Editors.)

NOVEMBER 22.

[St Cecilia's Day.]

MUSIC AND PRAYER.

FOR ever consecrate the day
To musick and Cecilia;
Musick! the greatest good that mortals know,
And all of Heav'n we have below.
Musick can noble hints impart,
Engender fury, kindle love,
With unsuspected eloquence can move,
And manage all the man with secret art. . . .

Musick religious heats inspires;
It wakes the soul and lifts it high,
And wings it with sublime desires,
And fts it to bespeak the Deity.
Th' Almighty listens to a tuneful tongue,
And seems well pleas'd and courted with a song.
Soft moving sounds and heav'nly airs
Give force to ev'ry word, and recommend our prayers.

When time itself shall be no more,
And all things in confusion hurl'd,
Musick shall then exert its pow'r,
And sound survive the ruins of the world :
Then saints and angels shall agree
In one eternal jubilee ;
All heav'n shall echo with their hymns divine,
And God Himself with pleasure see
The whole creation in a chorus join.

Consecrate the place and day
To musick and Cecilia :
Let no rough winds approach, nor dare
Invade the hallowed bounds,
Nor rudely shake the tuneful air,
Nor spoil the fleeting sounds ;
Nor mournful sigh nor groan be heard,
But gladness dwell on ev'ry tongue,
Whilst all, with voice and strings prepar'd,
Keep up the loud harmonious song,
And imitate the bless'd above
In joy, and harmony, and love.

JOSEPH ADDISON.

NOVEMBER 23.

OGIER THE DANE SURRENDERS HIS LIFE.

GOD, Thou hast made me strong ! nigh seven weeks
Have passed since from the wreck we haled our store,
And five long days well told have now passed o'er
Since my last fellow died, with my last bread
Between his teeth, and yet I am not dead.
Yea, but for this, I had been strong enow
In some last bloody field my sword to show.
What matter ? soon will all be past and done,
Where'er I died, I must have died alone. . . .

Get thee another leader, Charlemaine,
For thou shalt look to see my shield in vain,
When in the fair fields of the Frankish land,
Thick as the corn they tread, the heathen stand.
What matter ? ye shall learn to live your lives ;
Husbands and children, other friends and wives,
Shall wipe the tablets of your memory clean,
And all shall be as I had never been.
And now, O God, am I alone with Thee ;
A little thing indeed it seems to be
To give this life up, since it needs must go
Some time or other ; now at last I know
How foolishly men play upon the earth,
When unto them a year of life seems worth
Honour and friends, and these vague hopes and sweet
That like real things my dying heart do greet,
Unreal while living on the earth I trod,
And but myself I know no other god.
Behold, I thank Thee that Thou sweet'nest thus
This end, that I had thought most piteous,
If of another I had heard it told.

WILLIAM MORRIS.

NOVEMBER 24.

BLESSED BE THE NAME OF THE LORD.

O Lord, in sickness and in health,
   To every lot resigned,
Grant me, before all worldly wealth,
   A meek and thankful mind !

As, life, thy upland path we tread,
   And often pause in vain,
To think of friends and parents dead,
   Oh, let us not complain !

The Lord may give or take away,
　　But nought our faith can move
Whilst we to heaven can look and say,
　　Our Father lives above.

W. L. BOWLES.

NOVEMBER 25.

I HAVE been honoured and obeyed,
　　I have met scorn and slight;
And my heart loves earth's sober shade
　　More than her laughing light.

For what is rule but a sad weight
　　Of duty and a snare?
What meanness, but with happier fate
　　The Saviour's Cross to share?

This my hid choice, if not from heaven,
　　Moves on the heavenward line;
Cleanse it, good Lord, from earthly leaven,
　　And make it simply Thine!

CARDINAL NEWMAN.

NOVEMBER 26.

HECTOR PRAYS FOR HIS SON ASTYANAX.

THIS said, he reach'd to take his son, who of his arms
　　afraid,
And then the horse-hair plume, with which he was so
　　overlaid,
Nodded so horribly, he cling'd back to his nurse and
　　cried.
Laughter affected his great sire, who doffed and laid
　　aside

His fearful helm, that on the earth cast round about it
    light :
Then took and kiss'd his loving son, and (balancing
    his weight
In dancing him) these loving vows to living Jove he
    used,
And all the other bench of gods, "O you that have
    infused
Soul to this infant, now set down this blessing on his
    star :
Let his renown be clear as mine, equal his strength in
    war,
And make his reign so strong in Troy, that years to
    come may yield
His facts this fame when, rich in spoils, he leaves the
    conquered field
Sown with his slaughters :—These high deeds exceed
    his father's worth.
And let this echo'd praise supply the comforts to come
    forth
Of his kind mother with my life.

HOMER (Trs. George Chapman).

NOVEMBER 27.

CHRIST STILLING THE TEMPEST.

FEAR was within the tossing bark
    When stormy winds grew loud,
And waves came rolling high and dark,
    And the tall mast was bowed.

And men stood breathless in their dread
    And baffled in their skill,
But One was there who rose and said
    To the wild sea—*Be still !*

And the wind ceased :—it ceased ! that word
  Passed through the gloomy sky':
The troubled billows knew their Lord,
  And fell beneath His eye.

And slumber settled on the deep,
  And silence on the blast ;
They sank a's flowers that fold to sleep
  When sultry day is past.

O Thou ! that in its wildest hour
  Didst rule the tempest's mood,
Send Thy meek spirit forth in power,
  Soft on our souls to brood !

Thou that didst bow the billows' pride
  Thy mandate to fulfil !
Oh ! speak to passion's raging tide,
  Speak, and say, " *Peace, be still !* "

Mrs Hemans.

NOVEMBER 28.

THE LAST PRAYER OF ADAM IN EDEN.

Celestial, whether among the Thrones, or named
Of them the highest—for such of shape may seem
Prince above princes—gently hast Thou told
Thy message, which might else in telling wound,
And in performing end us.   What besides
Of sorrow, and dejection, and despair,
Our frailty can sustain, Thy tidings bring—
Departure from this happy place, our sweet
Recess, and only consolation left
Familiar to our eyes; all places else

Inhospitable appear, and desolate,
Not knowing us, or known.   And if by prayer
Incessant I could hope to change the will
Of Him who all things can, I would not cease
To weary Him with my assiduous cries;
But prayer against His absolute decree
No more avails than breath against the wind,
Blown stifling back on him who breathes it forth:
Therefore to His great bidding I submit.
This most afflicts me—that, departing hence,
As from His face I shall be hid, deprived
His blessed countenance.   Here I could frequent,
With worship, place by place where He vouchsafed
Presence Divine, and to my sons relate,
" On this mount He appeared; under this tree
Stood visible; among these pines His voice
I heard; here with Him at this fountain talked."
So many grateful altars I would rear
Of grassy turf, and pile up every stone
Of lustre from the brook, in memory
Or monument to ages, and thereon
Offer sweet-smelling gums, and fruits, and flowers.
In yonder nether world, where shall I seek
His bright appearances, or footstep trace?
For, though I fled Him angry, yet, recalled
To life prolonged and promised race, I now
Gladly behold though but His utmost skirts
Of glory, and far off His steps adore.

JOHN MILTON.

NOVEMBER 29.

THE PILGRIM'S SONG.

AND wilt Thou hear the fevered heart
    To Thee in silence cry?
And as the inconstant wildfires dart
    Out of the restless eye,
Wilt Thou forgive the wayward thought,
By kindly woes yet half untaught
A Saviour's right, so dearly bought,
    That Hope should never die?

Thou wilt: for many a languid prayer
    Has reached Thee from the wild,
Since the lone Mother, wandering there,
    Cast down her fainting child,
Then stole apart to weep and die!
Nor knew an angel form was nigh,
To show soft waters gushing by
    And dewy shadows mild.

Thou wilt—for Thou art Israel's God,
    And Thine unwearied arm
Is ready yet with Moses' rod
    The hidden rill to charm
Out of the dry unfathomed deep
Of sands, that lie in lifeless sleep,
Save when the scorching whirlwinds heap
    Their waves in rude alarm.

These moments of wild wrath are Thine—
    Thine too the drearier hour
When o'er the horizon's silent line
    Fond hopeless fancies cower,
And on the traveller's listless way
Rises and sets the unchanging day,
No cloud in heaven to slake its ray,
    On earth no sheltering bower.

Thou wilt be there, and not forsake,
　　To turn the bitter pool
Into a bright and breezy lake,
　　The throbbing brow to cool :
Till left a while with Thee alone
The wilful heart be fain to own
That He, by whom our bright hours shone,
　　Our darkness best may rule.

The scent of water far away
　　Upon the breeze is flung :
The desert pelican to-day
　　Securely leaves her young,
Reproving thankless man, who fears
To journey on a few lone years,
Where on the sand Thy foot appears,
　　Thy crown in sight is hung.

Thou who didst sit on Jacob's well
　　The weary hour of noon,
The languid pulses Thou canst tell,
　　The nerveless spirit tune.
Thou from whose cross in anguish burst
The cry that owned Thy dying thirst,
To Thee we turn, our Last and First,
　　Our Sun and soothing Moon.

From darkness here, and dreariness,
　　We ask not full repose,
Only be Thou at hand to bless
　　Our trial hour of woes.
Is not the pilgrim's toil o'erpaid
By the clear rill and palmy shade?
And see we not, up Earth's dark glade,
　　The gate of Heaven unclose?

JOHN KEBLE.

NOVEMBER 30.

[St Andrew's Day.]

O Scotia, my dear, my native soil,
  For whom my warmest wish to Heaven is sent!
Long may thy hardy sons of rustic toil
  Be blest with health and peace and sweet content!
And O! may Heaven their simple lives prevent
  From luxury's contagion, weak and vile!
Then, howe'er crowns and coronets be rent,
  A virtuous populace may rise the while,
And stand a wall of fire around their much lov'd isle.

O Thou who poured the patriotic tide
  That streams through Wallace's undaunted heart;
Who dared to nobly stem tyrannic pride,
  Or nobly die, the second glorious part
(The patriot's God peculiarly Thou art,
  His friend, inspirer, guardian, and reward!),
O never, never Scotia's realm desert;
  But still the patriot and the patriot bard
In bright succession raise, her ornament and guard!

ROBERT BURNS.

DECEMBER 1.

TERMINUS.

It is time to be old,
To take in sail :—
The god of bounds,
Who sets to seas a shore,
Came to me in his fatal rounds,
And said : " No more !
No farther spread
Thy broad, ambitious branches, and thy root.
Fancy departs : no more invent,
Contract thy firmament
To compass of a tent.
There's not enough for this and that,
Make thy option which of two ;
Economise the failing river,
Not the less revere the Giver,
Leave the many and hold the few.
Timely wise accept the terms,
Soften the fall with wary foot ;
A little while
Still plan and smile,
And, fault of novel germs,
Mature the unfallen fruit.
Curse, if thou wilt, thy sires,
Bad husbands of their fires,
Who, when they gave thee breath,
Failed to bequeath
The needful sinew stark as once,
The Baresark marrow to thy bones,
But left a legacy of ebbing veins,
Inconstant heat, and nerveless reins,—

Amid the Muses left thee deaf and dumb,
Amid the gladiators, halt and numb.”
As the bird trims her to the gale,
I trim myself to the storm of time,
I man the rudder, reef the sail,
Obey the voice at eve obeyed at prime :
“ Lowly faithful, banish fear,
Right onward drive unharmed ;
The port, well worth the cruise, is near,
And every wave is charmed.”

RALPH WALDO EMERSON.

DECEMBER 2.

THE SEASONS.

THESE as they change, Almighty Father, these
Are but the varied God.   The rolling year
Is full of Thee.   Forth in the pleasing Spring
Thy beauty walks, Thy tenderness and love.
Wide flush the fields : the softening air is balm ;
Echo the mountains round ; the forest smiles ;
And every sense and every heart is joy.
Then comes Thy glory in the summer months,
With light and heat refulgent.   Then Thy sun
Shoots full perfection through the swelling year :
And oft Thy voice in dreadful thunder speaks,
And oft at dawn, deep noon, or falling eve,
By brooks and groves, in hollow-whispering gales,
Thy bounty shines in Autumn unconfin’d,
And spreads a common feast for all that lives.
In Winter awful Thou ! with clouds and storms
Around Thee thrown, tempest o’er tempest rolled,
Majestic darkness ! On the whirlwind’s wing,
Riding sublime, Thou bidst the world adore,
And humblest nature with Thy northern blast.

JAMES THOMSON.

DECEMBER 3.

PII ORANT TACITE.

The turf shall be my fragrant shrine,
My temple, Lord! that arch of Thine
My censer's breath the mountain airs,
And silent thoughts my only prayers.

My choir shall be the moonlight waves,
When murmuring homeward to their caves,
Or when the stillness of the sea,
E'en more than music, breathes of Thee!

I'll seek by day some glade unknown,
All light and silence like Thy throne,
And the pale stars shall be, at night,
The only eyes that watch my rite.

Thy heaven, on which 'tis bliss to look,
Shall be my pure and shining book,
Where I shall read, in words of flame,
The glories of Thy wondrous name.

I'll read Thy anger in the rack
That clouds awhile the day-beam's track:
Thy mercy in the azure hue
Of sunny brightness, breaking through!

There's nothing bright above, below,
From flowers that bloom to stars that glow,
But in its light my soul can see
Some feature of Thy deity!

There's nothing dark below, above,
But in its gloom I trace Thy love;
And meekly wait that moment when
Thy touch shall turn all bright again.

Thomas Moore.

DECEMBER 4.

HYMNE DE L'ENFANT À SON RÉVEIL.

FATHER, to whom my father calls!
  Thou, whom upon our knees we greet:
  Whose name, so terrible and sweet,
My mother's gentle soul appals;

They say the burning sun, O Lord,
  Is but the plaything of Thy might;
  That, poised beneath Thy feet, its light,
As from a burnished lamp, is poured.

They say 'tis Thou that orderest
  The small birds in the fields to live,
  And Thou the little child dost give
That simple soul that knows Thee best.

Grant to the sick recovery;
  And to the needy beggar, bread,
  The orphan, where to lay his head,
And to the prisoner, liberty.

Full may my father's quiver be,
  Who Thee, great Lord, does fear and bless;
  To me grant wisdom, happiness,
And thus my mother joy in me.

Let me, though small, be free from guile,
  As in the Fane that child of Thine,
  Whose image o'er my bed does shine,
And ev'ry morn I see his smile.

Within my soul Thy Justice place,
  And on my lips be Truth, that so
  With fear and gentleness may grow
Within my heart Thy word, Thy grace.

ALPHONSE DE LAMARTINE.
(*Trs.* Editors.)

DECEMBER 5.

PRAYER is the soul's sincere desire,
   Uttered or unexpressed ;
The motion of a hidden fire
   That trembles in the breast.

Prayer is the burden of a sigh,
   The falling of a tear ;
The upward glancing of an eye,
   When none but God is near.

Prayer is the simplest form of speech
   That infant lips can try ;
Prayer the sublimest strains that reach
   The Majesty on high. . . .

Prayer is the contrite sinner's voice,
   Returning from his ways ;
While angels in their songs rejoice,
   And say, " Behold, he prays ! " . . .

Nor prayer is made on earth alone :
   The Holy Spirit pleads ;
And Jesus, on the eternal throne,
   For sinners intercedes.

O Thou, by whom we come to God,
   The Life, the Truth, the Way,
The path of prayer Thyself hast trod :
   Lord, teach us how to pray !

JAMES MONTGOMERY.

DECEMBER 6.

PRAYER FOR PEACE.

    ALAS! if it were known,
When, in the strife of nations, dreadful death
Mows down with indiscriminating sweep
His thousands ten times told,—if it were known
What ties we sever'd then, what ripening hopes
Blasted, what virtues in their bloom cut off;
How far the desolating scourge extends;
How wide the misery spreads; what hearts beneath
Their grief are broken, or survive to feel
Always the irremediable loss;
Oh! who of woman born could bear the thought?
Who but would join with fervent piety
The prayer that asketh in our time for peace?—
Nor in our time alone!—Enable us,
Father, which art in heaven! but to receive
And keep Thy word: Thy kingdom then should come,
Thy will be done on earth; the victory
Accomplish'd over Sin as well as Death,
And the great scheme of Providence fulfill'd.

ROBERT SOUTHEY.

DECEMBER 7.

GOD AND NATURE.

O GOD, Thy glory morn and eve display,
Who dost the soil with flowers, with stars the skies
   array;
 Earth's myriad discord rises in accord,
And her unnumber'd tongues unite to praise Thee,
  Lord!

Thou knowest all, unknown; unseen, dost see,—
O Thou, who settest bounds to all, who shall set
    bounds to Thee?
        On the light Thou movest,
        By the sun Thou seëst,
        Thro' the thunder speakest;
        Thine immensity
        Is th' illimitable,
        And eternity
        Is Thy point of time;
  With the lever of Thy finger
    Thou canst shake the stablish'd land,
And Thou holdest all the oceans
    In the hollow of Thy hand.
One breath of Thine can quench the heav'nly light,
One nod of Thine can mingle day with night.
  Thou, like a Monarch in his mint,
  Thy shining image didst imprint
    Upon a thousand thousand suns;
  The multitude of stars obey
  The names Thou didst upon them lay,
    And each his course appointed runs.
Thou smilest, and the universal face
  With radiance of the sapphire is adorn'd;
Thou noddest, and the fixt stars seek their place,
  And heaven's dome with myriad lamps is hung;
Thy finger pointeth, and the planets race,
  Eager to bear Thy tidings from the Court,
And Thy blue firmament is stretch'd in space
Most like a cloth of gold, whose fringes none may trace.

        PANAGIOTES SOUTSOS.
    (*Trs. from the modern Greek by the* Editors.)

DECEMBER 8.

CUM INVOCAREM.

Heare me, O heare me, when I call,
   O God, God of my equity!
Thou set'd'st me free when I was thrall,
   Have mercy therefore still on me,
   And hearken how I pray to Thee. . . .

O Lord, lift Thou upon our sight
   The shining clearness of Thy face,
Where I have found more heart's delight
   Than they whose stoare in harvest space
   Of grain and wine fills stoaring-place.

So I in peace and peacefull blisse
   Will lay me down and take my rest;
For it is Thou, Lord, Thou it is,
   By power of whose owne only brest
   I dwell, layd up in Safetie's nest.

Sir Philip Sidney.

THE LORD IS MY PORTION.

Servants of time—lo! these be slaves of slaves;
   But the Lord's servant hath his freedom whole.
Therefore when every man his portion craves,
   "The Lord God is my portion," saith my soul.

Jehudah Halevi.
(*Trs.* Nina Davis.)

DECEMBER 9.

A FUNERALL HYMNE.

O God, while mortal bodies are
Recall'd by Thee and formed againe,
What happy seate wilt Thou prepare,
Where spotless souls may safe remaine?
In Abraham's bosome they shall lie
Like Lazarus, whose flowry croune
The rich man doth farre off espie,
While him sharp, fiery torments droune.
Thy words, O Saviour, we respect,
Whose triumph drives black death to losse,
When in Thy steps Thou wouldst direct
The thiefe, Thy fellow on the crosse.
The faithful see a shining way,
Whose length to Paradise extends,
This can them to those trees convay,
Lost by the serpent's cunning ends.
To Thee I pray, most certain guide,
O let this soule which Thee obey'd
In her faire birth-place pure abide,
From which she, banisht, long hath stray'd.
While we upon the cover'd bones
Sweet violets and leaves will throw :
The title and the cold hard stones
Shall with our liquid odours flow.

PRUDENTIUS.
(*Trs.* Sir John Beaumont.)

DECEMBER 10.

The sober stillness of the night
　That fills the silent air,
And all that breathes along the shore
　Invite to solemn prayer.

Vouchsafe to me that spirit, Lord!
　Which points the sacred way,
And let Thy creatures here below
　Instruct me how to pray!

GEORGE CRABBE.

DECEMBER 11.

When I bethinke me on that speech whylere,
Of Mutability and well it way;
Me seemes that though she all unworthy were
Of the heaven's rule; yet very sooth to say,
In all things else she bears the greatest sway:
Which makes me loath this state of life so tickle,
And love of things so vaine to cast away:
Whose flowring pride, so fading and so fickle,
Short Time shall soon cut down with his consuming
　　sickle.

Then 'gin I thinke on that which Nature sayd,
Of that same time when no more change shall be,
But stedfast rest of all things, firmely stayd
Upon the Pillours of Eternity,
That is contrayr to Mutability:
For all that moveth doth in change delight:
But thenceforth all shall rest eternally
With Him that is the God of Sabaoth hight:
O! that great Sabaoth God, grant me that Sabbath's
　　sight!

EDMUND SPENSER.

DECEMBER 12.

THY WILL BE DONE.

ALL the tongues of Thy creation
    Sound, O Lord, their Maker's praise ;
And in one loud jubilation
    Earth and heav'n their voices raise.

Thou art Father, and the savour
    Of Thy mercy fills the earth ;
Inexhaustible Thy favour,
    And Thy wisdom knows no dearth.

Thou didst sow the soil with flowers,
    And the starry sky didst plan,
And didst order all Thy powers
    To make glad the heart of man.

Ah, but what may erring mortal
    Render for those gifts of Thine ?—
Let our praises storm Thy portal,
    From our lips Thy glory shine !

Take the heart which Thou hast given,
    Take the mind which is of Thee,
Let our sins be white as driven
    Snow, as fine gold let them be.

All astonied at the beauty
    Of Thy works is human eye,
And a thankful psalm of duty
    Is creation's psalmody.

Let our will be what Thou willest
    Till the limit of our days !
Thou our highest aim fulfillest
    To Thine own eternal praise.

A. R. RHANGABES.
(Trs. from the modern Greek by the Editors.)

DECEMBER 13.

HEARE me, O God !
   A broken heart
   Is my best part :
Use still Thy rod,
   That I may prove
   Therein Thy love.

If Thou hadst not
   Beene sterne to me
   But left me free,
I had forgot
   Myselfe and Thee.

For sin's so sweet,
   As minds ill bent
   Rarely repent,
Untill they meet
   Their punishment.

Who more can crave
   Than Thou hast done ?
   That gav'st a sonne,
To free a slave :
   First made of nought ;
   Withall since bought.

Sinne, Death, and Hell
   His glorious name
   Quite overcame,
Yet I rebell
   And slight the same.

But I'll come in
   Before my losse
   Me farther tosse,
As sure to win
   Under His crosse !

BEN JONSON.

DECEMBER 14.

As Thou hast touched our ears, and taught
  Our tongues to speak Thy praises plain,
Quell Thou each thankless, godless thought
  That would make fast our bonds again.
From worldly strife, from mirth unblest,
Drowning Thy music in the breast,
From foul reproach, from thrilling fears,
Preserve, good Lord, Thy servants' ears.

From idle words, that restless throng
  And haunt our hearts when we would pray,
From pride's false chime, and jarring wrong,
  Seal Thou my lips and guard the way:
For Thou hast sworn that every ear,
Willing or loth, Thy trump shall hear,
And every tongue unchainèd be,
To own no hope, no God, but Thee.
JOHN KEBLE.

DECEMBER 15.

Lord, when we bend before Thy Throne,
And our confessions pour,
Teach us to feel the sins we own,
And hate what we deplore.

Our broken spirits pitying see;
True penitence impart;
Then let a kindling glance from Thee
Beam hope upon the heart.

When we disclose our wants in prayer,
May we our wills resign,
And not a thought our bosoms share
Which is not wholly Thine.

May faith each weak petition fill,
And waft it to the skies,
And teach our hearts 'tis goodness still
That grants it or denies.

HENRY KIRKE WHITE.

DECEMBER 16.

MERCY, my Judge, mercy, I cry
With blushing cheek and bleeding eye,
The conscious colours of my sin
Are red without and pale within.

O let Thine own soft bowels pay
Thyself: and so discharge that day.
If sin can sigh, love can forgive.
O say the word, my soul shall live.

Those Mercies which Thy Mary found,
Or who Thy cross confessed and crowned,
Hope tells my heart the same loves be
Still alive, and still for me.

Though both my pray'rs and tears combine,
Both worthless are : for they are mine.
But Thou Thy bounteous self still be ;
And show Thou art, by saving me.

O when Thy last frown shall proclaim
The flocks of goats to folds of flame,
And all Thy lost sheep found shall be,
Let "Come ye blessed" then call me.

When the dread "Ite" shall divide
Those limbs of death from Thy left side,
Let those life-giving lips command
That I inherit Thy right hand.

Oh hear a suppliant heart, all crush'd
And crumbled into contrite dust.
My hope, my fear ! my judge, my friend !
Take charge of me and of my end.
                    RICHARD CRASHAW.

DECEMBER 17.

THE IMAGE OF GOD.

OH, Lord ! that seest from yon starry height,
Centred in one the future and the past,
Fashioned in Thine own image, see how fast
The world obscures in me what once was bright !
Eternal Sun ! the warmth which Thou hast given
To cheer life's flowery April, fast decays ;
Yet, in the hoary winter of my days,
For ever green shall be my trust in Heaven.
Celestial King ! oh, let Thy presence pass
Before my spirit, and an image fair
Shall meet that look of mercy from on high,
As the reflected image in a glass
Doth meet the look of him who seeks it there
And owes its being to the gazer's eye.
                    H. W. LONGFELLOW.
          (*Trs. from the Spanish of* F. de Aldana.)

DECEMBER 18.

PRAYER OF THE THEBAN ELDERS IN THE TIME OF TROUBLE.

DAUGHTER of Zeus, Thee first I invoke, immortal
     Athene ;
Our city's champion, thy sister, next,
Artemis high o'er the Agora's circle in glory enthroned,

Thee too, Far-shooter, Apollo !
Threefold averters of doom,
O now from heaven come forth to deliver us,
If ever, when hung o'er our heads
Menace of woe, at your behest
The flaming ruin was rolled away,
Visit us now !
Unnumbered woes, alas ! are mine to bear :
I see the sickness sweep our ranks along,
Nor weapon hath my thought
That can its breath avert :
For neither of the goodly earth
Prosper the springing fruits,
Nor women from the lamentable pangs
Of childbirth rise again :
But one upon another shalt Thou see,
Like flocks of feathered birds,
Swifter than fire that no man tames,
Swept onward to the shore,
Far west, of Pluto and the night.
Unnumbered dead !   A city perishing !
For children unregarded in the streets
Lie, tainting the air with death,
Unwept : and gentle wives,
And grey-haired mothers, pressing round,
Their sad petitions pour
Where the great altar, lifted o'er the crowd,
Stands like a seaward cliff :
And high and clear, with flutes in solemn dirge,
The wailing voices blend :—
O golden goddess, child of Zeus,
Have pity and send us Help,
Fair-visaged Help, with eyes benign.
And this fierce Ares, who,
Not now with brazen shields,
But with the blasting of his fiery breath,
Wakes worse than din of battle in our midst,

I pray that he far from my country's shores
Backward at headlong speed may turn and flee,
Either to Amphitrite's western bower
Under the great salt sea,
Or those inhospitable tides that rave
On rock-bound shores of Thrace ;
For what the ravined night at last lets go,
Day makes of this his prey :
But, O our Father, Zeus,
Lord of the lightning's flaming might,
Slay with Thy bolt the dreaded foe. . . .
Bacchus, I cry to Thee,—
Crowned with a golden diadem and girt
With shouting Mænads round,
Come to our rescue now,
With blazing pinebrand all aglow,
Against the God whom gods disown.

SOPHOCLES.
(Trs. R. Whitelaw.)

DECEMBER 19.

A SONG OF DEGREES.

WHEN the Lord turned again the captivity of Zion, we
were like them that dream.

Then was our mouth filled with laughter, and our
tongue with singing : then said they among the heathen,
the Lord hath done great things for them.

The Lord hath done great things for us ; whereof
we are glad.

Turn again our captivity, O Lord, as the streams in
the south.

They that sow in tears shall reap in joy.

He that goeth forth and weepeth, bearing precious
seed, shall doubtless come again with rejoicing, bringing
his sheaves with him. PSALM CXXVI.

DECEMBER 20.

SONNET.

LEAVE me, O love, which reachest but to dust,
And thou, my mind, aspire to higher things,
Grow rich in that which never taketh rust;
Whatever fades but fading pleasures brings.
Draw in thy beams, and humble all thy might
To that sweet yoke where lasting freedoms be;
Which breaks the clouds and opens forth the light,
That doth both shine and give us sight to see.
Oh, take fast hold; let that light be thy guide
In this small course which birth draws out to death,
And think how ill becometh him to slide
Who seeketh heaven and comes of heavenly breath.
Then farewell, world, thy uttermost I see:
Eternal Love, maintain Thy life in me.

SIR PHILIP SIDNEY.

DECEMBER 21.

FATHER of all which is or yet may be,
   Ere to the pillow, which my childhood prest,
This night restores my troubled brows, by Thee
   May this, the last prayer I have learned, be blest.
Grant me to live that I may need from life
   No more than life hath given me, and to die
   That I may give to Death no more than I
Have long abandoned.   And, if toil and strife

Yet in the portion of my days must be,
   Firm be my Faith and quiet be my heart!
That so my work may with my will agree,
   And strength be mine to calmly fill my part

In Nature's purpose, questioning not the end.
　　For love is more than raiment or than food.
　　Shall I not take the evil with the good ?
Blessèd to me be all which Thou dost send.

Nor blest the least, recalling what hath been,
　　The knowledge of the evil I have known
Without me and within me.　Since, to lean
　　Upon a strength far mightier than my own
Such knowledge brought me.　In whose strength I
　　　　stand
　　Firmly upheld, even tho', in ruin hurled,
　　The fixed foundations of this rolling world
Should topple at the waving of Thy hand.

The Earl of Lytton
(Owen Meredith).

DECEMBER 22.

We are part of an Infinite Scheme,
All that we are ;
Man the high crest and crown of things that be,
The fiery-hearted earth, the cold unfathomed sea,
The central sun, the intermittent star.
Things great and small,
We are but parts of the Eternal All ;
We live not in a barren, baseless dream ;
No endless, ineffectual chain
Of chance successions launched in vain ;
But every beat of Time,
Each sun that shines or fails to shine,
Each animate life that comes to throb or cease,
Each life of herb or tree
Which blooms and fruits and then forgets to be,
Each change of strife and peace,

Each soaring thought sublime,
Each deed of wrong and blood,
Each impulse towards an unattainèd good,—
All with a sure, unfaltering working tend
To one Ineffable, Beatific End.
Oh hidden Scheme, perfect Thyself, and take
Our petty lives, and mould them as Thou wilt!
All things that are, are only for Thy sake,
And not to obey Thee is our only guilt!
Perfect Thyself, and be fulfilled, oh great
Unfathomable Will, who art our Life and Fate!

There is hope, but nothing of fear,
Naught but a patient mind,
For him who waits with conscience clear
And soul resigned
Whate'er the mystic coming change
Shall bring of new and strange.
He looks back once upon the fields of life,
The good and evil locked in strife,
The happy and the unhappy days,
The Right we always love, the oft-triumphant Wrong;
And all his Being to a secret song
Sings with a mighty and unfaltering voice—
" I have been; Thou hast done all things well; I am
      glad; I give thanks; I rejoice! "

SIR LEWIS MORRIS.

DECEMBER 23.

FIRE of heaven's eternal ray,
Gentle and unscorching flame,
Strength in moments of dismay,
Grief's redress and sorrow's balm,
Light Thy servant on his way.

Teach him all earth's passing folly,
All its dazzling art
To distrust:
And let thoughts profound and holy
Penetrate his heart
Low in dust.

Lead him to the realms sublime,
Where Thy footsteps tread ;
Teach, O teach him so to dread
Judgment's soul-tormenting clime
That he may harvest for the better time.

RODRIGUEZ DEL PADRON.
(*Trs. from the Spanish by* Sir John Bowring.)

DECEMBER 24.

GOD IS LOVE.

For me
I have my own church equally :
And in this church my faith sprang first.
In youth I looked to these very skies,
And, probing their immensities,
I found God there, His visible power :
    Yet felt in my heart, amid all its sense
    Of the power, an equal evidence
That His love there, too, was the nobler dower.
For the loving worm within its clod
Were diviner than a loveless god
Amid his worlds, I will dare to say. . . . .
    Love which on earth, amid all the shows of it,
    Has ever been seen the sole good of life in it,
    The love ever growing there, spite of the strife in it,
    Shall arise, made perfect, from death's repose of it.

And I shall behold Thee, face to face,
O God, and in Thy light retrace
How in all I loved here, still wast Thou!
Whom passing to then, as I fain would now,
I shall find as able to satiate
  The love, Thy Gift, as my spirit's wonder
Thou art able to quicken and sublimate,
  With this sky of Thine that I now walk under,
And glory in Thee for, as I gaze
Thus, thus!   Oh, let men keep their ways
Of seeking Thee in a narrow shrine—
Be this my way!   And this is mine!

ROBERT BROWNING.

DECEMBER 25.

[Christmas Day.]

*THE PRIEST IN HOLY TRANSPORT THUS
EXCLAIMED:—*

. . . ACCOMPLISH, then, their number; and conclude
Time's weary course!   Or if, by Thy decree,
The consummation that will come by stealth
Be yet far distant, let Thy Word prevail,
Oh! let Thy Word prevail, to take away
The sting of human nature.   Spread the law,
As it is written in Thy holy book,
Throughout all lands: let every nation hear
The high behest, and every heart obey,
Both for the love of purity and hope
Which it affords to such as do Thy will
And persevere in good, that they shall rise
And have a nearer view of Thee in heaven.

Father of good ! this prayer in bounty grant,
In mercy grant it, to Thy wretched sons.
Then, nor till then, shall persecution cease,
And cruel wars expire.   The way is marked,
The guide appointed, and the ransom paid.
Alas ! the nations who of yore received
These tidings, and in Christian temples meet
The sacred truth to acknowledge, linger still ;
Preferring bonds and darkness to a state
Of holy freedom, and redeeming love
Proffered to all, while yet on earth detained.

So fare the many ; and the thoughtful few,
Who in the anguish of their souls bewail
This dire perverseness, cannot choose but ask,
Shall it endure ?—shall enmity and strife,
Falsehood and guile, be left to sow their seed,
And the kind never perish ?   Is the hope
Fallacious, or shall righteousness obtain
A peaceable dominion, wide as earth
And ne'er to fail ?   Shall that blest day arrive,
When they, whose choice or lot it is to dwell
In crowded cities, without fear shall live,
Studious of mutual benefit ; and he,
Whom Morn awakens, among dews and flowers
Of every clime, to till the lonely field,
Be happy in himself ?
                    The law of faith,
Working through love, such conquest shall it gain,
Such triumph over sin and guilt achieve ?
Almighty Lord, Thy further grace impart !

W. WORDSWORTH.

Nunc dies Christo memoranda nato
Fulsit, in pectus mihi fonte purum
Gaudium sacro fluat, et benigni
            Gratia Coeli !

Christe, da tutam trepido quietem,
Christe, spem praesta stabilem timenti ;
Da fidem certam, precibusque fidis
                    Annue, Christe !

                    DR SAMUEL JOHNSON.

DECEMBER 26.

Lord, with what courage and delight
        I do each thing
When Thy least breath sustains my wing !
        I shine and move
        Like those above,
        And—with much gladnesse,
        Quitting sadnesse—
Make me faire dayes of every night

Affliction thus meere pleasure is,
        And hap what will,
If Thou be in't 'tis welcome still.
        But since Thy rayes
        In sunnie dayes
        Thou dost thus lend
        And freely spend,
Ah ! what shall I return for this ?

Oh ! that I were all soul ! that Thou
        Wouldst make each part
Of this poor sinfull frame, pure heart !
        Then would I drown
        My single one ;
        And to Thy praise
        A consort raise
Of hallelujahs here below.

                    HENRY VAUGHAN.

DECEMBER 27.

TO DEATH.

Thou bid'st me come away,
And Ile no longer stay
Than for to shed some tears
For faults of former years,
And to repent some crimes
Done in the present times:
And next, to take a bit
Of bread, and wine with it:
To don my robes of love,
Fit for the place above;
To gird my loins about
With charity throughout;
And so to travel hence
With feet of innocence;
　　These done, Ile only cry,
　　"God, mercy!" and so die.

R. Herrick.

DECEMBER 28.

FROM EVERLASTING TO EVERLASTING.

When all Thy mercies, O my God,
　My rising soul surveys;
Transported with the view, I'm lost
　In wonder, love, and praise.

O how shall words with equal warmth
　The gratitude declare
That glows within my ravish'd heart?
　But Thou canst read it there.

Thy providence my life sustained,
    And all my wants redressed,
When in the silent womb I lay
    And hung upon the breast.

To all my weak complaints and cries
    Thy mercy lent an ear,
Ere yet my feeble thoughts had learnt
    To form themselves in prayer.

Unnumbered comforts to my soul
    Thy tender care bestowed,
Before my infant heart conceived
    From whom those comforts flowed.

When in the slippery paths of youth
    With heedless steps I ran,
Thine arm unseen conveyed me safe,
    And led me up to man.

Through hidden dangers, toils, and deaths
    It gently cleared my way,
And through the pleasing snares of vice,
    More to be feared than they.

When worn with sickness, oft hast Thou
    With health renewed my face,
And when in sins and sorrows sunk,
    Reviv'd my soul with grace.

Thy bounteous hand with worldly bliss
    Has made my cup run o'er,
And in a kind and faithful friend
    Has doubled all my store.

Ten thousand thousand precious gifts
    My daily thanks employ,
Nor is the least a cheerful heart
    That tastes those gifts with joy.

Through every period of my life
  Thy goodness I'll pursue,
And after death in distant worlds
  The glorious theme renew.

When nature fails, and day and night
  Divide Thy works no more,
My ever grateful heart, O Lord,
  Thy mercy shall adore.

Through all eternity, to Thee
  A joyful song I'll raise,
For O, eternity's too short
  To utter all Thy praise.

JOSEPH ADDISON.

DECEMBER 29.

[W. E. Gladstone born, 1809.]

Rock of ages, cleft for me,
Let me hide myself in Thee;
Let the Water and the Blood,
From Thy riven side which flow'd,
Be of sin the double cure,
Cleanse me from its guilt and power.

Not the labours of my hands
Can fulfil Thy law's demands;
Could my zeal no respite know,
Could my tears for ever flow,
All for sin could not atone:
Thou must save, and Thou alone.

Nothing in my hand I bring,
Simply to Thy Cross I cling;
Naked, come to Thee for dress;
Helpless, look to Thee for grace;
Foul, I to the Fountain fly—
Wash me, Saviour, or I die.

While I draw this fleeting breath,
When my eyelids close in death,
When I soar through tracts unknown,
See Thee on Thy Judgment Throne,
Rock of ages, cleft for me,
Let me hide myself in Thee.

AUGUSTUS TOPLADY.

DECEMBER 30.

OLD AGE.

As this my carnal robe grows old,
Soil'd, rent, and worn by length of years,
Let me on that by faith lay hold
Which man in life immortal wears:
   So sanctify my days behind,
   So let my manners be refined,
That when my soul and flesh must part,
There lurk no terrors in my heart.

So shall my rest be safe and sweet
When I am lodgèd in my grave;
And when my soul and body meet,
A joyful meeting they shall have:
   Their essence then shall be divine,
   This muddy flesh shall starlike shine,
And God shall that fresh youth restore
Which will abide for evermore.

GEORGE WITHER.

DECEMBER 31.

NEW YEAR'S EVE.

RING out, wild bells, to the wild sky,
  The flying cloud, the frosty light:
  The year is dying in the night;
Ring out, wild bells, and let him die.

Ring out the old, ring in the new,
  Ring, happy bells, across the snow:
  The year is going, let him go;
Ring out the false, ring in the true.

Ring out the grief that saps the mind,
  For those that here we see no more;
  Ring out the feud of rich and poor,
Ring in redress to all mankind. . . .

Ring out false pride in place and blood
  The civic slander and the spite;
  Ring in the love of truth and right,
Ring in the common love of good.

Ring out old shapes of foul disease;
  Ring out the narrowing lust of gold;
  Ring out the thousand wars of old,
Ring in the thousand years of peace.

Ring in the valiant man, and free,
  The larger heart, the kindlier hand;
  Ring out the darkness of the land,
Ring in the Christ that is to be.

ALFRED, LORD TENNYSON.

INDEX OF AUTHORS.

The names of *Translators* are printed in *italics*.